Reaper's Revenge

Death's Journal (Book One)

CV Reinhardt
09/01/2019

Published by: Artisan Publishing Guild, LLC
APGuild@outlook.com

CV Reinhardt

Reaper's Revenge

Death's Journal – Book One

By CV Reinhardt

Dedication

To the Storyteller in all of us. Keep doing what you do, it makes the children smile!

Love and Strength,
Christian V. Reinhardt

Author's note:

Hello and welcome to another day in Death's world. Today, however, our friend, Death, is learning there's more to himself than just a pretty face. In the story, there are several entries called Death's Journal, a few of them are from historical works, i.e.: the hero, Lemminkainen, and Gilgamesh... these entries are written in the style of the original author. Which, in the case of Lemminkainen, was quite a challenge.

I hope that you enjoy Death's new world. Cloudan Courstre, this side of douchie or not, is our rendition of the Grim Reaper. You probably shouldn't let him catch you reading this.

Love and Strength,

Christian V. Reinhardt

Reaper's Revenge
Section One
Chapter One - Cloudan

So few humans fully understand this world isn't supposed to be perfect; your expulsion in the beginning sealed that fate. However, the way you treat each other in this day and age is outrageous and simply draws attention to how screwed up your continued existence really is. Since forever and a day, I have been here, watching you. In some ages, like this one, I choose to interact directly with you. Why? I'm actually not certain.

The fear you have for me is justified, although little of who I am is actually known to you. It seems like each country, culture, religion and even subset of religion have their own ideas of who I am and what I mean to your world. Some see me as a scythe-wielding skeleton dressed in a black cloak. Some, as a benevolent saint, and others think I'm a puppet of the higher powers, wielding no influence of my own. They're all wrong. I, in fact, am a monster, ripping the souls from not only the ugly but also the beautiful, not only from the bodies of the forsaken sinners but the benevolent beings that walk in the footsteps of saints. Moreover, one day in the not so distant future, I will be taking yours as well.

In this effigy, I have chosen the name Cloudan Courstre, and although I'm a monster, I happen to be a beautiful one. Women and even some men who look upon my sculpted cheeks and shocking gray eyes become smitten with the true beauty a man can wield. Those unmoved by good looks, which, let's face it, aren't many, see my 6'1" sculpted and tattooed frame and assume I'm a professional football player. Not the American version, real footballers who run for forty-five minutes beating the shit out of each other without pads. But neither my good looks nor my physique are what make me special, that would be my taste in clothes, always just this side of douchie.

Currently, I have on low-rise form fitting black pants, a black tailored t-shirt under a black collared, baby blue pin-striped dress shirt which I wear open like a jacket with the sleeves pulled up, not rolled. I adjust my baby blue belt as I appear a block from my current destination and start walking. It's not that I can't just appear where I need to, I just hate it when one of you catch me materializing and I need to wash your minds of what you saw. Sometimes, I see things in there that are, well... disturbing, even to me.

Briefly, I pause my stroll through the streets of this once fantastic accomplishment of modern man and take in how far it's fallen into disrepair. There is garbage piled along the curbs and paint peeling from public buildings while people sit at home and live off the backs of others. Not having enough respect for their neighbors to give back, too worried about themselves and what everyone owes them to ask, 'What can I do for my neighborhood, state, country, or even my world?'

I laugh aloud at my play on a presidential quote and start walking again. I produce five smooth stones in my left hand and roll them in varying patterns, causing the symbols on my palm to stir pleasantly. Although for years the significance of these stones has been lost on you, I still leave a single memento each time I collect a worthy human soul. At some point in the past, humans noticed this and you began leaving my gifts on the graves of the departed as a remembrance. Step ahead to the 17th century and stelae, a fancy word for funeral art, began frequenting cemeteries.

The time for my work draws near as I walk up to the door of the deli and pull it open. Immediately, I'm hit with a foul sensory overload from the patrons. The foolish fears, unrealistic dreams, obvious regrets, and other unnamable emotions wash over me from those who will see another day, week, or year of life, as well as those less fortunate. I hear the thoughts of those who'll try to be more than they should ever dare to be, and those who will allow their meager existence to be enough. Alone, I see the one who could actually have broken free from all of this; the lying, pretending, the greed and abandonment. Instead, she sits, thinking of others, wondering why her help hasn't moved them forward and devising a new method to encourage them, but there's no more time for this new approach.

I shake my head, seeing the three ruffians who, minutes from now, will set this place on its ear. I look closely at each of them, they all have identical thin, black lines running across their faces, forming an 'X'. In addition to their face tattoo, each have platinum white hair, almost translucent. I try to glean the significance of their look from their minds but none of these lemmings seem to realize. The one leading this group stares back at the girl sitting alone at a table.

The anger in his aura is obvious as he turns back, "Hey, buddy, watch where you're going." He chides after walking directly into me and then runs his hands over his slicked-back hair, drawing even more attention to the X. He opens his eyes wide, tilting his head in a vain attempt to look tough. Instead, creating a poor impersonation of a confused dog.

"My mistake, friend, I was momentarily distracted. I thought that girl to be Kira, an old friend." I babble in a deliberate attempt to quell the situation, looking at the girl I'm there to reap.

He looks back at her again, then at me, glancing up and down, taking all of me in. "That ain't her name." His words a mumble and his thoughts a mess as he shoulders past me.

"Don't let it happen again." The smallest of the three tosses a rebuke my way, sounding fiercer than he actually looks with the smattering of Oppy freckles across the bridge of his nose.

"I'll make certain not to," I step to my left to allow the remaining two to pass. As they do, I look down to meet the shortest one's eyes, which are level with my Adam's apple. 'Asshats', I think as I walk to the counter where I take a position behind a green vinyl barstool. The little man behind the counter has three tables, yet to look at the stress he's under, you'd think he had twenty or more. I patiently wait for him to catch up and notice he has a new patron. While I wait, parts of me are pulled away, tending to other souls ready to pass into their next existence. At any given instance, I can be in a thousand places or more. Each of the souls my shades touch are known to me, their entire existence in a whisper on the breeze.

I check my reflection in the soon-to-be destroyed antique mirror behind the counter and adjust my sleeves. Thinking momentarily about the tattoos across the three boys' faces before I refocus on my purpose here, taking the only worthy soul, pulling it from this plane of existence and turning it over to a higher power. It doesn't matter which, they all call for my service and I, of course, answer. Delivering their followers' very essence to whatever afterlife 'They' feel is correct, I'm just a patsy for the higher-ups. At least today we'll be headed to the realm of the blessed. I can't even tell you how disconcerting going in the other direction is, although most of my trips these days tend to take me that way.

"Hello, I'm Roger and I'll be your server tonight. That's a very interesting bracelet, may I?" The little sweat-covered man tries to make up for the delay with a compliment. Isn't that cute.

"Pleased to meet you, Roger, and thank you, I've had it forever." I hold out my arm, allowing him to look down at what currently appears to be a charm bracelet, which, by design, pushes my douche level up a notch. Most of the time, my accessory appears as a simple leather strap tied around my wrist. This is what we in the supernatural realm call a magical artifact. As such, I can make it appear as anything I choose, even a living creature. It's rather fun to make it look like a snake. If, however, you were to look upon it in the Planes of Death, you would see what it really is, the souls of the unworthy who tried to make a deal with me. No, not after they're dead. Shit, everyone does that; it's like a rite of passage.

"Please can I have more time?"

"Actually, it's '*may*' I have more time. And no, piss off." My standard answer to all humans asking for anything... thousands of times a day this scenario plays out. I take no action against any of those humans. As I said, these requests are to be expected. However, the souls I carry around on my wrist are the morons who found a method of summoning me, which, yes, unlike fallen angels, I can be summoned. Once I stand before them, they attempt to barter with me for a plethora of things; money, love, talent, sometimes even magic power. Nothing pisses me off more than getting pulled off a beautiful golf course by some idiot wanting to be a rock star, or a cow wanting to be a model. Usually, it plays out like the dead asking for additional time.

"I have a wish that I want you to grant."

"No, piss off." As I said before, it's my go-to reply. If they drop it, so do I. That being said, most of those who have been committed enough in their research to bring me to their location can't just give up that easily.

They will typically follow with, "I'll give you my soul if you help me to... Blah, blah, blah." Even then, I give most of them another shot over the bow. After all, it's three strikes you're out, not two. I said most of them because a person can force me to ignore all rules of engagement if they use the term, "I order you", or equally as bad, "As I have summoned you, you must..." For those stupid enough to order me or make a third request, all bets are off. It doesn't matter what they ask me for at that point, I grant it, whatever the hell it is. Here's the kicker, I do the old switch-a-roo, walking away with their soul on my wrist, replacing it with one of my shades. As I said, I know every detail of who they are, so my shades passing as them is easy. Don't go thinking I'm welching on a deal, the contract is fulfilled. Hell, some of the best guitarists you've ever heard were actually one of my shades.

Later, when the Fates say their time is up and the scissors cut their thread, I release them to whichever god will have them. Once in a great while, the tortured of soul, losing its living body is enough to fashion it away from perdition. Not really, your fate is woven when you're born, I just like to torture troublesome assholes. To be fair, I wasn't always this way, but back when I was known as Thanatos, a King named Sisyphus messed with me. First, he shackled me with my own chains, not only stopping me from reaping him but also stopping all the other souls from being reaped as well. Creating havoc that I was later held accountable for. When I finally escaped, with the help of Ares, I took him to hell. Upon his arrival there, he managed to trick Persephone with a sad story and return to his body. Keep on pushing that rock, Mr. Know-it-all.

"Shit." Roger jumped back from looking at the bracelet. "I saw... never mind." As the Planes of Death grow close, some, perhaps like Roger here, become more sensitive to it.

"Too much acid when you were a kid?" I winked. "May I have a large glass of cranberry juice?"

"Of course." He left, giving several glances at my charm bracelet.

Five minutes later, he brought me a shot glass half full of an almost burgundy liquid.

"I asked for a large glass." I said.

"We only have one size for juice," Roger's voice grated on me with its articulated bitchiness.

"I'll tell you what, take forty-seven of these little things, fill up a real cup and bring that to me." He rushed away. I guess I didn't tell you, along with my beauty comes the ability to alter the alluring cast, driving fear into a person's being. Using it to get juice though, boy, I must be in a shitty mood.

"Here you go. Did you decide on any food tonight?"

"Actually, Roger, do you have any biscotti?" I asked, already knowing the answer.

"No. We do have muffins though."

"I'm certain the coffee shop on the corner has a couple of selections. Take this," I handed him a one-hundred-dollar bill. "And get me two, make certain they don't have chocolate frosting."

"I'm really not allowed to—"

"You can keep the change if you can do it in under fifteen minutes."

"O...K..."

"And, Roger, take the money from the till and leave by the back door." I added and then take a sip of juice as he walked away. If you're wondering why I sent him out the back door, it's because I really didn't want to hear his panicked scream as he ran in circles like his hair was on fire. Too many things are going to happen in the span of a few heartbeats. Besides, he wasn't going to die anyway, I wouldn't have been allowed to shelter a being from harm that way.

The shots from the passing van riddle the tables, the walls, and even the bar at which I sat. I walk unperturbed through the tumult, glancing over to see the beautiful old mirror disintegrate. People are hitting the deck, diving under their tables or taking cover wherever possible. The part in all this that irritated me is that my clothes joined the ranks of the bullet-riddled. Whereas, if I had just appeared, I could've spared my custom-made shirt.

"Get down, you idiot," a random stranger ordered.

"Yeah, yeah." I replied, reaching the single victim of the shooting. While her corporeal body had deceased; unlike movies, books, or even interviews with people who've had near-death experiences say they were floating above themselves or looking into a light. No, the girl was still locked inside her shell where her true essence has always dwelt. For some reason, I had to concentrate deeply to get the dead girl's name, "Terpsi, I call you forth." I held out my hand above her, the four symbols glowing.

"No, the shooting is still going on." She replied, and I lowered my hand, feeling the heat release.

"True, but, child, for you this matters not. Come to me." I held out my hand a second time, a greater heat emanating.

"What do you mean, it doesn't matter for me?" a white gray shadow of what she once was left her body. I took the hand, my magic coaxing her from the already withering husk to stand at her full height. In life, she was seen as beautiful; tall and thin, with long silky hair pulled back to accentuate the harsh features that most humans seem to find alluring these days.

"My dear, bullets can't hurt you, you're already dead."

"How?" she winced as the last shots ripped through the building.

"The first bullet they fired shattered the window, the second struck you directly in the heart."

"No. I was going to ask, how can you be talking to me if I'm dead?"

"I, my darling, am the embodiment of death. I'm here to take you to your next—"

"But all the hopes and dreams, all the hard work. I dance to…" she interrupted me, but as the emotions hit, she couldn't finish her statement.

"Your dreams of dancing are gone, like so many others snuffed out before their flame touched the kindling." I replied stoically.

"But what did killing me accomplish?" she asked after she gathered herself.

"It was a random act of violence, a freak bullet from a gun that hit you. I don't believe you were the target."

"Who did it?"

"One of the boys with 'Xs' on their faces."

"Who are they?" Terpsi asked, still looking around at the devastation. "One of them tried to strike up a conversation with me. Maybe I was rude, I was…"

"Part of the living, set that aside." I cut her off, "I need you to let that go, release this life so I can take you on."

"You don't understand, my death can't have been an arbitrary event. I'm here to insp—"

"Whatever you feel you were here to do is gone now. Those you tried to help need to move forward without your help." I cut her off again, I'd seen so many distract themselves with 'could've beens' that they end up missing their chance to go with me. "I want you to close your eyes and breathe in. What do you smell?" A tactic I've learned over the years which works well on those not ready to depart.

"Incense, sandalwood incense," she replied.

"Open your eyes." She did, the room was lavishly decorated with silk hanging from the ceiling. As she walked forward, an older woman moved aside a sheer of the deepest purple.

"Gran?" The girl rushed forward, releasing my hand, sending me from her paradise. Over the eons, I've come to know I can stay if I so choose, but why bother?

The smell of gunpowder and blood tickled my nose. I reached over to the table adjacent to the dead girl's and pulled the tablecloth with a flourish. I allowed nothing that could have stained the cloth to spill, everything else toppled over, crashing to the ground and bringing the customers out of their stupors. I covered the girl and walked back up to the bar.

"Oh my god, oh god, oh no. What happened?" Roger asked, running in from the kitchen.

"There seems to have been a shooting. Do you have my biscotti?" I asked.

"What?" he snapped out of his fit, "Oh, of course. Here," he held the bag to me, I took it and looked inside.

"Excellent, no chocolate. You should call the police, Roger, there's been a death." I pointed to the girl under the now blood-covered tablecloth. He rushed off to place the call. Five minutes later, the first police cars arrived.

"Who the hell covered the dead body?" The police detective who asked the question was tall and clean-shaven, over all, good looking. His blonde hair was longer than one would expect from a police officer and, more importantly, it was extremely out of date in a feathered cut. He wore a tacky, tan, trench coat, with a lapel pin of a laurel wreath, cliché enough to be a toga on a Greek god. His entire ensemble made me vomitous.

"That would be I." I said, not turning to face the room.

"And you are?"

"I think the proper thing to occur in a situation like this is for the detective—" I started.

"Lead Detective," he shot back.

"Oh, of course, the lead detective should introduce himself before trying to intimidate a witness or evoke his power of persuasion." I sipped my juice, which Roger had been kind enough to replace after my first glass fell, as another victim, to the X-faced boys' shooting.

"My name is Neirin, Detective Neirin Delphinios."

"Lead Detective." I muttered, placing my glass on the counter in preparation for what was to come next.

He spun the stool so that I faced him. "Now. Who in the hell are you, and why the hell did you cover a victim?" He pulled a small notebook from his inside pocket, with a pen attached to its side.

"My name is Cloudan, no specific honorific, just Cloudan Courstre. I covered her because I'm rather squeamish and didn't wish to look at the unfortunate soul any longer."

"He covered her while the shooting was still going on." The jackass who had told me to get down said.

"Actually, what I did was check on her while the shooting was going on. When I covered her dead body, I assure you, no more bullets were being fired. I'm simply not that brave."

"So, let me get this straight, you're a doctor?" The detective asked.

"Heavens no. I'm merely a good Samaritan, who wanted to—"

"Mess up my crime scene." The lead detective's eyes bore into mine.

"Precisely. When the shooting started, I thought, oh this is going to be fun, let's dance through a hailing of bullets and 'mess up' *Lead* Detective Delphinios's crime scene. You need to understand, she was dead, no one needed to see that. I was merely trying to keep the situation calm." I crossed my arms.

"By walking through gunfire?" he asked.

"At the time, I didn't know she was dead, I saw her body jerk and went to give aid."

"Very admirable." Lead Detective Delphinios replied.

"Thank you."

"Sir," a different police officer interrupted.

"One moment," the lead detective said to me and turned to the cop, obviously put out. "What can I do for you, officer?"

"She was holding this." He held a stone in his gloved hand. I smiled and reached for my juice.

"Ok, so bag it." He dismissed the officer. "Why the hell is she holding a rock?" He asked himself as he turned to face the victim.

"She was worthy." I said, placing the juice back on the counter.

"What?"

"Who? What? Are you talking to me now?" I looked around stupidly.

"I have a couple more lines of questioning." Lead Detective Delphinios returned his attention to me.

"Of course." I waited.

"Did you see who did the shooting?"

"Now there's the question I've been waiting for. Yes, I did." I couldn't help but goad him.

"Mister," he glanced at his notebook theatrically. "Courstre. This is an investigation and if you aren't a help then you're a hindrance. As in obstruction of justice, go to jail, do not pass go." His feathered hair bounced as he spoke, giving the effect of a 1970's sitcom beauty tussling her wreathed locks.

"White van, three men all with Xs on their faces."

"They did the shooting? Those gentlemen were sitting at that booth." Roger pointed to the booth next to the shattered window.

"I'll get to you in a moment, sir." Detective Delphinios said. "Any further description?"

I held up a finger as I finished chewing my biscotti. "They were all in their twenties, the youngest of the group did the actual shooting, he's around 5'6" tall, skinny, pale as a cadaver, freckle-faced and has pure white hair."

"Any tattoos or visible scars?"

"Aside from the X on his face?" I asked, shaking my head.

"Oh yeah, um aside from that."

"Not that I saw. The second assailant was a male, about 5'11", and a bit overweight. He also had white hair. Last one was the driver, well-built, maybe 5'9", also with pure white hair."

"Hold up, did you say they all had bleached white hair?"

"Perhaps not bleached, but platinum, yes." I replied with a yawn, stretching my arms theatrically.

"Your clothes, are those bullet holes?" Detective Delphinios asked.

"No, don't be silly, these are my church clothes." I said, straightening my collar.

"That's funny," Roger laughed in spite of the situation.

"What is?" Detective Delphinios asked.

"Church clothes… get it? They're holy." The waiter continued to laugh.

The detective let me leave after getting my contact information in case he had further questions or if the coroner's report turned up something hinky. That was his word, not mine, I almost changed it in my telling. Seriously, who the hell says hinky? I finished my juice and thanked Roger by putting another hundred-dollar bill on the table.

"You don't have to do that," he said.

"Actually, son, none of your tables are going to pay, and this will be a crime scene for at least a couple of days. Just say thank you to the rich douchebag that likes to throw money around." Detective Delphinios instructed.

"Thank you, please come again." Roger waved.

"That probably isn't a great thing to request." I muttered and left. The throng of investigators and paramedics packed the sidewalk outside the deli, along with the looky-loos, trying to determine if they knew the deceased. Pathetic. I hid amongst them and allowed myself to follow the next call for my services. As I teleported to the new location, I changed my attire before reaching a room which surprised me in two ways; first, it's only two blocks away, second, it's dark, so dark, in fact, I see no one, alive or dead.

Reaper's Revenge
Chapter Two - Cassiopeia

The darkness of the room was extinguished as a spotlight burned it into submission. She stood on a stage in a simple white sleeping garment holding a sheet of paper. After clearing her throat, she began.

"If I could explain one thing to you, it would be that anger itself is not the cause of evil, just as Christ was not evil when he lost control of himself upon the merchants in the temple. Anger, if kept in check, can be good, and in some situations, can even save your life. But when left unchecked, anger will cause you to do things, things you will regret, things that can't be undone." She allowed her frailty to remain exposed to her audience, her hands at her sides and open to those watching. She closed her splayed fingers, sweeping her arms forward in an arc until she formed a chalice in front of her. Drawing from an unseen well, she raised the cup to her mouth. Attempting to drink, she looked into her hands and appeared confused. Fluttering her fingers, the chalice broke apart and her hands fell to her sides, open to the audience again, showing that they, like her hopes, are empty.

"You, there," her voice vexed, she took a step toward her audience, pointing her finger accusingly at no one in particular. "You who piously judge the actions of others. Yes, you, sitting so innocently, it's you I reach out to. I need you to release me. My life is too full of mistakes to allow it to continue." Her words echoed in the darkness as the spotlight was overtaken once more for the duration of a lapping wave.

"Stop." On the other side of the stage, her thin body was silhouetted inside the white garment by a harsh light behind her. "Take a moment to look around you." She took a long breath and the spotlight once again went out. "Stop. Can you picture me in a pitch-black room, alone? Debating the meaning of it all, alone." Her voice seemed to travel side to side in the darkness. Suddenly, at center stage, there was a minor explosion and a brief flash of light showing the thin girl holding a gun under her chin.

"Was the flash and the crack unexpected to you? Did you feel the sound along with my essence rebound from the wall into you? Did it feel powerful? Could you hear the silence that followed? Of course, you could, it was so loud that it hurt. To fill the created void, you found yourself peering into the darkness, searching, pleading for more, didn't you?" The spotlight again shined on the thin girl, this time, her white sleeping garment was covered in a red stain. "Tell me, how do you feel now, alone in my room, knowing I'm no longer actually there? Not really." The light began to strobe and she was dragged from the stage by an unseen being.

"A figure, *the* figure, leaves the room with my very essence, leaving only a husk of who I was to the silence. Follow him! Don't lose this figure. Does he see you? That would be bad. He's there, just ahead of you, entering into the adjacent alley. Take measure to remain cloaked, can't you hear the silence that follows this creature? Like the gaping maw of an animal before it strikes? The junkies in this alley, so close to dying, can see only a shadow as it passes, yet they don't try to beg money from him. The rats smell him, yet they don't scurry to his feet to lick the blood, my blood, from the ground as it drips from his clothing. They know this figure is fear and oh so much more. But where am I?"

One last time, the stage was a victim to the darkness, until alternating red and blue flashing lights illuminated an empty stage, showing a white nightgown puddled and covered in a red liquid in the center. Her voice came from above now, "The silent scene is now broken by the sound of a siren. It could have been... so much more... what a waste."

"End scene," the house lights came up and there, in front of the stage, a woman, who may have been a wart that had fallen from the ass of a toad, sat. "Where was your fire, Cassiopeia? Where was your drive? That was flat, barely one step above terrible." Her nasally, prima donna, bitch voice fitted her physical demeanor.

"I'm sorry, Miss Mella. I guess I wasn't really up for this today." The actress climbed down from a small ladder, a slight sheen on her brow.

"I want you to think about motivation. What is this girl trying to convey?"

"Convey?"

"Oh, Cass, is that actually a question?" The acting coach's voice that started as nasally and bitchy now came off as disgusted.

"Please don't call me, Cass." She replied.

"My dear, you just had it, the emotion you were trying to convey was strength. That's what I want to see. The other piece you need to think about is in your writing. How are you trying to turn the scene?"

"Turn the scene?" The girl held back a grin as the instructor's face reddened.

"Ok, class, that's it for tonight, I'll see you Thursday." She gave no voice to answering the girl's confusion. "Remember, it's only three weeks until each of you does your single scene spectacular in front of a live audience. Practice, practice, practice. Use my advice; I won't always be here to guide you."

The thin girl walked from the stage, joining the other students as they filtered from the theatre.

Reaper's Revenge
Chapter Three - Cloudan

I sat in the auditorium watching the class leave as Miss Mella flipped through her notes, speaking to herself quietly. I waited patiently. Typically, I would've stolen a look into the future to see what was going to happen, but how many times do you get to observe an acting coach's death scene? I wanted to see it play out for myself. Go ahead and think I'm an ass, you'd be correct.

"Hello, is anyone there?" the woman asked as a measured amount of noise filtered down to her level.

"It is I, Romeo." The single line echoed, and then nothing else.

"Orphe, is that you? Stop playing around and show yourself." The fat woman stood from her padded seat with some effort.

"Bitch, I told you who I am." An almost demented voice replaced the whimsical one.

"I beg your pardon, how dare you refer to me in such a manner. Do you know to whom you're addressing?"

"I'd have to say, I couldn't give two shits."

"He really can't, he's physically unable." A different voice said and then gave a sharp laugh at his humor.

"Show yourselves this instant." Miss Mella screamed toward the rear of the auditorium. I decided to liven things up a bit and turned on the same light used to cast the girl on stage into a silhouette earlier.

"Dammit, Ricky, did you turn that on? It's god damn bright, shut it off." Romeo ordered.

"I didn't do nothing." A voice answered from behind the stage. Miss Mella turned around and faced the third intruder.

"It's 'I didn't do anything' ignorant buffoon." She corrected the empty stage and then turned back to see the two figures the spotlight was illuminating. Both figures were wearing kilts for goodness sake, one was red and black, the other dark blue and green. They also had matching Xs across their faces. "What exactly are you doing in my playhouse?"

"Your playhouse?" The voice, easily recognizable as the one who called himself Romeo earlier, asked. "I believe this falls into the Black and Tan side of the Quarters. So, we get full range to enjoy." One of the X-faced intruders stood in front and to the side of the other, his hands were resting on a braided belt slung over his hips. The top of his black hair was pulled back into a top ponytail, showing that the sides were completely shaven, which I have to say suited him. I couldn't help wondering if his cut and the kilt were perhaps to make himself look taller, as both were nowhere near five-foot in height.

"You'll never run roughshod over the arts," her flamboyant arm gestures and overly articulated pronunciations let me know this would be her grandest performance. "So many before you fiends have attempted to—"

"Shut the hell up." Romeo barked.

"Never, you'll never still free expression—" A gunshot flashed backstage, presumably from Ricky's pistol, doing what Romeo's words couldn't. The bullet shattering her larynx didn't allow her to finish her soliloquy, although it didn't even slow her continued pantomime. The gasps and overly dramatic flailing, pitching and head throws cascaded from seat to seat across nearly the entire front row. I would have to admit, it was quite a performance.

"What the hell? Shoot her again." Romeo ordered after the instructor's way over the top death scene stretched above his endurance level (no, that isn't a short joke). Ricky stepped forward showing that he too had black hair, possessed an X across his face, and was most definitely in the under-five club. His second shot put an end to Miss Mella's award-winning production.

I walked down to greet the newly deceased. "End scene. Miss Mella, I call you forth." Without delay, a hand left the confines of the dead body. Unlike the grasping ones that typically reach out to me, hers appeared with a slight bend of the wrist, fingers together. 'Even now,' I thought, 'she plays the role of a Diva.' I, like any gentleman must, bow and take the proffered hand. As if guiding her to a dance floor where the band patiently waited on us to start the music.

"And how well did my death scene play out?" she asked as we walked.

"You were very committed to it."

"Anything worth doing, dear boy, is worth fully committing to. Now, I must know, have my illustrious actions granted me a journey to Broadway or will I forever play the bordellos of hell?"

"Dear lady, I've never had someone so calmly ask me that." Instead of answering further, we exited down stage, straight down stage.

"Well, this sucks." She replied, losing all vestige of the grand lady.

"You've taken too much from people who came to you with their dreams exposed, giving not one real piece of advice."

"That's not true, I—" a figure immerged from the shadows, revealing a face I recognized from a reaping in 1865, John Wilkes Booth. As he walked up to Miss Mella, she redirected her statement, "Well, hello, sir."

"Your scene awaits, Madam." His hand shot out like a bullet from a derringer, grabbing a fist full of hair, he dragged her away kicking and screaming.

"Think, what motivation are you trying to convey in order to turn this scene?" I asked. Quickly, her middle finger extended. "That's close. Unladylike, but close." I returned to the playhouse, Romeo and his black-haired companions had already left. Miss Mella lay dead on her back, holding a stone that I hadn't left. "Odd," I shook my head and once again allowed myself to travel to a reaping, this time to a distant land. 'I'll return to this rapidly unfolding drama later.' I thought.

Death's Journal - Enkidu

Enkidu, who came to life when Aruru, the mother goddess of the mountain, formed him from clay and cast him into the wilderness, where he ran naked, enjoying life without the stigma of knowing what he was supposed to be. Why did the goddess form this specific man? Because she was ordered by Anu, the sky god and father of all gods, to deal with a specific issue.

The problem in one word: Gilgamesh, the king of Uruk and an overall jackass. Having been born a demi-god, Gilgamesh was the most powerful being alive. Flaunting his power with various antics, most of which were acceptable. Yet the citizenry of Uruk raised their voices to the heavens for help against this creature the gods had created, when he refused to allow husbands to lie with their wives on their wedding day until he, Gilgamesh, had lay with them.

Therefore, the valiant Enkidu was created and endowed with the strength of Ninurta, the god of hunting and war, to counter Gilgamesh in all ways. Interestingly enough, it wasn't through this strength that he tamed the king that so infuriated his people, it was through his friendship.

When I first ventured to the deathbed of Enkidu, many years later, he and Gilgamesh were all but brothers having gone on several epic quests, which unwittingly he shared with me. When he woke on the third crow of the cock, glorious Gilgamesh took his hand. "Brother," Enkidu said, "Do you remember why we sent out to chop down the cedar forest?"

"I do, but I would like to hear your telling." Gilgamesh replied.

"I was sad, I was becoming weak from being stagnant. You declared we would travel to the cedar forest, guarded by the one whose roar is a Flood, whose mouth is Fire, and whose breath is certain death!"

"Humbaba." Gilgamesh added.

"Yes, my brother, Humbaba. You calmed me, yet your mother, Ninsum, and the council, were not so easy to pacify." I saw then that Enkidu's eyes widened and his hands searched for something around his neck.

"Nimsum's necklace is safe, brother."

"Did you know she gave it to me and insisted that I keep you safe? The council also insisted that I promise to bring you back?" A smile touched his lips.

"And I thought it was my strong words that convinced them. Such a fool I was, you tried three times to stop me from chopping that first cedar." Gilgamesh lay his head on Enkidu's chest and a few tears fell into the tuft of hair.

"And it was my blow that killed Humbaba, sending the forest into tumult." Enkidu said.

"Not so much tumult as when we returned, brother."

"True, yet I tire, please return tomorrow." I watched Enkidu fall into a fitful sleep, waking on the second crow of the cock.

"You wake?" Gilgamesh sat as a doorstop, not allowing anyone to enter.

"Brother, do you remember the day we returned with the head of Humbaba and the way you rejected Ishtar's marriage proposal?"

"My stupidity at its height, had I found a kind way to bow out of that then you may still be going on grand adventures with me." Gilgamesh crossed the room, the tears flowing freely.

"The largest laugh of my life, never will an insult be so well crafted that the spoiled brat's father could not deny."

"But Anu gave into his daughter's wishes and sent forth the Bull of the Heavens to kill me." Gilgamesh pulled at his clothes and hair, and I have to admit, looked more human in that moment than ever before.

"Only after she threatened to release the dead to feast upon the living." Enkidu laughed until he spat blood. "The bull, I thought would be my end." The regret filling his posture.

"But you surprised that beast by grabbing his horns." Gilgamesh said. "Twas him or you, brother. Besides, it was I that drove my sword deep and removed his heart. And in doing so, I killed you, worthy Enkidu."

"Gilgamesh, again, you're wrong. I cut off his thigh and cast it in Princess Ishtar's face for cursing you. Never should you blame yourself for my death." And Enkidu fell into another fitful sleep.

When Enkidu woke on the first crow of the cock, Gilgamesh lamented, "None can wake on the first calling of the rooster and live."

"Brother, do you recall the celebration after we slew the Bull of Heaven?"

"I do but I want you to tell me."

"All the dancing girls and greatest warriors gathered to see the horns you had the artisans cover in gold and lapis lazuli. But the dream that came that night ended me." Enkidu's eyes moved, taking in several figures in front of him. "Anu, Enlil, and Shamash," he said in reverence. "I understand, it's I that must pay for the lives of Humbaba, and the Bull of Heaven with mine, so that Gilgamesh, my brother, may continue."

And with that, I walked up and took the noble Enkidu from his plane to the next.

Reaper's Revenge
Chapter Four - Cassiopeia

Cassiopeia stood outside the playhouse entrance with the rest of her acting class two days hence. "Miss Mella, open up, we're freezing." She lied, the night was beautiful at 72 degrees but they had all learned that their teacher wanted them to be performing, always. She pounded on the door, trying to convey terror. The truth was, she really was calm even while the rest of the group was beginning to allow the grip of panic to close around them. Cassiopeia knew the fear they felt was real, none of them were good enough actors to fool her.

"Her car is parked out back," a boy no older than fifteen exclaimed, running up to the group.

"Did you check the backstage door?" A tall stranger asked in a confident demeanor.

"He's not stupid." Cassiopeia snapped.

"I, ah, actually didn't," he said and ran off.

"Sorry." The thin girl turned, looking at the man who, although dressed casually in a pair of jeans, silver-gray t-shirt and a thin, black cardigan, looked as if the gods of fashion had placed each piece of clothing on him. "Do I know you?"

"I was here on Tuesday when you performed, perhaps you saw me in the audience."

"That's possible, although when I'm up there—" a scream from inside the building stalled her words and drove the gray-eyed stranger into action. Three shoulders thrown into the locked door and its jam shattered inwards allowing entry. "Orphe, are you ok?" she asked.

"It's Miss Mella who's not ok, Cassiopeia." The boy who had gone to check if the back door was unlocked ran back to the group. Turning, he pointed to center stage, "She's dead."

"Did you check for a pulse?" a different girl asked.

"Lin, he's not stu—" this time, the thin girl stopped her statement as she saw Orphe pulling his lips back in disgust.

"It would've been a bad idea to disturb the crime scene further anyhow." The stranger said.

"And just who are you and who said it was a crime scene?" Lin asked.

"Sorry, miss, my name is Cloudan Courstre. The blood on Orphe's shoes tells me it wasn't a natural death." The boy looked at his shoes and passed out cold.

"Oh great." Cassiopeia shook her head. "Someone call the police, I'll see to him." She bent and lifted his head off the floor. Ahead of her in the shadows, she heard a crashing, smashing noise.

"Here," the stranger who called himself Cloudan handed her a backrest from one of the auditorium chairs.

"Shouldn't disrupt the crime scene?" She took the cushion and placed it under the boy's head.

"What?" he winked.

"Orphe, sweetie, are you ok?" Cassiopeia asked.

"My shoes, the blood, oh god." He whimpered.

"Cloudan is cleaning them up for you." She said.

"I'm what?" he asked to a stern glare and head gesture that brokered no further questions, then removed the sneakers from the prone boy's feet, walking away to clean them. A blink of an eye later, he returned, setting them on the floor next to the boy.

"I told him you were cleaning them."

"And that's precisely what I did. They'd pass a coroner's inquest." He grabbed one and held it up for her inspection.

"Thank you. I have an aversion to blood." Orphe said.

"We noticed. The police will be here in fifteen minutes." Lin said. "They want us to go back outside."

"Why?" Cloudan smugly stood up. With his hands on his hips, he gave a little inflection in his voice.

"They don't want us to disrupt the crime scene," she mumbled.

"Come on, Orphe, let me help you up." Cassiopeia held out a hand, lifting the small frame easily.

"You're deceptively strong." Orphe said, walking out barefoot.

"Being dragged across the stage by the Grim Reaper in her performance showed me there's more to her than—" Cloudan's words were cut off as he grabbed the shoes still lying on the ground and followed them out.

"What?" Lin asked.

"In her scene, she's taken by the Reaper and then tells the audience to follow him as he leaves through the adjacent alley."

"Is that really what your scene is about?" Orphe asked.

"You saw the scene once and remember specifics like that?" Lin asked.

"Suffice it to say, I have a thing for the Grim Reaper," he tossed the shoes at the boy's feet.

"Thanks for cleaning them." Orphe knelt and put on the sneakers.

"Yes, that's what it's about; a defiant girl killing herself and having her soul taken away."

"If her soul is taken, why would the Grim Reaper leave by the side street?" Orphe asked.

"Some lore said the Reaper returns after delivering the soul to its resting." Cassiopeia replied.

"Who wrote the scene?" Cloudan asked.

"I read a story about the Grim Reaper, but I changed it to fit the one-person scene Miss Mella wanted us to do."

"It's creatively dark." He said.

"Thanks," it was obvious that Cassiopeia was not one to talk about herself. "Here come the police." The flashing lights were reminiscent of the way her play had ended.

"Hello again." Detective Neirin Delphinios said, exiting the last police car to arrive.

"Lead Detective." Cloudan replied coldly.

"Who found the body?" he turned to the others.

"I did. I went around, checking if Miss Mella's car was here." Orphe said.

"Then Cloudan asked if he checked the door." Lin added.

"I ran back around and the door was open, so I figured I would surprise everyone and come out the front." He continued.

"But we heard him scream—" Cassiopeia started.

"I didn't scream." Orphe stood up straighter.

"You most certainly did." Lin corrected.

"Well, I was kinda freaked out as I stepped in something sticky, so I turned on my phone's flashlight app." He shuddered.

"Ok, what happened next? You ran up and let them in?" Detective Delphinios asked.

"Cloudan busted in the door." Lin said.

"Oh, you did?" Instead of turning to the tall man, the detective looked over and saw the news vans pulling onto the street. "Oh, crap! Jenkins, O'Reilly, get a parameter set up quickly."

"Yes, sir." The two police officers jogged back to their car.

"Ok, so let me make sure I have this," the detective cleared his throat and popped the collar on his trench coat as he looked through his notebook, "Mr. Courstre told the boy to try the rear stage door and then broke in through the front." He asked and then waited.

"That's about right." Cassiopeia replied.

"Well, let me have contact information for each of you." After he collected the information, he said, "Don't leave town in case I have questions, especially you, Mr. Courstre."

"Of course not, sir." They all replied and then broke into their own directions.

"Do you know a good place to eat?" Cloudan asked, padding up to Cassiopeia.

"I do," she replied, continuing to walk.

"Care to share the information with a hungry shoe cleaner?"

"Not to be rude but I do have rules about talking to strangers."

"And yet here we are." His lopsided grin and twinkling gray eyes put her at ease.

"Why were you here tonight? I know it wasn't as it seemed; to save helpless damsels and Orphe," she asked, still walking, albeit slower.

"I came to sign up for the acting class."

"Seriously?" She finally stopped, turned, and faced Cloudan, who momentarily looked distracted.

"No, I wouldn't have taken lessons from your Miss Mella. I did, however, come to help." Cloudan said.

"Will you be taking over now that she's dead?" Cassiopeia asked.

"I didn't sign up for..." he started.

"Come on, we've all been working so hard."

"How about if I commit to it through the single scene spectacular?"

"That sounds..." She started.

"Only if we can name it something better!" Cloudan said.

"I think the flyers are already printed." Cassiopeia smiled.

"I think you're missing the extent to which I believe that name lacks the panache that will make people attend." He replied. "I mean, shit, I'll pay for new ones."

"That would be your prerogative. Miss Mella was a different sort," she said, turning and beginning to walk again.

"By the way, your scene, I found it—" he started.

"Hello," out of nowhere, a bright light turned on and a woman speaking into a microphone said. "I'm Clio Antiquity for WKDT news."

"No comment." Cloudan said.

"Just a few words, come on, what happened?" the reporter asked.

"I'll give a comment," A young man with tan hair and a thin black X across his face said.

"Excellent. Go ahead."

"Die, bitch." The newcomer drew a gun and shot the reporter between the eyes.

"Run," Cloudan pushed Cassiopeia in front of himself.

They began running, seeing a white van idling at the end of the side street they ventured down. Another gunshot echoed around the brick walls. "I hope the cameraman got my good side. Hey, where are you going?" A mocking voice asked behind them.

"Do you have a car?" she asked.

"No, I materialized here," Cloudan replied, but then sensing Cassiopeia's anger growing, he rethought his jackass statement, "Fine, fine, it's parked back there." He pointed to an alley just ahead of them.

"Glad to hear—" she stopped speaking as the van began backing up with squealing tires and then whipped onto the street they were still running down.

"There, the black Mustang," he pointed as they turned the corner and jumped in.

"What is it with you and black?" she asked as the muscle car fired up and shot out of the side street like a bird of prey diving in for the kill.

"You know what they say, black is the new black." He shifted gears and steered the car, losing the pursuing piece of shit van in a couple of heartbeats.

"Who is it that says things like that?"

"You know, 'they'. What is it about being called Cass that bugs you?" He asked as they drove, reaching a dead-end. "Shit." He turned left, trying to guess which way the van had gone. Two blocks up, the white van shot out of a blind alley, crashing into the driver's side. His car spun for a moment, then he cranked the wheel and hit the accelerator, gaining control. From there, Cloudan shifted into reverse and continued the progress from the now disabled van. Slamming his foot on the brake and clutch, he turned the wheel and shifted into second gear, progressing forward, quickly turning left and then right again.

"Perhaps that's a conversation for after we're safe." She said, "Did we lose them?"

"It appeared the van gave up the ghost."

"When they rammed us?" Cassiopeia asked.

"Yeah, with that amount of smoke coming from the engine, they weren't going anywhere." Cloudan explained.

"Oh, I get it, they probably cracked the block. Where did you learn to drive like that?"

"I played a stunt driver in a movie."

"Seriously?" Cassiopeia leaned in.

"No," he laughed. "Truthfully, I practiced in vacant lots when I got my first real sports car. Burned off dozens of sets of tires."

"W...why?" she asked in complete confusion.

"I, well... It really seemed important to understand how the car handled. But when you look at me like I'm a moron, I have no idea. I'll go with, it's an alpha thing!"

"Alpha thing? Turn left here, I work at the diner two blocks up."

"Are you certain you want to go to work? I mean, those guys really seemed to be after you."

"Want to? Of course not, need to is more to the point. Besides, I'm fairly certain they were after you," she chided as they pulled into the diner.

"Me? Why would they be after me?" he asked, trying to open his door and failing.

"Sorry about your car." Cassiopeia held the passenger door for the driver to get out.

"Don't worry about the car, why do you think they would be after me and not you?"

"First, your name is Cloudan." She held up a finger and then raised another, "Second, I'm sure it's an alpha thing. Third, things as pretty as you don't come out at night so they were definitely trying to crush out your light. Now, come in and let me buy you a piece of cheesecake."

"Never let it be said that this 'pretty alpha boy' turned down cheesecake, but I can't stick around tonight." The tall stranger said after walking around and looking at the damage to the antique automobile. He let out a small laugh.

Reaper's Revenge
Chapter Five - Cloudan

There's really no simple way of saying how great it is to be me sometimes. Right now, for example, I just destroyed a one of a kind car from the private collection of a former TV talk show host. You may be thinking that's not nice, and you would be right... remember I said I'm a monster? Ok, keep that in mind.

You see, I can't actually break the laws of physical magic. By that, I mean, I can't make a car appear from air, I can, however, summon a car that I've seen. At least I think that's how it works every time I do a cute little trick like this. I find out at some point in the not so distant future where the item came from. Tonight, I happen to know this car from a show the owner does showing off his collection. Later, when it ends up in his garage with all this damage, he's going to be quite confused. Perhaps I'll hide in the shadows to watch, it would be the best episode by far.

I thought back momentarily on taking Miss Mella to her resting, she did go out quite dramatically. Glad I followed the pull, there are so few times a death scene is fun, I mean, hell, once you've seen a human's dying throws, typically ending in a bowel movement, you've seen 'em all.

"Some other time then," Cassiopeia said from the curb, I hadn't realized she was still there.

"Absolutely," I waited until she left before I got into the passenger door. Working my way behind the steering column just looks too ridiculous to leave a good impression. A minute later, I was in and drove the vehicle around the corner, stopping, I scanned the area and then I was standing in the street.

"What happened to your car?" an obviously drunk man asked from his hiding spot next to a dumpster.

"Car-jackers." I said flatly.

"Bastards. This city's going to shit." He coughed into his sleeve.

"Empirical data suggests you're correct."

"Of course, it does." The old bum snapped.

"Who are you talking to?" The sound of a girl's voice came from the shadows.

"Just some pretty boy. Cover up, you're sick." His voice took on a harsh but sympathetic tone.

I ignored the various pulls that came for me and headed to the only spot I truly could relax in this world, the tip of the pyramid at Giza, and let my shades handle all the reaping for a while. The heat of the sun would've been too much for my normal black apparel, so I took the opportunity to change into one of my oldest outfits, a pair of powder gray linen pants along with a white linen shirt. When paired with my white baby harp seal sandals, I felt completely naked. By the way, I got my sandals well before the world decided it was cruel to beat seal pups to death with a bat, and wouldn't throwing them away mean the seal died for nothing?

The day turned to evening, turned to day and evening again when I felt a stronger than normal pull and looked ahead to see where it would take me. Finding the end destination was a locker room, I changed from my linen and sandals, into a black pair of flat front dress pants, a black collarless dress shirt with a loose dark teal and black diamond-pattern three-quarter-length jacket. Today, my bracelet took the appearance of twenty-one black O-rings and three teal ones. When I placed my solid black infinity scarf on, I allowed myself to be extricated from my surroundings, being delivered to a locker room.

From the odor I was assailed with, it was a men's locker room, and I was glad I changed out of my linen clothing as this stench would never leave them. Staying incorporeal, I walked in the direction of loud music. Glancing up, I saw a neon sign, Erinyes' Fight Club, glowing through the large upper windows. "Nice name," I continued my quest to find the music. The single person exercising to pop music was the reigning women's mixed martial arts champion. The twenty-nine-year-old fighter was torturing the double end-striking bag to the rhythm of both the music and the dancing of the elastic cords holding the bag.

"It's about time you showed up." She grabbed the bag as a shadow projected on the wall next to her. "Who the hell are you?" she turned and, for a second, I thought she saw me.

"Who were you looking for?" A red-haired man with an X across his baby face asked as he walked through me. I really hate that.

"My sparring partner, Justin." She said.

"Good, I thought I was in the wrong place. Justin called my dad and asked me to step in for him tonight." I quickly scanned through my shades' recent reaping, finding her deceased sparring partner.

"No one told me. Ok fine, come on, we have around half an hour before I have to leave." She stepped toward the ring, which was already illuminated. "The gloves and headgear are over there. I'm Brunnhilde by the way." She pointed into the shadows.

"I know who you are, I'm a big fan. Call me Skeeze. These are all so small," the ginger said from the shadows. "Do I really need to wear the headgear?"

"State rules say we can't spar unless you do and I'm not giving up my title for you to not feel silly."

"Fine." The young man returned to the ring wearing the proper sparring attire, right down to the shiny, padded shorts.

"Ready?" She looked at the well-built guy getting in the ring, now shirtless, he even had muscles on his nipples.

"Ding-ding." He smiled and put in a mouth guard. They danced around for a while. As she hit him, he flexed and absorbed the shots. "Nice tattoo," he pointed at her chest-piece of a crow.

"It's my daughter, well, to remind me of my daughter. Throw a couple, don't just let me hit you." Her words were garbled yet clear. I shook my head not believing a girl could be so stupid and continued to watch.

"Ok," he threw a couple of soft jabs.

"Seriously? I have a title match coming up, I need—" her words stalled as his arm swept her guard away, sending her sprawling and he hadn't even hit her. "Damn, you're strong." She said as he helped her up.

"Ready?" he asked.

"Ding-ding." She smiled as he got into a fighter's stance and started forward.

"I can't watch this." I muttered, yet didn't turn my head.

"What did you mean by, remind you of your daughter?" He said.

"She died a while back. Come on!"

"Dead, ok, good." His punch toward her left cheek found air as she pulled her head and shoulders right. 'Crack', a gunshot sounded and her ear exploded.

"What the hell?" Brunnhilde put a gloved hand to her left ear. Skeeze followed up with a left jab, she dodged again, 'crack' a second gunshot and her right ear flew off in a flowering of blood.

"Now that hadda hurt." I watched in amazement as the woman remained standing.

"Why?" She looked at her white gloves, both covered in blood.

"Why is it good she's dead?" he asked.

"That, and why did you just shoot my ear?" Brunnhilde asked.

"Good because I like kids. The shots because the red and white have a bet with black and tan. Now, come on, Champ, let's do this." Skeeze grinned, throwing an uppercut that Brunnhilde easily pulled back from. The next 'crack' from the unseen gun whistled along the part in her hair, leaving a red trail behind.

"You sick bastard." She spun, connecting the back of her leg with the back of his, sweeping them from under him. She was on him in a heartbeat, throwing left and right haymakers into his grinning face. When it appeared she actually hurt him, he threw a head butt, shattering her nose.

I waited, knowing it wasn't going to be long now. He stood up, lifting her nearly unconscious form into a standing, albeit tottering position.

"Who are the red and white?" Brunnhilde asked.

"Good girl." I listened for new information.

"We are the red," he touched his chin with the thumb of his glove. "Our sister, Side, in this are the whites." This time, he touched his left eye.

"You're white." She said. I knew she was stalling, hoping someone would've heard the shots.

"Bitch, does this look white?" he shook his hand, allowing the glove from his left hand to skitter away, and touched his red hair between the padded helmet. "Red as fire!"

"Ok, you're a white ginger, so wha—" the hand still in the thinly padded glove connected under her left eye. She dropped to a knee.

"And the champ goes down." I did my best commentator voice, watching Skeeze throw off the second glove and reach for her.

"Oh no, not yet," he pulled her dark ponytail and for a moment, it looked like she would just let him pull it out. "Anyway, it's not about the quarters, it's about the Sides." He gave two jerking tugs on her ponytail, this time, she stood and spat in his face, he threw another punch. Without the padded glove, her eye burst open. The blood from Brunnhilde's forehead, ears, nose and now eye ran freely down her body. Surprisingly, she spat a second time. Using her entire body, she pulled free of Skeeze's clutching hand as he threw another punch at her face, she dodged it. 'Crack' the sound of the gun echoed as the small circle briefly separated the flowing blood down her forehead.

"Pug, you god damn idiot. Did I look like I was done with her?" Skeeze turned, looking at the red-haired guy who stood, pulling his hair back out of a ponytail. The X on his face was different than Skeeze's, it was colored red from the bridge of his nose down to his jawline. The red triangle gave him a perpetual frown.

The fifth 'crack' of the gun made the longhaired ginger smile, "Oh, and you were so close to passing your initiation." He mocked the fallen initiate as he packed up his rifle. I walked over to the fallen fighters.

When I was two feet away from the bodies, a ghostly figure jumped up and spat in my face. I had only seen one other soul launch from its body like this. As rare as it was, it startled me. "Asshole." Brunnhilde was shaking.

"Hold up, hold up, I'm not with them." I held my hands up in surrender.

"That hadda hurt... Eww, the champ goes down." She said in a pretty good impersonation of me.

"Wait, you heard me?" My confusion mounted and I took a step back.

"Yes, I heard you, I'm not deaf."

"Did you see me too?"

"Seriously? Are you completely stupid? Of course, I saw you."

This was new, in thousands of years, I had never been seen prior to a reaping. "Brunnhilde, I'm sorry to tell you but you're—" I started.

"Dead, yeah I kinda guessed that while leaving my body after getting shot in the forehead, you really are an idiot."

"Sweetheart, you do understand I can send you to hell to face perdition, right?" I asked coldly.

"Look at that." She grabbed my face, turning it toward her body. "You let that happen, you stood here and made fun while it happened, you're a monster." Even with the shouting, for the first time, I saw something other than anger in her, she was burdened.

"In that you're correct, I am a monster. I've seen more souls die than you can even imagine. Good people and bad."

"So, you've what? Become insensitive to it?"

"Most likely, yes. I—"

"Children look up to me. They see me as a role model. Do they need to see this?" she pointed at her dead body. It truly was a gruesome sight.

"I'm not the one who decides how you die. Just as I didn't have a say in how you lived."

"Then what's that?" she pointed at my right wrist. The souls of the tricksters that tried to play games with Death floated about it.

"Different." I stated flatly.

"Different my left ear, oh wait, I don't have a left ear, you let some sick bastard shoot it off while you made jokes. Were you ever human?"

"Brunnhilde, look, let me take you—" I tried to get the situation back in control.

"NO. Fix this." She made circles with her hands, "All of this."

"There's no fixing it, not then and especially not now."

"You never answered me, were you ever human?"

"I don't know, I honestly don't remember it if I was. Look, my job is stupid simple, I take the dead to their afterlife, be it perpetually hot or consistently perfect. There are NO do-overs."

"How do you know? Can't you try? For all the little girls that look up to me and for all the damage," again, she pointed at her corpse and paused. "That's going to do."

"The outcomes of all things to come are hinged on me not altering what the Fates have foretold. Mine is the hand of Death and none shall I sway from their demise."

"What the hell is that supposed to mean?"

"I don't know, I didn't write it, I think it was from Shakespeare or something."

"I'm not going." She crossed her arms and cocked her head, showing contempt for the situation.

"Don't say that, you don't understand what that truly means." I put all the authority in my voice I could, and then focused my thoughts, allowing her a view of those who ventured aimlessly around us. "The ghosts you see have no memories of life as a mortal, just an anger of not being, pushing them forward. You don't want to end up like that." As the ghosts started toward us, I focused them away again.

"I'm not asking not to die. I'm asking to die with a single shot." Her words echoed strangely in the empty gym.

"Wh..." I closed my eyes and pictured the scene, remembering the feelings I had at that moment, all the senses I experienced, right down to the smell. I concentrated, feeling the symbols on my palm grow cold. I looked down to see a strange blue glow growing brighter.

As if in reverse, it all played backward, the ghost jumped into her body, the bullet that killed Skeeze went back into the gun, the scene went faster and faster. The bullet that killed Brunnhilde, the punches into her face, her ears repaired, all the way back to Skeeze getting into the ring.

"Ready?" She looked at the ginger getting in the ring with a bit of disgust.

"Ding-ding." He smiled and put in a mouth guard. They danced around for a while. As she hit him, he flexed and absorbed the shots. "Nice tattoo," he pointed at her chest-piece of a crow.

"It's my daughter, well, to remind me of my daughter. Throw a couple, don't just let me hit you."

"Ok," he threw a couple of soft jabs.

"Seriously? I have a title match coming up, I need—" her words stalled as his arm swept her guard away, sending her sprawling and he hadn't even hit her. "Damn, you're strong." She said as he helped her up.

"Ready?" he asked.

"Ding-ding." She smiled, still looking at me as I began climbing into the ring.

"What am I doing?" I muttered.

"What did you mean by, remind you of your daughter?" Skeeze got into position.

"She died a while back. Come on!" Brunnhilde said.

"Dead, ok, good." His punch toward her left cheek found air as she pulled her head and shoulders right. Impossibly fast, I pushed her. 'Crack', a gunshot sounded and the bullet hit her in the center of her forehead. Brunnhilde crumpled to the ground dead, again.

"Pug, you idiot. Did I look like I was done with her?" Skeeze turned, looking at the red-haired guy who stood, pulling the rubber band from his ponytail.

'Crack' the gun bucked and the initiate dropped dead on the mat beside Brunnhilde. "Oh, and you were so close to passing your initiation." I watched Pug for a moment as he broke down the rifle and packed it.

"See, now the little girls will just think I was shot, and not defiled." Brunnhilde bounced on her toes.

"I didn't know I could do that. I don't even know if I should've done that." The pull, which I expected, came. When I ignored it, a shade stood at my side.

"That was pretty weird." Brunnhilde said.

"Take my hand." I held out mine and she took it. We appeared in a desert. I looked around, confused. She smiled and looked at a meadow in the center of burning trees, I heard the sound of hoofbeats and a large steed took air over us.

"Sigurd!" She released my hand and ran toward the young man, and I stood in the gym again.

I was alone with the memory I could make things different. People didn't need to live until the end of their torture. The images of all the people I let die screaming rushed through my mind, and I grew angry with myself. Angry for the dark humor of thousands of years. Angry for the uncaring attitude I showed the good people as they came to me afraid. I knew they deserved better. Angry for the excuses of not having the power to change it, when all along, I actually did. 'What else can I change?' I wondered. The sound of talking close by broke me from my revelry. I moved to find Pug on the cell phone.

"Look, I know that Sides wanted this punk initiated, but he totally screwed up the job. I had to end his miserable existence before he screwed up something important."

"Did you take care of him?" I heard the voice on the other end of the phone ask.

"Sur, he isn't wearing our colors." Pug replied.

"Dude, are you stupid? He's as ginger as you and I."

"Oh yeah, consider his X gone." He hung up the phone and walked back up toward the ring. "He's as ginger as you and I... Blah blah blah," he mimicked as he grabbed a wet towel from a clothes hamper. Getting in the ring, he avoided stepping in the blood as he bent over the body, "Not a bad shot," he smiled at the hole in the center of the dead boy's forehead. Pug moved Skeeze's head back and forth as he scrubbed the X from his face.

"Must be mascara or something?" I mused, continuing to watch him finish scrubbing. The sound of sirens in the distance caught his ear, he perked up and stopped his movement.

His cell phone rang and he almost jumped out of the ring. "Goddammit, what?"

"Get Skeeze's cell phone before you leave and don't you think about talking to me like that again." Sur said.

"Sorry, cops are on their way." Pug replied.

"Get it and get out. Did you take care of Skeeze?" Sur asked.

"I'm trying."

"What? Dumbass, just send him home."

"Oh yeah, I'm stupid." He scoffed.

"That's an understatement." Sur cut off the call. I grinned, seeing the look on Pug's face. I turned to see the lights getting closer. When I looked back, the well-built ginger was tip-toeing around the ever-spreading blood on his way to get the cell phone. Only Brunnhilde's body remained in the ring. I searched through memories of my shades, nothing. "Ok, what in the hell is going on?" The sound of Pug rummaging through Skeeze's discarded jeans, he removed the phone and his wallet. Starting to leave, he paused and began searching once more, this time in his socks and shoes.

"Ha." He pulled a watch and a ring from the shoe. "Always loved this ring." Pug stood up and walked out the back of the gym as the police sirens arrived at the entrance.

"Cut that pretty close." I said as I ventured up to the catwalk that surrounded the upper windows of the huge building. I watched the initial police come in and find the dead body. As the rest of the festivities occurred, I lost track of how many of my shades came and went. I watched until the woman, whose words had bitch-slapped me into understanding, made me realize I had more power in the way things played out than I ever thought. Now I just needed to determine whether this newfound knowledge was something that should ever be applied again.

My phone vibrated. Removing it from my pocket, I noticed a text message from Clotho Decimaskuld, my clothier, *'The last sweater you returned had an oddity to the thread I didn't recall from when I spun it. Be careful.'* I shut off the phone and decided I needed some cheesecake, so I teleported to the parking lot across from the diner. As I started to walk, a ringing in my right ear forced me to sit on the curb and cover my ear. When it finally subsided, I ran my hand through my hair and stood up.

Reaper's Revenge
Chapter Six - Cassiopeia

She stood at the cash register, thanking the patrons as they left. While some of her hair had escaped from the braid which fell to the middle of her back, she still looked as put together as Cleopatra on a good day.

"Ah, you're back for the cheesecake?" Cassiopeia asked when she saw the tall man walk into the diner.

"I told you I wouldn't miss it, I just had a life and death situation to deal with." Cloudan smiled, progressing past her and into the diner.

"You mean life or death?" She asked when she walked over with a menu a couple of minutes later.

"I'm sorry?" he looked up from his cell phone.

"You should be, I really hate people texting while I'm talking."

"Well then," he pushed the power button on the flashy piece of electronic wonder and tucked it into his pocket. "Better?"

"Much. Thank you." She handed the menu to him, "When you walked in, you said you were dealing with a matter of 'life and death'. The saying is life or death."

"Did I really? Must have been a Freudian slip, you see, I kill people for a living and—"

"Shut up, so do I." she smacked him on the shoulder. "What a kawinkydink. I'll be back with your warm tea in a minute."

"How did you know that's what I wanted?" Cloudan asked.

"First, your name is Cloudan. Second, though you've done well masking it, you still have a bit of a British accent." The thin girl walked away from the table with a huge smile on her face. As she waited on several other customers, she occasionally stole a glance at the man who saved her life the previous night. It had been a whirlwind of insanity. She couldn't stop thinking about how calm Cloudan had been. Handling the panicking group when they found Miss Mella and then when the crazy X-faced guy shot the reporter just feet from them.

"What do you have against my name?" He asked when she returned with his tea.

"I'm just playin' with ya. I can stop if you want." Cassiopeia replied.

"No, actually, I don't think I want you to." Only the corner of his mouth pulled up before he looked at the table.

"Good because I have an entire shtick about that scarf and that white streak you put in your hair."

"White streak?" he heard the comment about his infinity scarf and changed his comment, "Hey now, this was handmade for me by—" he started.

"You look like a douche."

"This side of douchie?" Cloudan held his thumb and index finger an inch apart. She shook her head and moved them closer together.

"About that much." She laughed, her hand was warm and he smelled cinnamon on her breath.

"Miss, could I get a check?" A woman sitting at a floor-mounted stool asked and then spun back to the counter.

"Absolutely, ma'am," she removed her hand, leaning in to whisper, "That's Urania. She's grouchy." Giving a wink, Cassiopeia walked over to the woman, searching for the check in the front pockets of her vintage diner uniform. As she stepped around the counter, two young men with pure white hair walked in, the Xs across their faces made her take an involuntary step backward.

"Sorry, didn't mean to spook you." The young man in the front gingerly reached a hand out, thinking she had slipped.

"It was entirely my fault. I was trying to find a check in these impossibly deep pockets. Please take a seat, I'll be with you momentarily."

"Thank you." They both said and went to sit.

"No rush, we have a third and he's parking our van." The one that had steadied her earlier said.

"Actually, Egg doesn't eat much, can we get—" the larger one started.

"Bebo, the young lady just said she'll be with us momentarily. Sorry, miss."

"Peia, they call me Peia." She said, walking back with menus.

"Pleased to meet you, I'm Dodger, this is Bebo and that steely-eyed rogue is Egg." He pointed to a man who definitely didn't look like a petite eater. The monster's shoulders barely fit through the opening after having ducked to not hit his chin on the door jam. His curly white hair went to the center of his chest and was emboldened by the strange powder-blue pearl color of his eyes and the left quarter of his face which was filled in with white.

"Give me a dozen eggs over easy, a dozen sausage links, six slices of toast and a cranberry juice." The deep voice carried across the entire diner, even though he spoke softly.

"Doesn't eat much?" she smiled at Bebo.

"Ok, that may have been a fib." He laughed.

"Miss, my check." The same woman demanded in a strong bitch voice.

"Right away, ma'am." Cassiopeia said over her shoulder.

"After she finishes taking our order," Egg softly replied.

"I was waiting for my check before you and your gang bangers even came in."

"Sorry about the delay." Cassiopeia handed the woman her check.

"I've got it. It was my fault she was delayed." Egg said.

"I don't think so." The woman reviewed the bill and dropped a twenty on the counter. "Keep the change." With a sneer, she leapt from the bar stool and stomped from the diner.

"And what will you have, Bebo?" The thin girl tried to get the now insulted group to forget about the foolish woman.

"Actually, Peia, I think I've lost my appetite." Egg glanced out the window at the departing patron.

"Friends," Cloudan said from the rear of the diner. "I must apologize for my ex-wife. You see, we just found out our only child has leukemia."

"She's your ex-wife?" Dodger asked.

"You weren't even sitting with her?" Bebo commented.

"She's a bitch, that's why the term EX comes before wife." The group all laughed. "Please let me buy your breakfast, I would hate for our troubles to affect your dining experience."

"Your offer in the midst of your tragedy is very moving, thank-you." Egg's voice carried to Cloudan.

"Ok then, Bebo, what can I get for you?" Cassiopeia asked, realizing that this man had just saved the life of another stranger. Two hours later, the 'Whites', as she had heard them refer to themselves throughout the night, had finished eating and Cloudan picked up the rather substantial check, adding a fat twenty percent tip.

"Good luck to you and your kid. Sorry I can't wish that bitch ex-wife of yours the same." Egg said and they walked out together.

Death's Journal – Distrusted Oracle

So many of the souls I've reaped over the years have had interesting tales associated with their living years. I've met a wide assortment of beings; evil, good and everywhere in between. But an oracle that was cursed to not have her prophecies believed was bizarre, even for me.

Most of the deceased have a very limited desire to communicate with me before I release them to whatever will come next for them. Today, however, Cassandra greeted me like an old friend desiring to hear how the years since we had last spoken had unfolded.

I did, however, need to coax her from her fallen body. "How did a daughter of Troy end up so far from home?"

"Several years ago, back in my homeland, I had fallen asleep in the temple of Apollo when I dreamt of a mighty snake entwining me." As Cassandra began her story, we appeared in a temple with a small girl in front of us.

"Who are you to s-s-sleep in s-s-such a plac-c-ce?" It hissed, looking into his victim's eyes.

"I'm the daughter of a king and Queen, a priestess of this temple, and as such, I've pledged a vow of life long chastity to Apollo." The girl's words came in small exclamations as the coils constricted. Her large brown eyes weld over.

"How does-s-s that give you the right to s-s-sleep here?"

"I've given my entire life to..." she remembered not finishing this statement.

"What was-s-s your reas-s-son to do s-s-such a thing? Nothing is-s-s done for nothing."

"And who are you to accuse me of ulterior motives?" Cassandra said as the snake laughed at her. When his laughter subsided, he unhinged his jaw and engulfed her as if she were no more than a rabbit.

"I remember my bones cracking as the snake pulled me into the darkness. I knew this would be my final living moment." The elder Cassandra said, looking up into my eyes.

"Vile being!" A deep voice carried to every inch of the shrine, including inside the snake's stomach. "Unless you release your hold on this girl, I will cut you open and take her from your corpse. Thereafter, I shall have the uniforms of all my priests and priestesses fashioned from the skins of your ancestors." She felt the muscles reverse and moments later, she sat beneath the statue of Apollo.

"I apologiz-z-ze for the mis-s-stake, Pries-s-stess-s-s. I've given you the gift of unders-s-standing prophec-c-cy to make up for my rude behavior."

"I want no gifts from you, snake!" The girl stepped away from the creature.

"Here is where I made the mistake that would change my life," the woman next to me pointed as the girl version of her cringed. "The discharge from inside the vile being, as Apollo called it, had dropped into my mouth," as she said this, the girl spat a green ooze from her mouth, which landed on the statue of Apollo.

"You dare spit upon my statue after I saved your miserable existence?" The carved edifice of Apollo came to life, grasping her face, forcing her mouth open and then spat into it. "The gift the snake had given you is now a curse upon you."

"A curse?" she asked the embodiment of the god she had sworn herself to.

"While you now understand prophecy, you will go through life seeing the events of the future and attempting to warn those around you. Yet no living being will believe your visions, you will be looked upon as a mad woman for all time." Apollo stepped back onto the plinth, retaking the form of a statue.

"I hate that self-righteous prat." I mumbled.

"Prat he may be but in regard to the curse, he accomplished exactly what he wanted to. Over the months and years to come, I went from merely being misunderstood by those around me to, as Apollo had said, being viewed as a truly mad woman. My father, King Priam, locked me in the temple room to keep me safe, and, of course, to save himself from humiliation. My twin brother was allowed to visit me. After much pleading from him and rejections from me, I caved in and taught him the art of scrying the future. Luckily, Apollo's curse didn't carry through to him and his visions weren't ignored." She smiled.

"We should move on from these memories." I held out my hand with its faint glow, which she stepped away from.

"Please, not yet, I want to tell someone that will believe me."

"Very well." I said.

"I saw many things, all but one of my visions were ignored as rantings. Oh, that they would've ignored my vision of Paris being my lost brother as well."

"Didn't that prophecy allow your family to reunite? Wasn't that a good thing?" I countered.

"Had Paris not been accepted as my brother and a Prince of Troy, he and Helen would never have met. She would never have ventured to Troy after the Spartan war, and all those lives would have been spared."

"You saw Helen as the cause to the war between Troy and Greece?"

"I did, I even attacked her when she stepped from the boat upon her arrival. Though the people all came to her defense." Cassandra said.

"But, Helenus, your brother. You said that you taught him to see the future as well. Why didn't he warn them of what would happen?" I asked.

"He joined me in warning Paris from venturing to Sparta, the fool ignored us both. When he saw everyone ridiculing me for the same predictions he was having, he wasn't going to offer himself up for that. Besides, I wouldn't allow it."

"What other visions did you have?"

"I saw the horse was nothing more than a trap."

"The horse?"

"The giant horse effigy, a gift of the Greeks. I saw it would open and spread death. My father and the rest of them continued their feasting. I even tried to burn it, the fools stopped me. I also saw the fall of our gods, and a war between other gods and a myriad of enemies like dead men, giants, and monsters."

"Interesting. Such challenges, yet you continued on." I offered some encouragement.

"Even through Ajax the Lesser's violation, I forced myself to move forward. Yet as my oath to Apollo was ruined through these actions, Eurpylus was never burdened with guilt for gifting me to King Agamemnon as a bed warmer for his cold trip back to Greece. Which, of course, is how you, lord of death, ended up before me. The king's wife, Clytemnestra, and her lover, Aegisthus, killed him in front of me. Before turning their blades on me."

"I see that you left a gift back in Troy which will repay Eurpylus for his kindness to the King." I commented.

"The chest?" She asked.

"Yes, lady, even now he opens it and his wits will be lost to him."

"He will get his mind back and save children in maidens from being sacrificed in the process." Cassandra lifted her eyes to me for the first time.

"I believe you." This time, she reached out a hand, which I took.

Reaper's Revenge
Chapter Seven - Cloudan

"Cloudan," Dodger stopped walking after we were all out of the diner, "You really seem familiar."

"We literally bumped into each other at the deli on Baker's Way a couple of days ago."

"Holy shit, I do remember." Bebo said.

"You guys got so damn lucky leaving when you did."

"How so?" Dodger asked.

"About two minutes after you left, there was a drive-by." I said.

"Actually, no, as we left, Oppie saw something and he chased them."

"Brave of him." I said.

"Dead of him." Egg replied, "Funeral's tomorrow. Surprising that all those bullets were fired and only one person died." Well, there's the answer, he was disappointed that he hadn't killed more.

"I'm so sorry to hear about your friend." I searched my shade memories for scooping up the soul of the White. Once again, nothing. Something completely off was going on.

"Nice of you to say, Cloudan, but some people aren't worth—" Bebo started.

"What the hell, dude? He was a White." Egg's hand shot out hitting the other, the resulting thump sounded as if he'd hit a bass drum.

"Well, almost." Dodger added.

"Yeah, almost a White and we'll see him off with respect."

"Sorry, Egg. You're right." Bebo did a good job not showing the pain he was in.

"We'll see you around." Egg offered his hand to me and I shook it. Surprisingly, he didn't try to crush mine. They got into their van and drove off.

"How in the hell didn't I feel the pull for that stupid kid?" I wondered aloud, walking onto the side street where, days earlier, I had made the wrecked car vanish.

My phone vibrated, I opened it and read the text, 'Your presence almost broke a thread. The cloth is showing many flaws in Destiny of late, you must appear before us for a fitting.' Clotho Decimaskuld's typical cryptic text was still reeling in my head when a thin voice captured my attention.

"Can you spare a few bucks, I'm rather hungry?" The same old man I saw by the dumpster a few days earlier asked.

"No, piss off." My standard reply felt forced, what the hell is going on? I refused to think about it, teleporting instead to New Orleans, more specifically, outside Clotho Decimaskuld's lavish boutique, Yggdrasil, a place known to few and frequented by even less. The entrance in the Corridor of Inevitable Outcomes is only visible to those who can pass the test of the living bronze jester. He sat at the corner of St. Ann and Decatur patiently waiting as the horse-drawn carriages past by with tourists, and those unlucky enough to stumble into a road apple, greeted the shoe shiner. "I need to see the swans of Uror." I whispered and dropped a twenty into his tip jar.

'Jingle.' The bells on his fool's cap rang out as he inclined his head, allowing the entrance to appear in the center of Jackson Square. A giant Ash with a makeshift bridge crossing the waters of Uror's well, and through the three elephantine roots supporting the tree above the still pool. Below the monstrous trunk, two swans swam, maneuvering around the roots without creating so much as a ripple, just as they had when the mythical tree along with the well resided in Asgard, the home of the Norse gods.

"Good morning, Holuspa. Good Morning, Havamal. Where's Nidhogg wrapping himself these days?" I tossed a handful of croutons to the progenitors of all swans and cautiously continued across the bridge.

"Thank you, Cloudan." They scooped the squares from the water.

"As always, he's hanging out by the root to Niflheim, but he's thinking about going to Jotunheim." a squeaky voice said from up on the trunk.

"Good morning to you as well, Ratatoskr. Did you say he was headed to Jotunheim? I wouldn't imagine a Wyrm would do well in the realm of ice and Frost Giants."

"The unnamed eagle said he didn't have the guts to go there for fear his frozen tail would make an ideal toothpick for one of them." The squirrel chattered.

"Let me guess, another secret you shared with him?" I asked.

"Now, Cloudan, would I do that?" Ratatoskr asked.

"I'm not accusing you of anything, I think Loki would have tricked him into becoming a toothpick, without an issue."

"The fact that you would even compare me to the Prince of pranks… Is an honor." He said.

"You haven't named that eagle yet?"

"Not my place in this, Cloudan."

"Did you tell him Ari like I said?" I asked, continuing to walk toward the trunk of the tree.

"He said to name him what he is would be foolish." Ratatoskr said.

"And remaining, 'The Unnamed Eagle' isn't?" Prior to my foot reaching the landing at the top, a door opened in the side of the tree and Ratatoskr scurried away.

"Come in, Cloudan. We've been expecting you." The shirtless man sitting alone among three chairs beside a loom sang. His prodigious girth would put a bull walrus to shame. Not a single hair could be seen on his glistening, oiled body as he held a thread outstretched from his left fingertip to his right nipple.

"Clotho?" I asked.

"You always get it wrong the first time. Your pandering amuses us." His voice, like a mother trying to calm an upset child, was melodic. As my eyes blinked, the man shifted to the seat on my right. Just as quickly, he held the thread between the blades of silver shears and away from his long beard which covered his dozen or so chins. "Well, I'm not amused by him at all, he knows very well you are Decima." His voice and apparel were now those of a small girl. The frilly collar of the dress curled out from under his fat earlobes.

"I'm sorry my poor attempt at repartee displeases you, Skuld."

"Enough, sister." The fat man now sat in the first seat, his voice that of an old woman with burned vocal cords from years of smoking unfiltered cigarettes, one of which hung from his lips. The greasy matted hair covering his head cascaded over his shoulders, leaving stains on the white tank top, commonly known to humans as a wife-beater. The ribbed material was stretched so thin, it was practically transparent. "What have you been up to, Cloudan?"

"Performing my duties." I replied.

"And perhaps more?" There was no delay in the question as the man went from my left to the far right, as the hair from atop his head melted down to his chin, and as the tank top flowed into the petulant girl's dress.

"Forgive me if I close my eyes," I did. "This rendition of you, Fates, is still difficult for me to grasp, seeing you as three women fighting over an eyeball was easier to follow."

"Oh, and this incarnation of you is—" Skuld started.

"Sister, this isn't the time for your old rivalry." Clotho coughed, I pictured her cigarette falling from her lips.

"You are, of course, correct, Uror."

"Sister, we need to maintain separation of the old worlds, call her Clotho. Please." Decima chided.

"You are correct, when my anger rises, I forget myself." Skuld replied.

"Cloudan," Clotho facilitated the conversation back on task. "Something has recently happened, the thread I have spun is not the same thread that Decima measured and Skuld cut."

"Sounds like you have a quality control issue."

"Consistent in any form you are in, you have a smart mouth." Decima's soothing voice could insult in a manner that it felt like a compliment.

"Have you had any strange challenges?" The voice behind me was familiar and I spun, opening my eyes.

"Alcestis?" The woman dressed in the black of mourning stood, "Nothing so challenging as the arm bar Heracles used on me to return you to King Admetus."

"Abomination!" The voices of the Fates shrieked, I turned and saw all three forms of the huge man almost confused in a continuous state of metamorphosis, from bald in a dress to shirtless with long hair and a beard.

"I will leave but, Cloudan, you must know all nine worlds feel something is amiss. You must pay attention to the signs of not only this plane, but the others as well."

"Go!" Decima yelled and the strong wind came from inside the boutique, blowing the veil from the face of the woman in the entrance, revealing sadness incarnated.

"Those that have lost the chance to die have no place here." Skuld screamed. The figure vanished. I also took the hint and allowed the next pull for reaping to depart. A car was headed for a 16-year-old girl, Dana, as I appeared.

"Not today." I concentrated to stop the vehicle's progress. I bent over to lift the girl, finding myself frozen.

"Cloudan, I want you to watch the specifics of what your actions will do." Skuld's voice echoed in the area. Events began to progress at what may have been 100x speed. The girl left the near accident, learning that life was short. She returned to school and promptly worked at stealing her best friend's very religious boyfriend, Jasper. Years moved forward, she broke the boy's heart and left him. The vision at that point split away from Dana and followed Jasper for a few years as he started to drink, lost his job, and eventually became so disenfranchised that he assassinated the Pope when he visited America. The events zoomed out further, the Newspaper headline, 'Jasper David Shaw kills Pope', the Pope's funeral, political leaders speaking out against Americans, and the first bombs going off at several populated American events. Ending with the mobilization of troops launching into what appeared to be WWIII. "Cloudan, everything you change has an effect on the world. This action, as you can see, will have vastly larger repercussions than just changing the way a fighter dies."

"Christ." I walked away, stopping when I was clear of the oncoming car's path and released time. Dana's eyes found mine just before the car reached her. I stepped up holding my hand out to the child. "Dana Murtain, please come to me." For some reason, I closed my fist over the glowing symbols.

"I would rather not, I saw you consider saving me. You allowed me to die." She said through her sobs.

"Dana, I saw some…"

"I don't care what you saw, you gave me hope for a moment." Dana stepped from her husk.

"You can still join your family, take my hand. Hate me later." I attempted again.

Before the glow began, she asked, "What did you see?"

"If I'm 100% honest, will it help you?"

"It would," Dana looked at her body, lying in the road.

"I saw the death of a Pope and World War III, caused by the way you treated someone after changing your life after I saved you." I held out my hand and allowed her to see the magic pulsing, "This is the last time I can reach my hand to you."

"Ok." She took my hand and we appeared in a mountain retreat at a large family gathering.

"Dappers!" An old man in ugly shorts said.

"Doppos!" She waved with her off hand. "I don't hate you." Her hand released from mine and I stood outside the deli where I had left the man with his hand out earlier. I wiped my eyes and started to walk from the alley.

"So, how about it, do you have some spare money for a hungry bum?" the old man said walking from the shadows.

"I do but how could I be certain you'd buy food with it? I could, however, go around the corner to the diner and get you something."

"Ha, that's the best blow-off line I've ever heard." The old man said. "Two points."

"Perhaps not, this city is going to shit."

"I thought that was you. I'm Devon by the way." He proffered a hand.

"Cloudan, I'm pleased to meet you. See you in a moment." I walked away, leaving him wondering.

Reaper's Revenge
Chapter Eight - Cassiopeia

"Oh, you came back." Cassiopeia walked up.

"I did, you're most observant, *Peia*." Cloudan grinned.

"They look out for me. Fake talent scouts and pretend agents like to prey on pretty little girls. Besides, there's a Calli here already and it would get confusing to have a Cassi. So, Peia it is." She stood with a hand on her tilted hip.

"Makes sense. Hey, wait, I thought I was the only pretty thing out at night."

"Ah that's true, but you see, I'm not out." Correcting her posture and standing straight-backed, she took out her pad of paper. "More cheesecake?"

"Only if you can magically turn it into chicken noodle soup."

"You shouldn't say that too loud, the cook may actually try."

"Oh, ok. May I have two bowls of chicken noodle soup to go? I'll need two spoons as well, please."

"Of course." She headed off and returned minutes later with a bag much too large for two bowls of soup.

"I didn't actually need two crockpots of soup."

"Well, I'm assuming this is for Devon, the bum in the alley, and the girl he's looking after, Cheyanne."

"Observant and perceptive," Cloudan replied and then closed his eyes as if a wave of dizziness hit him.

"Are you ok?" Cassiopeia reached out a steadying hand.

"Fine, thank you for asking." he held out a hand for the check.

"On the house." She waved her hands in front of her.

"Peia, you have another visitor." Calli said from the front of the diner.

"Be right there, Calli," when she turned, the tall man placed three folded hundred dollar bills on the table.

"For goodness sake, it's Detective terrible jacket, is there a back way out of this place?"

"I'll show you," she pointed at the table. "This is too much."

"You had better pick it up or someone else will. Use it to get your car out of the shop, you'll need it." He said, heading in the direction of the alley.

"I didn't say my car was in the shop, and what do you mean, I'll need it?" the thin girl inquired as she chased him into the alley and straight up to where the old man sat.

"Hello again." Devon said. "I didn't know if you'd be back, and hello to you, Peia."

"Hello, dear, how is she feeling today?"

"Cheyanne? Strong as an ox." He said while taking the bag from Cloudan.

"Peia, are you coming in to meet with this police detective?" Calli's voice called from the doorway.

"I'll be right there." She replied but as she did, the tall handsome stranger said something she couldn't make sense of.

"Devon, I'm here for Cheyanne."

"You can't have her, she's—" he started.

"She's sick, I know. That's why I'm here."

"The soup, it'll make her better. You'll see." Tears rolled down his cheeks.

"You know it won't, Devon, not this time. But, the cheesecake may make her give you one last smile." Cloudan pointed to the bag.

"What did you manage to get us today?" the girl was no more than sixteen with lungs full of pneumonia, making her sound old and frail.

"Soup, bread, and cheesecake." He said.

"Not that terrible cherry kind from the diner?" The girl pulled up her nose and started to cough.

"No, the white chocolate raspberry kind your Mena used to make. You remember, with the crushed dark chocolate crust?"

"Um, Cloudan?" Cassiopeia tried to interject.

"Seriously?" Cheyanne took the container from the bag and opened it. The street light illuminated the styrofoam container. "Oh my goodness, it is. Thank you!"

"Don't thank me, he told me it was your favorite." She looked at the old man with teary eyes and gave him a hug, breaking into another coughing fit.

"Can't you take me instead?" He looked over his shoulder as he hugged the girl.

"Um, Cloudan?" Again, Cassiopeia tried to get his attention.

"It doesn't work like that, no."

"Take you instead of what?" Cheyanne asked

"Eat your pie, sweetheart." Devon leaned her back against the wall. When her coughing stopped, she took a couple of bites.

"It's really good, thank you." Cheyanne smiled up at Cassiopeia and the old man, the crushed cookies in her teeth making her look even younger and more childlike. She leaned against the wall and her eyes closed.

"Cheyanne, I call you forth." Cloudan held his hand out to the girl.

Reaper's Revenge
Chapter Nine - Cloudan

Cheyanne's essence rose from her body. Before I grasped it, I saw Devon and Cassiopeia locked in frozen grief, staring at the dead girl. I shook my head at how close I was to revealing myself. 'Idiot,' I thought and took the small hand in mine.

"Why is your hand glowing?" Cheyanne asked.

"It's my death magic, I guess you could say." As I spoke, she turned my hand over, looking at the symbols that could have been burned in eons ago, I didn't even remember.

"What do these mean?" she touched the symbols.

"You're quite inquisitive. They each have a literal meaning, 'Need, Harvest, Human, and Death', I think it's my ID card."

"The Grim Reaper."

"Precisely." I smiled at her and we appeared next to a cabin along the banks of a small but fast-moving river.

"What? How?" Cheyanne asked.

"This is the cabin where you spent the better memories of your life." As I said this, the screen door creaked open. An old man with a bulbous nose walked out and looked over at us.

"Poppy!" She ran across the grass and leapt into the air. I turned away before he caught her, other souls needed harvesting tonight.

Having learned long ago never to rematerialize where I helped the dead to their resting, my invisible visage was across the street from the alley. Dumbstruck to be staring at detective Delphinios already talking to Devon and Cassiopeia, I waited and listened. "He was a tall, thin, good looking guy?"

"Yeah, and he had on a blue and black sweat—" Devon started.

"I told you, detective, it was Cloudan!" Cassiopeia interrupted.

He held up a finger to her and she stepped into the shadows, "And you said he held out his hand, she died, and then he disappeared? You actually saw him disappear?"

"Not exactly. I offered for him to take me," Devon's tears started again.

"You already said that. Did you see him touch her?"

"No, he was behind me, well, us, but he took her and vanished." The old man said.

To the side, Cassiopeia held her arms tightly across her chest, rocking side to side. "Yeah, how the hell can someone just vanish? And then she was holding this," she held one of my stones in her left hand. "What the hell is it? Who the hell can do that?" She interjected, ignoring the finger still raised to her.

I didn't like the tone of the conversation, I gave her a slice of cheesecake! This cop was really starting to piss me off. After seeing Alcestis, I simply haven't been able to think straight. A pull came and I ignored it, guilt was biting me like a weaning puppy and I gave up thinking puppies were cute a long time ago. I turned and started to walk, teleporting to Trafalgar Square in London. Sometimes people-watching helped me to get out of my headspace, "What else can I change?"

"Pardon?" A busker in front of four giant lions asked.

"I said, if I can change the way someone dies, what else can I change?"

"Useless Grockel. If it's all to pot, just take a step back and figure where it went tits up, then ask who it was that tol' ya it 'ad to be that way,' Easy as pie." He replied.

"Grockel? I'm not a tourist." I replied, tossing a Cockney brogue back at him.

"Rest stands mate." The busker plugged his guitar in, "Now, piss off. Oh, tips are scrummy." He pointed to the guitar case.

"Sure," I threw a 20-pound note into his case. As I walked away, I tried to remember who told me the rules of reaping. Then laughed aloud, "Rules." I increased my pace, opening myself to the lost-ones, ignoring the begging of clusters that gathered until I saw the ghost of a man sitting by himself. "Back, now!" the majority did, allowing my path to the individual man to clear. Taking no notice of the looks from the living. I asked, "Who were you in life?"

"I was Keradeg, I fought in the service of King Athelstan in the Battle of Brunanburh."

"Did you die there?"

"I was wounded there, aye. It was here that the sweats took me." He replied.

"Tell me, Keradeg, what do you see before you?" I ordered.

"You, Lord Ankou." He replied.

"Why did you not come with me last time we met?"

"I believed not that I had died. I thought you nothing more than the trickster, trying to steal my soul." The warrior stood and looked around. "I've sat in this very spot since the moment I realized I had been wrong. Can you take me home, Lord Ankou?"

"I honestly don't know. Keradeg, come to me." I reached out my hand and forced the symbols to spark to life. They did, but in an orange hue I had never seen. With this new glow, the call to where he needed to go overwhelmed me as never before. His hand grasped mine and a small village appeared before us, of people sitting in a circle around a statue of the warrior, holding hands.

"My husband, where have you... how did you..." the woman seated in front of the statue's face took several tentative steps.

"He became lost on the journey home," I said. "Please forgive me that I could not find him sooner." I released his hand when the woman embraced him.

I appeared at the edge of an area known as the Burrows by the locals, due to a failed five-star restaurant that still stood in all its splendor, an illuminated monument to a better time. "I'd wondered when I'd see you lot again." Looking through the window at four waif thin men, their tan hairstyles varied but they shared the same X across their faces. The shooter of the reporter, the driver, and the passenger in the van that T-boned me in the mustang. Two of them were restraining a female mime, bizarrely enough. "I thought I'd seen everything." I went over to join their party.

"Ornatanro, what in the name of the forest mother is going on?" The driver of the van from earlier asked as I glided through the wall.

"Listen, I told you the contest is simple, the women need to die in a specific order." Ornatanro replied. The tan color paint from the tip of his nose in a triangle up and over his forehead gave him a bird-like quality. His head twitched as small spasms of irritation hit him, adding to his bird-esque appearance.

"Why?" the shooter asked, his tan hair was long but pulled into a man bun.

"Alirila, even if I was answering to the Leshy, I would say the same thing... I don't know the plan, only the rules. The teams are informed who is to be killed on the list. When one of the teams marks a target, they have to kill them before the next target can die. That reporter was supposed to die last, or close to it." Ornatanro said.

"But we get the points, right?" Alirila asked.

"Ornatanro, what kind of goofed up initiation is this?" One of the two not holding the mime who I had not seen before asked.

"A fairly short one." He then pulled a gun from under his long waistcoat, shooting all three of his companions directly between the eyes. "Yes, we get the points. You just don't get it! We don't kill anyone without permission," he looked at the earlier speaker. "And you two are no better than Ajatar! You failed our lady by losing him and letting him mess up her plan." His chiding of the dead men completed and the gun holstered before the bodies had even known they were dead.

'Our lady?' I pondered the comment. I waited but there was no pull for these three as their bodies melted into the floorboards. 'No souls, no souls again.'

"What the hell?" the mime jumped back.

"I knew you could talk." Ornatanro said coldly.

"What ah just happened to ah them?" she asked in the broken English of an Italian.

"Don't play stupid with me, Thaila, they went home."

"How ah, do you know my name?"

"I tell you what, if you can make me laugh, I won't kill you." Ornatanro said.

"Well, this just got even more interesting." I crossed my arms and waited.

"I, ah, don't understand." Her head rocked back as the bullet found the same spot at the bridge of her nose and between the eyes as the three other victims. This time, the crumpled body had a soul and the pull came.

"I really am a great shot," the last of the Tans said while holstering his pistol.

"Thaila, I call you forth." I reached out my hand to her, palm down. The moment we began our departure, I glanced a figure in black outside the window, looking in. The brightness of the sun shining on the hills of a vineyard was overpowering.

"This, ah, is my father's vineyard." She turned and looked at me. In my distracted state, I said nothing. "Who are you and, ah, how did we get here?"

"I, my dear, am the embodiment of Death. This is where you will spend your afterlife." I felt the shadows sensing us, and they started to take form beneath the vines.

"There must ah be a mistake. I've ah spent my life making people laugh."

"Mimes don't make people laugh, they're actually creepy. Besides, that isn't why you're here, patricide is an unforgiv—"

"Are you joking? My father beat and forced himself on my mother routinely, not to mention what he did to women in his employ, and other women in the village he did the same to, or worse." All trace of the accent was gone.

"I don't make the determination where you spend eternity, the higher powers judge you. Did you know those men that killed you?"

"Screw you, as if I would sleep with beings like that!" The shadows formed into a man in his forties, his meaty hands reached out, closing around her arm. "Please, don't let him take me!" Memories of a tortured childhood flooded into the forefront of my mind. I could smell the burned skin after the man had put a cigar out on an older woman I assumed was her mother. I could taste the tears mixing with snot running down Thaila's face and into her mouth as her mother's unconscious body lay naked across her lap.

Her memories cleared from my thoughts as the shadow pulled her from my grasp. I returned. "Are you kidding me with that one?" I closed my eyes and looked up into the heavens. "Anyone would've killed that vile dog for what he did! To hell with your stupid doctrines; people are more confused than your unwavering gospels understand. Can't you see that? Can't you change?" I stopped screaming and remembered the black figure outside and bolted from the building. In the side alley, I allowed myself to become visible as I walked onto the sidewalk in the front of the building and promptly stepped in a huge pile of dog shit. "Seriously? I mock the heavens and this is my punishment?" Laughing, I scraped the foul-smelling substance from my shoe and onto the curb. When I saw it was useless, I took a step back and summoned a new set of clothes; two-tone black, vertical striped pants with a loose-fitting two-tone black horizontal striped dress shirt, and simple flat black shoes. My wrist was once again adorned with a charm bracelet.

My mind led me back outside the diner looking in at Cassiopeia, wondering what in the hell was going on. When a supernatural being such as Death is the most normal thing on the streets, this world is going to hell in a handbasket. I subtly checked with a few of the patrons walking out of the diner to see if I was invisible to them. "Hey, you useless piece of future worm food, can you see or hear me?" Satisfied, I ventured in and straight up to the coffee stand where Cassiopeia was talking to her cliché 70's sitcom waitress co-worker.

Reaper's Revenge
Chapter Ten - Cassiopeia

"**Peia,** you need to snap out of this." Calli said, patting and reshaping her hair.

"I know." She said.

"I'll tell you this, sugar. You haven't been so *blah* since before I told you about that acting class my neighbors were taking. More to the point, it was definitely prettier in here when you were getting visits from the incredible disappearing man." She winked and chomped her gum.

"True." Cassiopeia smiled, "Back to the moths." She fluttered her hands like wings, flying away from her co-worker and back to her customers.

"Kid," she tapped her watch, "You have to go to that acting class."

"He's not gonna show." She said.

"Well, if you don't go, you'll never be able to get passed whatever you thought you saw." Calli shot back.

"Devon told me the same thing." Cassiopeia replied.

"Sure, and didn't he see the same thing you thought you saw? You need to at least ask him where he went."

"Gotcha." She said. "If he shows, I promise I'll ask." She tossed her apron under the wait stand and headed out.

"Are you certain we still have class?" Orphe asked twenty minutes later as Cass walked up.

"I told you, after the issue with Miss Mella, Cloudan told me he was..." she started.

"Issue? You just referred to Miss Mella getting murdered as nothing more than an issue." Lin cut her off.

"I'm not your old teacher," Cloudan opened the theatre door. "Over-acting is not allowed."

"Looks like you were right, again." Orphe said.

"I didn't mean to leave you standing." The subtle apology covered both situations to Cass.

"Shit happens." She pushed her way in, "We need to get to work."

"Ok then." They all walked down to the front. "Lin, I believe you are first."

"Oh, I'm well... ok, fine." She stepped up the stairs and waited.

"No lights or outside bullshit. I want you to run through the dialog. Oh, and I want to see your face at all times."

"Excuse me?"

"I'm not here to help you run around the stage. I'm here to make you understand how the message you're conveying needs to be directed. I won't interrupt you when you go through it the first time." Cloudan said.

"Ok, so my scene is..."

"Lin, if I can't figure out what it is about without you setting it up, this isn't the right scene for a single-person show." He said.

"Oh, I guess that makes sense." She blushed. "I'm sorry."

"No reason to apologize." Cloudan replied.

Lin looked at the stage and took a deep breath. "It's the dreams of your kisses that make me stay awake until I pass out. Every night, I know you'll be there, making me remember what we had and what I threw away. When I wake and look at myself in the mirror, I'm disappointed to find I'm one of those people who felt no shame or regret that I broke your heart. But why? Because I couldn't face the changes that I needed to make, that I should've made. My fist-like grip on addictions which I chose not to release. Feeling they were more important than love, real love.

The largest of which, the cuts on my legs that I want to stop adding to, until the song of my knife calls to me again. Why can a blade make me feel alive when oftentimes I don't? Why do I judge my every action so harshly that each disappointment manifests into new physical scars, again and again? The lines that let me know I will never be worthy of a true connection. With the difficulty of commitment set aside, I need only seek the temporary fulfillment of the blade, which will eventually dull as well. Why could I not accept your love, relinquishing the glow of future scars, and the shine of the blade? My lamentations sequestered, for my unworthiness requires tribute to be paid, once more, by a glinting blade." She looked at the stage and waited.

"Christ, Lin," Cloudan's eyes were wide open in surprise.

"That's not really a proper response, Cloudan." Cassiopeia chided.

"No, I suppose not, I honestly didn't expect that. It was really good," He said.

"I think that was a compliment." Cass held a thumb in the air.

"I think so too." Lin smiled.

"Only real pointers I have, if you are standing still to your audience, try not to rock in place. So, do you have lights and other such 'justificatif'?" he threw a French accent on the final word.

"Sorry?" the girl blushed in her confusion.

"Lights, sound effects... to support your presentation." Cloudan's arms gestured wildly.

"I'm the only one who added that crap to my scene. I didn't know how else to make it play out." Cassiopeia said.

"Then maybe we can add some theatrical pauses to allow the audience to understand you're not using a metaphor. You're not actually a cutter though?"

"No? Should I go again?" Lin asked.

"How about if Orphe and Cassiopeia run through theirs first." He replied.

"My turn then?" the boy stood and walked up to the stage.

"Yes, sir." Cloudan rolled his shoulders and sat up straight.

"Good job, Lin." He high-fived her on the way past.

"Thanks. Break a leg."

Orphe stepped to the edge of the stage and took a ragged breath before looking down, and then looking into the audience. "Sandy isn't going to tell me why I'm not the right guy for her. Just like Veronica, Tina, Daisy, and Judy didn't. They just broke up with me and moved on. When I look at their social media pages, which none had the intelligence to remove me as a friend from, they have new love interests. What is a love interest?" He looked at the palms of his hands, trying to determine the difference between them. "Critical thinking tells us that we need to be able to question what we read, everything we hear, and absolutely everything we see. An intelligent person does not simply accept things at face value. We ask, 'what?' 'Where?' 'Who?' And even 'When?'" He turns his hands over, still searching for something. "If you find something that seems odd or out of place, an inquisitive person can't stop without looking again. We ask, 'how and why?' Turning stones over and replacing them with new ones, and asking, 'what if?' Sometimes we can get caught up with the analysis of things, why couldn't I make them happy? How can I change and become the person they need me to, in order to fulfil them? Or what if that new love interest wasn't around anymore? Pushing you... ugh, me, to ask the final question. What do I need to do next?" He looked down again, this time his left hand held five smooth stones, which he rolled in various patterns. "And who gets which stone?"

"Twist ending, nice. Maybe Miss Mella was better than I gave her credit for." Cloudan said.

"No. Actually, Cassiopeia has been the primary coach in the class." Lin said.

"You shower me with too much praise," Cass swooned. As she did, the lights in the entire theatre went out.

"I wonder if the police told the power company that Miss Mella died?" Orphe asked.

"More likely, Miss Mella forgot to pay the electric bill?" Lin added.

"Everyone, follow me. Get your cellphones out and let them light the way. Apparently, there are no emergency lights here either. That's a code violation and a half." Cloudan led them all outside, closing the door behind them. "Lin, Orphe you did great."

"Thanks." They both said.

"Do you have a ride home?" he asked.

"I drove us both," Lin pointed at the small two-seater across the road.

"Did you drive?" Cloudan looked at Cassiopeia.

"I walked. My car is back at the diner. It's only..." She started.

"I'll walk with you, I'm not going to have one of my students get killed by an X-faced hooligan on my first night teaching."

"Good call." Orphe said, "I'd offer for her to sit on my lap, but we all know what would happen."

"Orphe!" Lin punched him on the shoulder, "Pervert!"

"What? I was saying she'd fall in love with me and her life would be ruined. What were you talking about?" He leaned away from her and grinned.

"Come on, let's go." She walked off in the direction of the car, a sliver of the conversation trailed back, "That is not what you meant…"

"Are they related?" Cloudan asked after the arguing pair were in the car.

"Yes, brother and sister. Oh, hey, you got rid of the white stripe in your hair. Good call. You know I really can walk back to the diner myself. Besides, if we see a dead body, you'll just disappear." She poked as they began walking.

"Come on, that's hurtful! I already apologized for leaving you alone." Cloudan retorted.

"You did? When exactly did you do that?"

"When I opened the door to the theatre. What did you think I meant?" he raised an eyebrow.

"Well, I thought it meant sorry for leaving us waiting to start the class." Cassiopeia said.

"That was just being fashionably late." His lopsided grin came out, tickling her forgiveness.

"Speaking of fashionable…" she started.

"Here we go." Cloudan stopped and put his hands on his hips.

"What? I was just gonna say you look pretty tonight." She said.

"Pretty?"

"I mean, shit, I can't say handsome, you're wearing a blouse." Cassiopeia rolled her eyes.

"It's a custom-made shirt." He replied.

"With a charm bracelet." She grabbed his hand and looked at it, "Actually, that's kinda cool. Did you hear that?" she stood up straighter.

"What?" Cloudan stopped and listened.

"A cat." Cassiopeia walked up to the storm drain, "There's a cat stuck down there."

"Good, I hate cats."

"Cloudan?" she waited.

"Close your eyes." He said.

"What?"

"If you don't close your eyes AND turn around, I'm walking away." Cloudan said.

"Fine." Cass closed her eyes.

"And turn around," As she started to turn, he became incorporeal, dropping through the drain cover and seeing the cat that actually was stuck in a small trap someone had put down there. He pulled it into his plane and then returned to the street. The cat hissed loudly when he returned to proper form.

"Oh my god." She said, turning around. "How did you… Never mind, I don't care. We need to let it out."

"You'll need to do it, I don't save cats."

"You just…" she stopped and leaned over the cage as the creature almost turned itself inside out, howling, spitting, and scratching at the bars. "Maybe we can leave it here for animal control." Taking a tentative step back, "it may have rabies, and we don't want an innocent kid to get hurt."

"I told you, I hate cats." Cloudan started walking away.

"Beshee!" the voice of a small girl cried out. "You got her out!" She ran up and threw her arms around Cloudan's legs. "Thank you, thank you, thank you." She let go, grabbed the cage and was gone, just like that.

"I hate kids even more than cats! For god sake, look at my pants." There was a dirty face print on his thigh. "What the hell was the child into?"

"Storm drain goo I suppose, maybe even old kitty litter." She said.

"Don't you laugh, these pants cost..."

"Oh, don't be that guy!" Cassiopeia threw her hands up and walked away.

"I ruined my shoes and slacks, but you call me that guy?"

"Duh!" she shrugged.

"Maybe I should just leave you to the soulless X-faced guys while I clean up." He mocked.

"Soulless, what does that even mean? Of course they have souls, black as the darkest ebony." Cassiopeia said as he caught up.

"Same thing." Cloudan replied as they turned the corner next to the diner.

"Why did you freak out when Lin gave her one-woman show?"

"It was really dark, she doesn't look dark. Bitchy, but not dark." He said.

"What do you mean dark?"

"You're just goofing on me, like you did Miss Mella that first night I saw you."

"You could tell?" she asked.

"Um, you're not that good an actress." Cloudan struggled to hold in a laugh.

"Why did you ask her if she was a cutter?" Cass stopped and looked at him as they arrived across the street from the diner.

"Too much detail for someone to share. It just of easily could've been Orphe, but one of them understands that song." He attempted to brush the face print off his pants in the street light.

"Now look who's dark. It's mustard, you can't wipe it off."

"Oh, man, you're right." He stopped wiping.

"How much were they?"

"I'm not telling you, I don't want to be that guy."

"When you're asked, you can answer. That guy offers the cost of everything, whether he's asked or not." Cassiopeia replied.

"Good to know, they were $800.00." Cloudan averted his eyes.

"That's not too bad." She shook her head.

"Really?" he raised his eyebrow and looked at her.

"No, not really! That's more than I made in the last two weeks." Cassiopeia slugged him in the shoulder.

"You know you do that a lot." Cloudan said.

"Punch people?"

"Yes, quite aggressive."

"Oh, does little ol' me scare the tall, dark stranger?" she put her hands together as if making the church's steeple from the kid's game. Placing her index fingers under her chin, she batted her eyelashes innocently.

"I wasn't going to lie." Cloudan replied. When she looked confused at his change of topic, he went on, "The price of the pants, I wasn't going to lie about it."

"Ok, I'll give you that." She stopped and squared up to him. "Can I ask you about Cheyanne?"

"If I promise to explain it in full detail at some time in the near future, can I get you to trust that I didn't hurt her?" he asked.

"I'll consider it." She turned and walked into the diner, leaving him there with an open mouth.

Reaper's Revenge
Chapter Eleven - Cloudan

I looked around at the empty streets as I walked. I marveled at how the visual barrage during the daylight hours transformed into an olfactory attack when the sun went down. I watched Cassiopeia walk into the diner, chuckling to myself about her departure. I considered following her in, but then I saw that asshat lead detective. I changed my destination and walked around the deli into the alley to see Devon.

"Devon, how are you holding up?" I asked.

"Fine, I still wish you could've taken me. By the way, that self-righteous prat cop just walked into the diner." The old bum replied.

"I saw him. She's happy where she's at, that's not just words. I promise you."

"I trust you wouldn't lie about that." He wiped a tear. "So, what did you need?"

"Wait, what?" I asked.

"You didn't come over here to smell my lovely breath," he grinned. "Or give a buddy a hug."

"Do you want to make a few bucks?"

"Of course, booze costs money and I love booze. Especially now that I'm not taking care of..." he paused, "Who do you need me to kill? That cop?"

"Nothing like that. I just need a little delivery," I explained what I needed and gave him two hundred dollar bills. I feel two pulls, both in the same direction. I take it as a hint and follow.

The destination this time was a small observatory on the outer edge of the city. Years ago, a local college took money from a rich alumnus and built it. He did it primarily to assuage his guilt for all the terrible things he did in life. He may have been guilt-free but that bastard is still frying for his sick actions. As I lope through the halls looking at the photos lining them, I feel a third and then a fourth pull close to me and I continued walking forward. I found the two who had already died lying on the steps leading to the stage. They were no more than girls, maybe twelve years old. I sent my shades to assist them.

"They didn't have to die if they'd just listened." Romeo was standing with his black quarters, yelling at Egg, Bebo, and Dodger.

"I don't even know why you're here." Ricky added.

"Yeah, why are you here?" Romeo asked.

"We obviously didn't hit our target, why are you?" Egg said.

"We were told the hit was happening, so..." he swept his arm, taking in the room. "To our surprise, the doors opened and the woman who was supposed to be dead let our mark in."

"Look, we delayed our hit, we had an opportunity to get a free meal, so we figured 'what would the harm be postponing a few minutes?' We knew where she worked." Egg pointed at Urania.

"What?" the woman scurried away, hiding at the side of the stage.

"How could we know you'd go shooting innocent little kids if we let her get to work?" Bebo added.

"Butterfly effect biting your conscience?" Ricky asked.

"Piss off!" Egg shot back.

"Well, if you did what you committed to, those little ones would still be standing on the street. Ricky would've hit the teacher bitch out there." Romeo yelled.

"I said, piss off." Egg picked up and threw Romeo up onto the stage and through the podium, turning it into kindling.

"Enough, just do it already, the order in these two doesn't matter." A woman's voice ordered from over the auditorium speakers.

"Don't hurt Miss Poly!" One of the girls cried out just before Ricky's gun fired. The woman standing protectively between the X-faced intruders and the children in the audience fell over, dead. I called another of my shades as Ricky walked up to the observatory's stage and helped his fellow black up.

"Can we take their mark since they got hungry?" Romeo asked and then stood up, pulling his arms out of the helping hand.

"Screw you." Egg shot Urania who was still cowering at the side of the stage. Wanting to see this play out, I allowed a shade to cover her reaping. "Who the hell do you think you are?" Slowly and steadily, he turned the gun on Ricky shooting him twice. As if reading Egg's mind, Dodger shot Romeo. Nothing, I felt nothing at all.

"We ain't killin' you," Egg poked Alouc in the chest, sending him sprawling. "Because you didn't kill the kids." Dodger said.

"Romeo didn't kill the kids either." He said from the ground.

"He condoned it. Do you?" Dodger sighted his pistol on the last of the blacks. A scream from the children in the audience surprised me, so I looked at them and followed the direction of their scared faces. Ricky and Romeo were melting into the stage.

"Be on your way." The woman spoke over the speakers again.

"As you say, Sides." The four remaining men went off in two directions. Alouc turned two or three times, looking first where his fallen comrades had been and then at the innocent dead girls Ricky had killed.

"Children, stay in your seats, the police will be here soon." The voice ordered over the speakers.

Deciding to follow Alouc into the quiet streets where I cast my shades out, finding no police notification of this shooting were in the works. I watched to see which direction the short man was heading in and then ducked out of sight. Taking a corporeal form again, I concentrated summoning the cell phone I had seen Urania use at the diner and then dialed 911. When I heard the operator answer, I dropped it outside the front entrance to the observatory. Vanishing again, I ported ahead to catch my quarry. Despite the length of his legs, he was keeping an insanely good clip. So, I cheated a bit. As I said before, it's good to be me. He stopped and entered a vacated subterranean parking center without turning on any lighting.

When I passed through the opening, all wind or air movement of any kind ceased. I was assailed with the smell of decay and filth in the complete and utter darkness. "Damn." I took a stabilizing step sideways. "I guess he just followed his nose." I continued progressing forward, feeling the ground heading downward along the ramp. The darkness had to be a magical field of some sort. After five minutes of doing my best not to bump into anything, I felt the tight space around me open to a much larger one.

Just as suddenly as the stagnation ceased and the air movement began, I wished it hadn't. I gagged as foul odors hit me from three distinct directions along with a deep growl that reverberated in my chest. 'Dogs, big dogs,' unconcerned, I mused, knowing that in my invisible state not even the most empathetic canine was able to sense me.

The 'clunk' of a disconnect switch being thrown followed by the 'buzz' of all the lights in the area turning on revealed that I was completely and utterly wrong. Not only could the three, well over two-hundred-pound Rottweilers see me, but apparently, the forty or so short, X-faced bastards with black hair could as well. To make matters worse, a rope that I hadn't seen synched around my ankles, snaring me, hoisting, and dangling from the ceiling, upside down. What the hell is going on?

"You can't capture me, I'm fucking Death!" I blurted.

"So? I'm a fucking Dwarf." the only black with the right side of his face painted in stepped up.

"No, I'm the reaper of souls, the one that will eventually take you to your final resting."

"Listen to him, boys, 'I'm the reaper of souls.'" He did a horrible impersonation of me, his voice was much too effeminate in his mimicry, I knew I didn't sound like that.

"That, quite literally, was the worst impersonation of me I've ever heard." I said.

"Whatever, pretty boy. Oh look, his wallet fell, Alouc, get that for me."

"But ah, Xalos," he didn't move.

"Don't worry, laddie, if he makes a move for you, 'Her' pet will tear him into tender morsels."

"Don't you mean pets?" I looked at the three huge dogs while my wallet was scooped up and handed to the group's leader.

"Well," he read my identification, "Cloudan, what you're seeing is an illusion. Our Lady doesn't like to draw attention to her protector, but if you're death, you should be able to see through it."

"I really am the embodiment of Death."

"Not to us." Xalos said flatly.

"Ok, seriously, who the hell are you and how did you see me?" I asked, my dander starting to rise.

"Apparently not the Dokkalfar that get put into kid's books, you've got quite a potty mouth."

"Dokkalfar? Dark Elves?"

"Very good. Someone get Death a cookie. As for how we saw you? We didn't, the dog poop that you stepped in gave you away." Xalos explained.

"I changed my shoes!" I said.

"It doesn't matter, we have a great sense of smell." Alouc said.

"And it's a magic rope you're hanging from. That's what made you visible again." Xalos pointed with his massive hand.

"Why in the hell are you living in a dilapidated parking structure?" I have no idea why that question popped into my head. With all the murders being committed in the city, you'd think I'd ask about them first. Maybe because I was upside down, yeah, that's my answer and I'm sticking to it.

"With assholes in the world like Thor, we don't want to be tricked into turning into stone just because his daughter is a babe." He said.

"What? Thor? This is too much, there's no Thor." I said.

"I know, Jörmungandr took care of that tool at Ragnorok, but there are still assholes *like* Thor. Which is what I said." Xalos crossed his arms.

"I could keep up this witty repartee all night, but I have duties—"

"Heh-heh, he said duty." An anonymous voice said.

"Anyways," I tried to get control, "Why are you killing people?"

"Now, that's the right question, not why we're living in an underground garage." Their leader said.

"I know but I am spinning around upside down after all." I told you, I'm sticking to it.

"Sides made a bet that the black and tan couldn't—" Xalos started.

"I know, I got that, but how is it that creatures from mythology and magic are part of a bet like this? I mean, what the pixies and sasquatches are against you and the merfolk?"

"You're kind of a douche." Alouc said.

"I keep hearing that. But at least I'm not murdering innocent kids."

"What?" Xalos looked over at Alouc.

"I was going to tell you, Ricky and Romeo killed two girls. Then Egg and Dodger killed them."

"I would have to say, if they hadn't, I would have." The enormous, red-haired man said, walking into the room. "So, don't get your beards all twisted."

"Speaking of Ragnarok, Surtr, what are you doing here? You're not even on our team." Xalos asked and the three dogs stepped away from me and toward the huge ginger, growling.

"Shut up, ya stupid beast." He punched the center dog under the chin and all three flew head over hindquarter through the air. Beyond all my imagination, the three Rottweilers merged into one giant three-headed dog.

"Holy shit, that's Cerberus." I gasped.

"Look at that, he does see. Perhaps he's more than a pretty boy I'd like to punch in the face. More than I can say for you, Surtr."

"Watch yourself, pipsqueak, or you'll go the way of Romeo."

"My name is Xalos Blood Fist and I will not be threatened by the likes of an overgrown piece of kindling." He raised a forged steel fist, anodized with a red hue to look like blood.

"I thought it was blood stump that you were called!" Surtr replied.

"Enough! Surtr, be off." A woman in black robes said as she bent over the whimpering multi-headed dog. "And let him down," then she and the beast were quite simply gone.

"As 'Her' says." The ginger disappeared and the remaining group lowered me to the floor.

Getting back to my feet, "Xalos Blood Fist? That sounds a lot like a Dwarf name. What happened to your hand?" stupid questions seemed to be my thing today.

"It should. I am the King of the Dwarves. A foe from long ago took my hand."

"I thought you said you were Dokkalfar?" My mind raced through all the mythology I knew, remembering that dark elves were the dwellers beneath the realms and it came together. "Surtr? His men call him Sur." I mumbled, letting the pieces fall into place, "Didn't he die in Ragnarok?" I asked, knowing the answer.

"No, he made a pact with Bergelmir and his wife. The arrangement protected the couple from being attacked, ever, as long as Surtr could call on them one time to pull him out of the fire. Destroying everything with that damn sword after he killed Freyr, just for him to then get pulled out of the devastation."

"Inter..." I started.

"This is not a history class! Return him," A female voice ordered from somewhere.

"As you say, Sides." The Dwarf king made an odd hand gesture.

Again, I found myself outside the café. My mind was running through these new revelations; dark elves are here killing people to win a bet, and Cerberus is here guarding 'Her'. At least I know why I'm not cashing in their souls, comic book characters don't have them.

Death's Journal – The Real Romeo and Juliet

Each journal entry I've made has left me with an off-putting emotion, not sadness or sorrow, and certainly not regret or contrition, just a rebarbative sense of loss. Regret, of course, can't enter into this, mainly because it's my job to take souls to their final resting. But, when true love never gets the chance to flourish and a young couple never gets to walk on the beach holding hands as the waves lop over their naked feet, it's the universe that has lost the opportunity to develop new constellations.

Writers through ages have retold the story of Pyramus and Thisbe. Some may have thought they were retelling a William Shakespeare original story, but I asked him directly when he went to his resting if he based Romeo and Juliet on the fated couple of Ovid's Metamorphoses.

"A good writer bases his work on other's projects, but a great writer allows his work to resonate with amazing pieces of history." Was his answer.

The one and only time I've reaped two souls at the same time, knowing they would be heading to the same location, the neighboring villas where they grew up in Babylon. This time, however, without annoying parents forbidding their love. It was the parents that really made the would-be lover's story different, and the parents who no one has told the tale of, until now.

While Mr. Shakespeare had his Montagues and Capulets, the family names in his most famous play,

Ovid's recount of these families never appeared in the Metamorphoses nor any follow-up documents. As the Reaper, I do know and will write it in this journal for those in the future. Pyramus was from the line of Qahwa, and Thisbe was a Dallah. The parents of the fated teens were as thick as thieves when they were teenagers themselves. The reality of it, Nutesh (Pyramus' father) and Enusat (Thisbe's father) grew up as neighbors. Additionally, Alittum (Pyramus' mother) and Gemeti (Thisbe's mother) were raised in the same home as sisters, although not really related.

What could possibly cause these families, who grew up so close, to hate each other so much that they forbade their children to even speak? Money, of course. They entered into a joint venture that failed. The saddest part? The business venture they entered into was a combining of their family businesses. The Dallah family were smiths, specializing in brass, silver, and gold. The Qahwa family were growers of coffee berries. Combining the two trades made a specialty shop serving a hot beverage in a custom pot.

During the first few years of the shop, the two families were treated as equals by their patrons. But after a few of the sophisticated pots were purchased and displayed in prominent leaders of the country's homes, the Dallah family gained notoriety and decided that they deserved a larger cut of the profits. Though it hurt, they agreed that harvesting and roasting of the berries wasn't bringing in the customers quite as much as the people wanting to purchase the decorative pots. So, they agreed to change the split to 60/40 in favor of the fancy pots.

When the Dallah's decided that they wanted to change the split for the third time, this time to 80/20, Pyramus's parents could no longer just go along. Yet, as the shop was part of the Qajwa farm, the family graciously packed up the pots and asked their greedy ex-friends to leave. The feud that followed led to the deaths of the two smitten teenagers. Ages later, the coffee shops on every corner could settle the argument, the owner of the beans were the one who were worth more in that relationship.

Reaper's Revenge
Chapter Twelve - Cassiopeia

The night continued to surprise Cassiopeia as the police officer heading the investigation into all the deaths in their town was waiting in the diner when she returned from her acting class.

"Good evening, Lead Detective Delphinios." She greeted him with a cup of coffee.

"Good evening," he smiled but all she could see was the horrible trench coat. "I hate to pester you, but I was wondering if you've seen Mr. Courstre recently?"

"Actually, no, sir. The last time was when the girl died. Has something happened?"

"We found his fingerprints on a cell phone outside the observatory."

"Where Urania was killed?" She asked.

"Along with others, yes. And it was her phone we found his prints on. Wait, how did you know her?"

"She was a regular. Actually, Cloudan saved her from some of those X-faced guys the other day. I'm certain there must be a reasonable explanation for his fingerprints being on the phone." Cassiopeia said.

"I'm surprised you want to give him the benefit of the doubt when you saw what he did to that girl right outside this diner." The words had no sooner finished coming from his mouth when his cup of coffee spilled into his lap.

"Oh dear," she grabbed all the dry towels from behind the counter and handed them over to him.

"Peia, did you leave the lights on inside your car?" Calli walked in from the front, pulling with her the strong smell of menthol.

"I don't remember turning them on, it was light outside when I got here." She reached into her purse behind the coffee stand, grabbed her keys, and walked out to check. Padding across the street to her car, she couldn't help but glance back at the alley where her would-be savior had performed a strange disappearing act right as Cheyanne died. Maybe he was afraid of dead bodies. It's not like he got close enough to the sick girl to kill her.

'Honk.' A car horn blasted in the silent night.

"Sorry!" she waved a hand at the car, acknowledging her stupidity having stopped in the middle of the street. Stepping onto the sidewalk near the parking lot, she saw that her interior lights were indeed on. Cassiopeia used her car's remote to disable the alarm, momentarily bringing her headlights on, violating the purity of the dark night and revealing a shadow. The shadow appeared to be that of a man, his face was never illuminated as the headlights were only briefly lit. As the lights gave way to the overpowering darkness, all his features melted into the very shadows from which he came.

Hitting the panic button on the remote almost instantly brought the lights and the horn on in a random flashing pattern. To her surprise, there was no sign of the shadow, he had vanished that quickly, leaving her alone in a parking lot full of fear. The alarm had accomplished half of its job, scared away the intruder, yet as though there was no big deal about a car alarm going off, people walked by the parking lot and didn't even look twice. She started back to the car when she saw it, a basket sat on the hood of her car. Her direction of travel quickly stopped and she headed back to the diner.

The detective was still dabbing the coffee from his lap when she came running in. "There's someone, well, there was someone. Now there's something on my car."

"It'll be fine, let me call for some support." Detective Delphinios turned on his phone, dialing. "I need the bomb squad at my current location.

"Bomb squad?" Calli squealed.

"One never knows."

"True, I guess. So, I hear all police have a reason for joining the force. Why exactly did you become a cop?" Peia asked.

"It's not really the right time." He replied.

"Come on, we have time until the bomb squad gets here."

"I'll say that's true, there usually is a story that caused those who succeed as police officers to join. I'm no exception. I grew up in a small town in Georgia that had less than 1500 people, it was called Sparta."

"Like the battle of Thermopylae?" she asked.

"Yes, same name. In the town, there were several clicks, but everyone had to band together to show that we were united where it mattered. That basically meant the people who shouldn't have been athletes needed to be." Neirin said.

"I understand. There weren't enough kids in my senior class to perform the traditional senior play. We had to recruit the juniors to help." Peia said.

"When I was a senior, I was pretty much a god in the community. I know that sounds horrible, but..."

"You don't need to explain." She said.

"Thank you. The funny thing was, as god-like as I thought I was, there was a boy who was a freshman my senior year, his name was Hy. He almost started a turf war between us and the counties North, South, and the West. If there wasn't a huge forest to the East, I'm sure they would have gotten in line."

"Seems like you thought him more than a god?"

"I did, in fact. With him, I felt I truly understood what it meant to be human. If I had understood the depths of the jealousy I would feel for what we had, I may have stayed a god, being worshipped by others." He let a small laugh escape as he played on his earlier statement. "At our home opening football game, a girl from North county, Boreas, along with the children of the wind decided to kidnap our school mascot." Neirin said.

"Children of the wind?"

"It's what they called their little click."

"Odd, go on, did they steal your mascot?"

"No, our crew of miscreants banded together."

"Nice."

"When we made it to homecoming, we decided that we needed to work together again and welcome our rivals from the South. My personal goal was to put an end to the boasting of their Captain, Tham or something. He was punished but good."

"Boom." She smiled.

"That just made the game in the West for all the marbles. I asked Hy to stay after practice and work on routes. We worked until we were both stupid tired, but made the call to run the new route called 'quoit' a couple of times before calling it quits. On the third time, he ran to the back of the end zone, and Zeph, a cheerleader from the West Breezers, blew in and tripped Hy. As he fell, his head hit the uprights," He took a deep breath.

"Oh shit! And?" Peia put her hands up to her mouth.

"He snapped his neck. He was dead before the ball landed on the ground next to him." His eyes teared up.

"I'm so sorry. What happened to her?"

"There were 150 people that gave witness she was in the gymnasium of her school, leading a pep-rally."

"But…" she started.

"If it was cut and dry, then I probably wouldn't be standing next to you now." Neirin cut across her. "Here comes the bomb wagon. I better get suited up." Fifteen minutes later, the Lead Detective wore the heavy armor as he approached the car. Taking a pair of tongs from beneath his vest, he poked at the top of the basket. In the moonlight, it appeared to move. "I need some light shining over here sometime tonight." The sarcastic tone was not his usual way of behaving. Liked by all, his level head had saved many of them from death more times than he could remember, though they all remembered quite well.

"Sorry, Sarge. Er, I mean, lead detective." The young man addressed his old boss while turning the LED light in his direction.

"It's ok, David, I didn't mean to snap." Neirin remembered that before he had left the bomb squad to become a detective, the young man had all but lost his nerve when an accidental detonation caused a teenaged boy to lose his legs and a girl to lose her life. David had made a simple mistake; after he cut a tripwire, he released it from his needle-nose pliers before giving it a solid bend away. The wire sprung back into place, 'Boom'. Neirin had helped David through the first stages of coping with his mistake, but he knew the rest was up to the young man.

As the light came up, the shadow inside the basket melted. The napkin covering the contents definitely moved. "I think it's alive." He pulled a second set of tongs from under his vest. Grabbing the napkin in two places, he pulled it back, "Shit". Neirin fell backwards onto the concrete, pulling the basket from the hood of the car, throwing his tongs, and waving his hands trying to scatter whatever was flying around his facemask.

"Sarge, it's just butterflies." The laughter surrounded him.

"Butterflies?" Neirin continued to wave his arms.

"Yeah, there must have been 100 of them." The third member of the group, a blond-haired burly woman, removed her helmet, trying her best to stifle a laugh. She had been videotaping and after seeing his non-smiling face, she resumed.

"Who the hell puts 100 butterflies into a basket?" Finally gathering his composure, he stood.

The young officer stepped back and spoke quietly, "There is a note in the basket, sir."

"Thanks, David," Neirin collected his tongs and gingerly lifted the paper-clipped note lying on the side of the downed basket. "Clear. Tessy, you shouldn't have taken off your helmet until I gave the all-clear."

"You're right." She stopped videotaping again.

"What does it say?" David asked, distracting the lesson.

"It's for Cassiopeia. Give me a pair of cotton gloves." Neirin said and held out a hand. When he got them, he walked across to Peia, "Please put these on, I need to save the note to check for prints."

"Ok." She put on the gloves and curiously took the note, removing the paperclip and unfolding the paper.

'Cassiopeia, I enjoyed our walk from the playhouse. I do commit to you that I will explain everything about Cheyanne, but for now, please trust that I didn't harm her in any way.

The moths are a collection from around the world. The green one was a Comet moth from Madagascar. The green and black one is a Lime Hawk from Canada. The green, yellow and purple ones are Oleander. The white, brown and orange are garden tigers. And, finally, the pink and yellow are rosy maple moths.

Don't worry, they are all sterile, so none of the local fauna is in danger. I wanted to show you there are many beautiful things that come out at night. I hope you found this beauty of the night basket interesting.

Cloudan

PS – please scratch the paperclip here.

When she finished reading the postscript, she rubbed the paperclip across the words and the note burst into flames. Disappearing in a heartbeat.

"What the heck just happened?" Chief detective Delphinios asked.

"Um, fire." She replied.

"Did it say who this was from?"

"The letter didn't say. It simply said, 'Enjoy the moths.' Weird, huh?" Cassiopeia tried to play aloof.

"Very. I think I should escort you home and make certain everything is ok."

"I still have a couple of hours left on my shift."

"Oh, sugar, I can cover the rest of your shift, I'll punch you out at closing." Calli winked.

"Alright then, I guess we can leave now." She glared at her co-worker and started to head over to her car now that it had been 'cleared' by the bomb squad.

"Stay here until I get my cruiser." He walked off.

Cassiopeia walked to her co-worker. "Calli, what the heck are you thinking?"

"Peia, sweetie, you need to do one of two things; either see past that detective's clothing and realize he has the hots for you, or forgive that sexy bad boy for whatever happened in the alley. Promise me you'll think about it? Here he comes," she pointed with her cigarette at the police car driving up the road.

"I will, thank you." She replied.

"Be nice, offer him a beer for his troubles." The cigarette flicked out of her finger as she went to take a draw on it, landing in a puddle. "Damn, that was my last one." She walked into the diner.

"I'll follow you." Cassiopeia said.

"You really don't have to do this, Detective Delphinios."

"Peia, everything has been going to shit in this town and if I didn't double-check this and something happened to you, I couldn't forgive myself. By the way, call me Neirin."

"I'll try to keep it under the speed limit, Neirin." She walked over to her car and began the short seventeen-block drive to her apartment.

After parking, Neirin walked her to the door. "Thank you. I do have to admit I feel safer with you here. All those X-Faced hooligans out and about is rather unnerving." She said.

"Peia, I need to look through the apartment. Please open the door and stay here."

"I... um... it's kinda messy."

"That really isn't what I'll be looking at." He smiled, indicating the door.

"Be careful, my cat is a terror." Cassiopeia said, and then unlocked and opened the entrance. He entered the apartment with his gun drawn. Less than five minutes later, he came back out.

"All clear, I think." The detective put his gun in his holster.

"You think?"

"Well, you said it was messy." He stepped to the side and she looked in on an immaculate living area.

"It is." She put on a great poker face and leaned over to pick up the cat. "I can't believe you didn't claw his eyes out, Bast." The white cat purred loudly.

"She tried." He smiled, "There is one more thing." He led her to the fireplace. On the mantle was an illuminated globe with a stick and cocoon with an engraved wooden base.

"Yes?"

"What is it?"

"It's art."

"The plaque says, 'The new beauty of the night'. I don't understand." He said.

"As they say, art is in the eye of the beholder. I just thought it was interesting and I wouldn't be able to go from day to day without the light from her."

"Interesting, well, I think you're clear in here. I need to run down to the station to see if they found any prints on that basket."

"Goodnight, Neirin, and thank you again."

"It's my job. Goodnight to you as well." He left, she locked the door behind him and walked back over to look at the cocoon.

"Bast, I can't believe you didn't tear the deliveryman up for real." She set the cat down.

Reaper's Revenge
Chapter Thirteen - Cloudan

"She tried." I said as the cat twisted itself around my ankles, rubbing its scent gland on me.

"Cloudan, why did you clean my apartment? Was it too messy for you?" Cassiopeia asked after she heard the detective's car drive off.

"Only a little." I stood next to the fireplace looking at the cocoon.

"Beyond that, you tipped a hot cup of coffee in a policeman's lap—" she started.

"A lead detective's lap." I still didn't look away from the globe.

"Smart-ass. Did you also knock Calli's cigarette out of her hand when she was talking about Neirin?"

"It's a terrible habit."

"Actually, I agree with that." She walked around the rooms of her   partment   nervously. "You changed the kitty litter?"

"That's why Bast didn't attack me, she was happy. I also took out the trash." I replied.

"Smart-ass. Based upon your posturing over here, I'm guessing you want me to ask what that is?" she walked across to the room.

"I'm so glad you asked." I turned and watched her walk up. "This is a surprise."

"All that build up and that's all I get, 'It's a surprise'? You're something else."

"I know right," I put my hand on my hip, dropped my chin to my chest and gave my best male model pose, looking at her with my cheeks sucked in.

"Don't ever do that again." Cassiopeia shook her head.

"Should I have turned right?" I turned my body counterclockwise and looked at her again.

"Stop, stop, stop! You're a nut job." She put her hand under my chin and pushed it up.

"What? Isn't that how *Neirin* works his trench coat for you?"

"Seriously? You're jealous?" Cassiopeia chuckled.

"Don't chortle at me. Besides, I don't know if I actually can be."

"Did you just say chortle? Who the hell says that these days?" she asked.

"Me. Duh!"

"Oh yeah. But what did you mean by, 'You don't know if you can get jealous?"

"There's a lot about me that you don't know." I took a serious tone.

"You mean there's more than you being the Grim Reaper?"

"You really are amazing, how did you figure it out?"

"Devon told me about the handsome guy that got carjacked. Then Neirin saying you were present when Miss Mel, Urania, and even that dancer, Terpsi, died last week. Coincidence can't actually be that, um, well... coincidental. Besides, no real person can disappear."

"Hey, I am real! And you forgot Cheyanne, and the fact that your Neirin thinks I killed all of them."

"He's not my Neirin, he's just a cute cop that doesn't have a chance of catching the sexy suspect."

"Sexy?" I probed.

"Douchie, but yes, very sexy," she got on her tiptoes and kissed me.

Her lips were moist and warm, so many wrong things could happen right now. Time to leave. I honestly tried, but then asked, "Cute? You think he's cute?" I pulled back and looked disgusted.

"I refuse to answer another question until you show me what the Grim Reaper actually does." She crossed her arms and waited.

"I'm fine with that. If you're up for it, take my hand." I held it out with a smile.

"Fine." She took it and the room spun away. Quicker than the blink of an eye, we were in a rundown tattoo parlor. "Where are we?" she whispered.

"They can't hear you. We're in London. I have these, well, tingles I guess you could call them. They tell me about deaths, I've learned over the kajillion years to know which are worth looking in on."

"What is this place? Who's gonna die? Are they famous?" The rapid-fire questions shot from her.

"I'm not going to tell you who dies."

"Ooh, a game." Cassiopeia said.

"Sure, if you say so. Let me set the stage. When celebrities and 'A-Listers' appear at events, the enveloping lenses of the paparazzi are always seeking nip-slips or dress-left flops of the year. These same people have life-changing events where they need to be more than just noticed. It's at these times they become ordinary people searching for the best. Many have come to realize they can't rely on the standard high-end clothiers to perform the miracles they once could. When they truly madly desire to end their search with a humbling benediction, they know there's only one person to see, the Couturier. They have shops and domiciles in Hollywood, Paris, Venice, London and Dusseldorf, yet they've been known to make house calls for the proper dispensation. If ever asked, they call the Auberge la Rise hotel in New York City home." I paused.

"Dear god, you sound reverent." She cocked an eyebrow.

"Hush. I'll give you a word of advice, if you're lucky enough to be granted an audience with the Couturier, understand today their name could be Aiden-Elijah, and tomorrow they may be known as Aiden-Emilia. Do not presume to know who they are in their whimsical, artistic, and sexual fluidity. Never, however, should you address them as A-E. Unless you wish the meeting to end rather abruptly. Your best bet is to allow them to lead you to whom they're associating with at the present time."

"Fat chance there. I'm a clique, waitress, wannabe actress." Cassiopeia replied.

"Come on, upstairs."

"Shit! No one would guess the opulence of this place." She said, looking around the room.

"That's truer than you can imagine. No person is ever allowed in. Well, except them, and they own the building." I pointed at the figure laying alone in the bed, naked.

"Can you throw a cover?"

"They're awake, I think they'd notice."

"Fine," she kept her eyes busy looking around the room. "Is this the person you're reaping?"

"I already said, I'm not telling. Just so you know, to enter the flat, an individual would need to walk through the 'By Appointment Only' parlor, and then past a bouncer guarding the rear stairs. They had three such bouncers who would allow the building to burn down around them before leaving their post, guarding each of their dwellings. Additionally, they had two bodyguards who traveled everywhere they went. Interestingly enough, they didn't know who around them were their bodyguards. Their assistant, Paimon, handled such details." I continued.

"You're in love with him, er, ah, them." She corrected the pronoun-ization error. The phone rang. Getting from the bed, they stopped in front of the full-length mirror, posed briefly and then kept walking. "Are you sure they aren't you?"

"Hello." The Couturier answered the phone and then hung up and sauntered over to the kitchen.

"What the?" Cassiopeia looked at me.

"If I were to guess, their voice wasn't perfect." watching them grab a tepid bottle of water from the pantry. "See. And they won't drink cold water, it gives them a bloated feeling." He explained as they took two sips, replaced the lid, and set the bottle on the counter. Bending to remove an ice tray from the dishwasher, which they poured the remaining water from the bottle into. Placing the newly filled tray on a small shelf in the freezer, and removing the ice tray that was already on the shelf, emptying it into the sink.

"Please let them be the one that gets killed." She shook her head as the phone began to ring again. She smiled as they danced across the flat to it.

"Hello." The Couturier answered, this time, their voice was perfect.

"Yes, hello, I'm terribly sorry, I must have disconnected you earlier." The voice on the receiver was very deep and articulate.

"Actually, it was on our end. Who are you and what do you need from us?"

"I have a movie premiere that requires a bit of..." The deep voice started.

They hung up the phone a second time, "Blighter." They walked to the wardrobe.

"You're about to see the magic." I squeezed her hand, giving a shake of excitement.

"Speak to us." The Couturier opened the wardrobe, ignoring the phone that started to ring a third time.

"Seriously, they're not going to answer it?" Cassiopeia asked as the phone stopped ringing.

"Not for someone who couldn't even answer a simple question. Besides, Wardrobe's performing and no one is allowed to interrupt such an important diva."

"When we're corporeal, I'm gonna bitch slap you." She blinked repeatedly, looking like an animated GIF. Forty-five minutes later, the silk and taffeta teal, thigh-length, outerwear were selected as the leading role for the day. A black silk and charmeuse jumper, along with half-calf chinos, would take the supporting role, and gold leather loafers would close the look. "Ok, shit that's nice."

"Nice? They didn't need peripheries like socks or decorations like earrings or a watch. This is a perfect example of how the devil is in the details, and how editing fashion and not piling on is what made it all come together."

"Ok, yeah. I see it." Cassiopeia nodded, watching the Couturier set their phone to forward calls to their cell phone, "Are we leaving?"

"Nice catch. Yes, he set his phone to an Australian country code."

"Au revoir, Wardrobe." They let the touchpad read whatever data from their face it needed to open the door and they stepped onto the cast-iron spiral staircase.

"Someone dying soon?" She asked, tapping an imaginary watch on her wrist.

"I may have brought us too early. Just sit back and relax, we have nothing but time." I replied.

"Good morning." A handsome man in a pair of overalls the color of seaweed that drifted from a swamp and a lime green t-shirt said from a barber's chair. His jet skin was as fresh as the day he was born, and his off-putting light violet eyes made everyone around gangrenous with jealousy.

"Good morning to you, Leraje. We don't think we knew you were coming in." The Couturier said.

"I'm waiting to get a tattoo. Was thinking of a centaur shooting a bow." A hint of a French dialect came through.

"Too obvious." A woman with dusty-blue hair walked up.

"Oh my goodness. Her makeup looks like an artist placed every detail on her with a single-haired brush." Cassiopeia fawned.

"And now who's the one in love?" I poked.

"Ah, Paimon, you cut me to the quick." The man in green smiled.

"Why are you here?" Their assistant asked in such a way that brokered no further Tom foolery.

"I have a beautiful makeover that needs to take place," Leraje replied.

"Have the Em-ex call me, and I'll check availability." She shifted her hair behind her ear and put on a pair of oval glasses with carbon-fiber frames. The ovals were on an angle that made them look diagonal to her face, giving an illusion of eye-rolling. In this case, the illusion was most likely accurate. She opened her organizer and pulled out a card, holding it out to him.

"Tell us about this makeover." They ignored her and turned to the now standing visitor.

"Sair," she responded with the only honorific they recognized.

"Yes, Paimon?"

"There are several requests for the Couturier's talents." She said.

"Then let them wait a bit longer. Leraje has never let us down when looking for fun new assignments." They said as the visitor sat back down.

"What country is the fun supposed to be in?" She looked down and over her glasses.

"England, not London, but England." Leraje said.

"Not Manchester, they don't go to Manchester." Paimon said.

"Ok, yeah, I know that, but this time will be different." He shrunk back into himself.

"What happened in Manchester?" Cassiopeia asked, now being pulled into the drama.

"There was a footballer who created a pronoun-a-paloosa."

"Why? Who cares about personal pronouns?" she replied.

"Apparently, a fair few soccer fans." I said.

"Sair, I must insist. There is still a warrant for..."

"We know, Pai. Sorry, Leraje, that is not one we can do."

"Ok," the guns came out of his sleeves as he pushed off the chair he had been sitting in. Out of nowhere, a large man was between the shooter and the

Couturier, who had been twirled by Paimon to give a secondary layer of protection.

"Come to me, Leraje," I said in my best dramatic voice, I watched Cassiopeia as my palm glowed, she didn't seem to notice.

"Who killed me?" he asked, looking down at the knife sticking from the neck of his dead body.

"Paimon did as she moved the Couturier away from your bullets." Cassiopeia replied.

"Smart girl." He smiled momentarily as the world dissolved to a slum, "Not here, flay me every day for eternity, but don't leave me here."

"I do not make the call as to where you reside." I released his hand and we were in Cassiopeia's apartment.

"Oh my god, oh my flippin' god, that was intense." She said. "Offering to be flayed alive, what do you think happened to him where we dropped him?"

"I don't try to understand, I just ignore bargaining attempts."

"Really?" She got on her tiptoes and kissed him again.

"That little kiss could be construed as an attempt to strike up a bargain with me. Death can't be bargained with."

"Come on... Seriously?" she raised her left eyebrow and licked her lips.

"Yes, really." I held out my right arm and took the illusion away from the souls I had imprisoned there.

"What the hell is that?" she stepped back and the cat went nuts.

"The souls of the simpletons that attempted to blackmail me."

"Hold up, did you just call me a simpleton?"

"I need to leave, there's too much going on to sit around lusting after something I can't have." I said.

"Lusting?" Cassiopeia prodded.

"Hush you. By the way, if that light goes out, your surprise dies." And I disappeared, heading to see my clothier.

The bronze jester was sitting on his bucket unmoving. I walked up and sat on his lap. 'Jingle.' The bells made a slight sound and I found myself on a small island in the middle of a river, in near-perfect darkness.

"Ok, sorry, I was just kidding around. I need to see the Swans of Uror."

'Jingle.' Jackson Square Park was back, the tree was in the middle.

"Where the hell did you send me? Actually, never mind." I headed to the giant ash tree.

"Cloudan?" Ratatoskr cut me off from crossing the bridge.

"Yes, that's correct. I'm Cloudan." I threw a fist full of croutons to the doves.

"Aren't you the sweetest!" Havamal said. "Did you make these yourself?"

"I did, but don't let it be known I did something nice."

"Why are you here, Cloudan?" the squirrel chittered loudly.

"You stupid squirrel, they know I'm here." I said.

"Of course they do. There is nothing they don't—
"

"Get out of my way." I started forward.

"Methinks you have forgotten yourself again." The squirrel began reforming, gaining mass and losing most of his fur. A few short seconds later, the squirrel had become a rhinoceros with a furry tail twitching spasmodically. The horn that he grew from his snout was jet black and longer than I was tall.

"You know, when a squirrel changing into a rhino isn't even in the top five strange things that have happened in a day—" I stopped my statement as the door began opening and the rhinoceros climbed the tree like a champ. "That actually may have made the top two, though."

"Come in, Cloudan. Come in." Clotho started to cough.

"Whatever do we owe this magical surprise to?" Decima's melodic voice asked when the folliclychallenged oiled Fate came into view.

"Dwarves." I said.

"Are you talking about Dokkalfar?" The fat man vanished from the center chair and took up the four-hundred-pound bearded, little girl visage.

"Yes, Skuld, and may I say, your beard looks like it's longer than ever. I was captured by Dwarves."

"Dokkalfar." She repeated her correction.

"Yes, I was captured by Dokkalfar."

"Why did you go to Svartalfheim?" Clotho rasped out a question in reply, after taking the body to the left chair.

"What? I didn't even know that was possible. Is it actually possible?"

"Yes," she answered between coughs.

"I knew I could take the roots to Jotunheim and Niflheim. Oh, by the way, did Nidhogg go to Jotunheim? I know the unnamed eagle was taunting him."

"No, although he thought about it for at least a we—" Skuld started.

"Enough." Decima stole the body.

"I was talking!" Skuld pulled it back, its visage in front of me becoming blurred.

"Things need to move forward." Decima pulled it back. Based upon past experiences, these arguments could go on for a while. I took in a deep breath to sigh, then coughed, the tainted odor of giant wet dog was unmistakable.

"Cerberus was here recently." I stated.

"Perhaps." Skuld replied.

"That wasn't a question. Why is Cerberus playing pet to Alcestis?"

"It wouldn't, as a guardian of the underworld, a place she has never dwelt." Clotho started to shake the long greasy hair out of her face.

But when Skuld stole the body, the movement that continued sluffed the long beard instead, "Besides, we haven't seen the abomination here since she last visited you!"

"The guardian has always served one woman, you know that." Clotho's hair finally fell back from her face.

"Was Cerberus here with Sides?" I asked.

"In the old days from the well of Urd's well, you could travel to the center of Niflheim via the Well of Hvergelmir. Or to the heart of Jotunheim through the Well of Mimisbrunnr, most know it as Mimir's well. From these points, you can reach all but the ninth world. Only Asgard was connected to Midgaurd via the Bifrost bridge." This time, Decima facilitated the conversation back to my earlier topic.

"Yes, that's as I recall it," I allowed her to direct the conversation. Forcing a topic with these three was never easy. "Yet I thought we were isolated from the other worlds when the bridge fell during Ragnarok."

"And how is it that we are with you?" Skuld's voice was goading.

"The tree of life shifted?" I asked.

"Several odd things happened after the Bifrost fell. Things that none could predict, not even the keeper of the seers." Clotho said.

"The Volva?" I asked.

"No, brother, those were mine." Skuld answered. The use of the term brother in such a relaxed manner bothered me.

"Ok then, the keeper of the Ora..." I started.

"Mimir's well is unreachable, it shifted to Asgard, which no one can get to." Clotho cut me off.

"That's why you smell wet dog." Decima rolled the conversation back again. "Cerberus was here, yes."

"And to which of the worlds did they go to? And why are the others on this world?" I was having a hard time tracking the various yarns they were spinning.

"Who, Cloudan?" Clotho asked.

"The Dwarves, the whites, the reds, which are apparently fire giants, the tans, Cerberus, Alcestis, and Sides - whoever that is." My head was reeling and I knew this peculiar version of the Fates wasn't going to tell me anything. I had to ask.

"The prophecy has begun," Decima stood from her chair and took a step toward me.

"We can't give you information to stop it." The oiled body transformed while walking into Skuld, and walked past me.

"Where are you going?" I turned to watch the monstrously large man walking down the ramp just as the dress changed into jeans and a tank top.

"The roots of Yggdrasil require a dirt treatment from the well." Clotho walked down the ramp, a plume of smoke in her wake. I found myself back outside the diner again.

"Oh, hello, Cloudan, I didn't see you walk up." Calli stood outside smoking her menthol cancer sticks.

"What day is it?" I asked, seeing Cassiopeia inside the diner.

"Thursday, the day after you were here last. Are you ok?"

"I'm," I paused, in reality, I really didn't know how I was feeling. "Yeah, I'm fine. But you sound a bit sad though." I replied.

"My sisters are playing at the Scallop Dome, they even sent me tickets."

"Playing at the dome? Does that mean your sisters are the Daughters of Memory?"

"You know their music?"

"I love them. Why does that make you sad?"

"I really need to work, so the tickets are going to go to waste. Hey, why don't you take Peia? I can handle the diner, it's pretty slow."

"Only if you let me reimburse you for the tickets."

"I told you, I didn't pay for them."

"If you only take the face value, it's not scalping."

"That's really sweet, I really could use the—" her words faded off as she reached into her apron, digging around for the tickets I assumed. "Oh no, it's too much," her head shook as she looked at them, "they say two hundred and fifty dollars—"

"Sold." I opened my wallet and pulled out five, one hundred dollar bills. "Besides, I'm a rich douchebag that loves throwing money around, you'll make me happy." I held the money out to her.

"Maybe a little less of a douche if you keep treating that girl right." She handed me the tickets and took the money. Tucking it neatly into the apparent wallet older women have in their brassieres.

Reaper's Revenge
Chapter Fourteen - Cassiopeia

Cassiopeia stood near one of the back tables, catching the eye of the tall man she had kissed the night before as he entered the diner. Death, she couldn't believe she'd kissed Death and it wasn't a metaphor. "Good evening." She said, momentarily ignoring the ridiculously thin woman asking if they had goat milk for her chai tea.

"Well, I never." The customer blanched.

"Never? Really? Any idiot who would actually enjoy goat milk in chai tea should have at least once by now." Cloudan said, not looking away from the waitress. "Let's get out of here. I have a surprise for you."

"The last surprise is still, well, I still don't know what it is, but the light is still on." She walked away from the table, leaving the pertinacious asses with their mouths agape.

"And it better stay that way." He smiled.

"Um, Miss, I didn't get to give you my order. Hel-ooooo!" Said the man that sat at the booth wearing an overly matching flower print blazer and pants, the gold and black pattern of which was inverted on his vest.

"Are you trying to look avant-garde?"

"I... Um..." the man didn't know how to reply to Cloudan.

"I hate to be the one to tell you, it's coming off as boyband kitsch. And I think you're just a bit too old to be in a boy band? But, I tell you what, if you had green pants that matched the leaf under the flower, you may actually have a nice look." Cloudan reached out and pointed to one of the small leaves, "This one, not the stems." He linked elbows with Cassiopeia and pulled her from the diner.

"Sorry about the confusion, folks, I'm Calli…" the door closed and the words were drowned out.

"You're terrible." Cassiopeia punched him in the shoulder. "He's a good tipper."

"Probably because it's 'Non-conformist' to go into the mean streets dressed like a moron and over tip your waitress."

"Duh. Do you really think the green pants will make a good look?"

"Duh." He rolled his eyes, "But will he listen?"

"I think if anyone else had said it, no. He did, however, take in your ensemble," she moved her arms up and down and then made a twirling motion with one hand. He took the hint and turned in place. "A black, unlined blazer, with black on black patterning on the pocket and the collar." She looked closer, "and you made fun of him? This is paisley." They started to walk again.

"Actually, there is a print much like a bandana with undertones of paisley. Bottom line, this is Bohemian done right."

"A black t-shirt," Cassiopeia continued.

"A flat black t-shirt." He replied.

"Sorry, a very flat black t-shirt. Black jeans, not distressed. A tan belt, and shoes. Is matching the colors fashionably correct?" Cassiopeia asked.

"The answer yes is SO only part of it." He put a valley girl flare on the word 'so'. "If done properly, the pattern in the belt and shoes should match as well. If I have an alligator shoe, wearing a belt without a pattern isn't actually correct even if they're both the same color."

"You're kinda ridiculous." She smiled up at him. "So, where are we off to?"

"First, we need to find you some clothes because I won't be seen with you in that shabby diner girl image... It was so two months ago. And we don't have time for the Couturier, although I would love to see what he would do with you. That not being possible, how about we pop off and find you something in Paris?"

"That's just stupid," Cassiopeia was dazzled by the brightness as they were suddenly walking down the Rue Vieille du Temple. "Are you kidding me?"

"You teleported with me just yesterday. Why the freak out?"

"No, we did some form of astral projection yesterday. This was actually teleporting." She said excitedly.

"Well, we're here for some sustainable clothing choices then a glass of wine and then we head back for the surprise." Cloudan smiled at the complete joy on her face. They walked into a shop and a thin man with ebony skin ran out of the back room waving his hands at the girl.

"Sortez! Toute de Suite!"

"Pardonne moi?" Cloudan stepped forward.

"Monsieur Cloudan." The man's face broke into a toothy grin.

"C'est mon ami, Cassiopeia."

"English please," Cassiopeia pinched the underside of Cloudan's arm.

"Sorry, dear," the man began speaking in perfect English, "Your friend likes to play the pretentious snob."

"You do know I can speak English, right?" Cloudan asked.

"Yes, yes, go sit down, you lovely ass. Oh, wait, you didn't tell me what you're going to be doing so I can help her."

"We have a painting lesson under the tower," he looked at his watch. "In just under an hour. After that, a nice glass of wine, and then we'll see a concert."

"A concert?" Cassiopeia interjected.

"Hush, you. You can help her, right?" Cloudan asked.

"Of course I can. I have many grand ideas."

"You're a saint." Cloudan replied, leaping up onto a wooden stool.

"For quite a while now actually. Cassiopeia, I'm Maurice." He proffered a hand and they shook. "I'd say you're a size eight or so?"

"She's from the US, not the UK." Cloudan said from the stool.

"Sorry, dear, that would mean you're a size four or so?"

"Yes, sir." Cassiopeia smiled and Maurice took her hand.

"Silly conversions make everything different. This way, I'll have you on your way in no time." True to his word, forty-five minutes later, her clothing was transformed and they left the boutique.

"Are we really going to a painting lesson and a concert?" Cassiopeia asked as they walked. "This outfit is amazing. Who was he and how do you know him? I've never done anything like this. Do you take girls on dates like this often? I imagine you do. I don't—" she was speaking a million words a minute.

"I'll answer all your questions if you can slow them down a bit." He winked.

"Sorry. This is just insane."

"Not insane, just… ok, maybe a little insane. No, in all my time in this form, I've never let a human know who I really am."

"What do you mean in this form?"

"As far back as humans have been worshipping gods or a God, there've been versions of Death." Cloudan said. "By this form, I simply mean I don't have wings or the head of a jackal any longer yet I've tried to distance myself from the living."

"Well, I'm glad you stopped that foolishness."

For two hours, they had a private, extremely uptight tutor. After catching Cloudan drawing boobs on a stick figure for the tenth time, he kicked them out, smocks and all.

"Cretin!" he yelled, throwing an orange at the departing couple.

"But I stopped putting towers on the male stick figures." He said to Cassiopeia a while later.

"That's true, I don't know why he would have gotten upset."

"It's time for the concert anyhow." Instantly, they were swaddled in darkness.

"What happened to my smock?" she asked, looking down at the outfit Maurice had put together for her.

"Back at your apartment with the god-awful uniform," he winked. "So, you like that outfit? I wish I could have taken you to my clothier but I don't think you would have handled that reality quite yet. I mean, shit, I can barely handle him, er, ah, her, I umm, them."

"How do you know Maurice?"

"I took his soul about 1800 years ago. After his beautification, he set up shops all over Europe—" Cloudan started as they walked into the Scallop Dome.

"Beautification? He actually is a saint?"

"Oh good, we have time for a drink before they seat us. "Yes, he's a saint." He said.

"How is he here if he died?"

"Upon the beautification of a saint, they are offered the opportunity to return to earth to continue to inspire. Most say no, he accepted the offer. And as he's the patron saint of weavers, and other things, he loves making clothes for pretty girls."

"And you were worried about me meeting your tailor?"

"Clothier, and yes. Very."

"What are they, the Fates fighting over an eyeball as they fit you?" Her laugh was real and full of fun.

"Two glasses of 2005 Amour Champagne, please." Cloudan spoke with the bartender.

"I'm sorry, sir, we don't have anything that pricey on our—" she started.

"Here, pour us two flutes and sell the rest at a minimum of $100.00 a glass." He handed her a beautiful white-topped bottle along with two, one-hundred-dollar bills.

"I think I can do that." She stepped back, popped the cork and poured.

"You didn't laugh."

"I'm sorry, about what?" Cloudan asked.

"I asked if your tailors were the Fates."

"Clothiers, and yes they are." He touched his glass to hers. "But they no longer fight over an eyeball. They fight over a four-hundred-pound male body."

"Ok, now you're just making fun of... You're serious?" she changed her comment halfway through, seeing the look on his face.

"Please make your way to the auditorium, the concert will start in ten minutes." A woman in a white silk gown announced.

"Let's make our way." He held out an arm, she looped her hand through and they walked.

Death's journal – Lemminkainen

And there, on the bank of the river, Tuonela, a hero in his final death throws grasped at a snake biting his chest. While across the river, a blind man laughed as he unstrung his bow. Thus, beginning one of the most memorable reapings of all my requests from above.

Walking forward, I reached out my hand, "Step forward, hero Lemminkainen of the islands. Hear my words, Kaukomieli, together we shall travel onward from the plane of your mother to the Realms of Tuonela."

The typical hand reaching toward me when I called the dead forth was this time replaced with a man leaping from his shell to the side, raising to a knee. He held his bow in hand, an arrow already notched and aimed at my chest. "Why would I leave this plane with you or any other?"

"You have passed, and I am your guide to the tombs." I touched my hand to my breast. "And this is not the target for your arrow, nothing beats within." I created an opening in my armor, showing the hollow void. "Besides, my friend, what if you need that single arrow later and you wasted it on me?" I motioned for him to look behind him as the blind shepherd tossed his dead body into the black waters of the river.

Silently, the sable-haired hero watched as the current carried his empty shell into the grasp of Tuoni's son. The creature lifted it from the river and tossed it on the rocks beside him. A moment later, the beast began attacking the corpse. After several strikes of his giant axe, he had chopped what used to be Lemminkainen into several unequal pieces. Each axe blow caused sparks and chips to fly from the stone the fallen hero lay upon. The impacts, I noticed, caused no reaction in Lemminkainen, only when Tuoni's son cast the pieces into the water with a great laugh did he finally speak.

"Alas, that I had listened to the advice of my mother. I should never have strived to woo a maid of higher station. Never should I have taunted the daughters of Sahri." He turned and strode passed me to the river bank. I followed.

"But," I said, "You chose to allow your lusts to drive you."

"Alas, that I ever took my sable locks to be derided by the virgins of the Sahri planes and pastures." Spoke Lemminkainen.

"Many men hate the station they're born into, be it one of lower or one of higher." I felt the need to help him come to terms with his mistakes. Why? I couldn't be certain.

"Alas, that I toiled as a shepherd under the sun by day and made merry with the maidens with braided Tresses each night." He continued to pace the river's edge, watching the pieces of his body sink.

"To work and enjoy its fruits is nothing to be ashamed of." I consoled.

"Alas, that I saw the maid of beauty, Kyllikki, that first time. Losing all vestment of sense, I stole the pleading maid of beauty."

"It is not my role in all of this to forgive the transgressions of..." I started.

"Alas, that I could take back the threats I cast at the maidens with braided tresses, to kill any future husband they would have if they told my actions."

"Lemminkainen golden hero, don't banish your soul Kaukomieli. Follow me to yond tombs of pleasure, forget these concerns and come with me." For a second time, I held my hand out to him, this time, in the darkness, the symbols burned like the torch.

"Alas, that I brought Killikki to my mother's dwelling, even while the years passed in supposed happiness and I ignored my lust for the battles. The desire for the dance did not escape my wife." He pulled at his clothes and turned back in the direction we had come.

"All men must reach a point of transition in their days, and with it comes the trifling concern that you've chosen a sullied path." Still, I attempted to ease his troubled mind.

"Alas, that I heard the cruel tidings of the maid of beauty's betrayal with her trip to the gathering of strangers where she posed as a maid with braided tresses." His hand stopped pulling at his clothes and cradled his face, the hero stood still, less the racking of his shoulders as he silently wept.

"The jealousy of others sharpens their tongues to allow intentional wounding."

"Alas, that I turned from my promise and prepared to leave." Lemminkainen's hands wiped his tears away. "Whoa, that I discredited the foreboding dreams of Killikki, choosing instead to polish my mail of copper in my desire for the mead of conquest instead of the stale beer of contentment." As he spoke, he mimed the actions of his words, polishing imaginary armor, drinking from an imaginary mug and finally tipping the mug as to pour what remained of the stale beer to the earth.

"Those who feel their affections cast aside act as irrationally as a child, stop this torture and second-guessing, in the end, it will do you no…"

"Alas, that my dishonor clothed me in heavy armor and accessorized me with spear and broad sword. To the north, I would campaign for the gold of Lapland." He interrupted me and began the marching of lamentation up and down the river again. "Alas, that I ignored my gray-haired mother's warning of the Pohya witchcraft and their star of evil."

"Setting your sights on an enemy you could not hope to defeat alone?" I couldn't stop myself, I followed him more closely, I needed to help him calm his ranting to allow him to move to the next realm.

"Alas, that I motivated the heroes of my homeland with my soliloquizing of fortunes to be earned following me to Lapland to fight the wizards there." His keening for the men he lost made him stop, again dropping to a knee. "Alas, that I used that cursed incarnation of lightning and flames, stilling the witches' mouths with dust and ashes and banishing their heroes to everlasting torment."

"The song you sang, the song of witchcraft banished all your enemies save one, ancient minstrel, Kaukomieli." I stayed my third attempt to reap this man, which as history dictated, would be my last.

Came the reply from Lemminkainen, "Alas, that I spared the life of the blind shepherd, asshat before leaving Layland to steal my second wife in Pohyola, the fairest daughter of Louhi." He raised slowly from his knee and turned quickly, pointing to the distant sky.

"The believed transgression of your wife made you embark on these quests, the jealousy of the others cut you again."

"Alas, that I had turned from the quests for her daughter's dowry. Ending in a mere swan to be killed on the river of death seemed simplistic."

"That is no mere swan," I laughed in spite of myself.

"Alas, that I did not police my footfalls, which alerted the wretched, blind shepherd to my arrival to the banks of the Tuonela river, where he sat in wait with a bow to shoot a serpent arrow to bite and kill me." On the bank, his rant finally completed, he dropped to his buttocks and looked up at me.

"Lemminkainen, splendid hero of many adventures, take my hand, the third time offered, I cannot extend again, Kaukomieli." I proffered for a final time. This time, the glow from my palm drew his attention.

As he took my hand, the words, "Still your reaping, Death," echoed along the banks of the river, originating from the intended victim of the third quest, floating gracefully on the top of the raging current. Days past and I found myself still unable to leave. The hero sat quietly on the banks of the river, holding Death's hand. Until all movement in the area seemed to still and a frantic woman with a five-hundred-foot-long copper shafted rake, with teeth a hundred fathoms long and forged of the strongest metal, appeared and walked along the river.

"Mother?" he stood questioning, attempting to pull from my grasp as the woman waded into the water. A moment later, she started walking along the bank, pulling the rake along the bottom. "Death's Guide, you must let me go to her."

"Lemminkainen, in this you must hear me; this is the time for you to show the patience that you ignored in life. Only then, Kaukomieli, may you prove worthy of the gift of another chance."

Before he could do anything more, his mother pulled several pieces of his dismembered body from the black waters, "From these fragments, I will bring life back to my golden hero."

"Now?" He looked longingly to run to her and ease her grieving.

"You'll know when." I said as his mother attempted to weave the right spell. Failing several times, she called for spellcraft help from Suonetar, the weaver of life, also from the maiden in the ether, and, finally, from Ukko, the creator of all.

When things fell silent, "Death, you said if I showed patience, you would give me another..." he started.

"I? No, not I. That is far outside my abilities. The opportunity will come from the same one you asked many favors from on your journeys. Secondarily, it has come from your intended victim," I nodded at the swan. "Never have I delayed my reaping like this." The answer had only just left my lips when a magically infused honeybee buzzed passed my ear in this land of death, followed by Lemminkainen and his mother vanishing before my eyes.

"That was played well," the swan flew from the water up to me, splitting into two before landing next to me.

"Holuspa? Havamal?" I smiled.

"Those, young death, are the names you will give us many ages from now." The swan on my left said.

"Truly, we are as unnamed as the Nameless Eagle." The swan on my right added.

"We will see you again, near the roots of Yggdrasil." They said together.

"Bread is always welcome, though croutons have much more flavor." The voice echoed but I couldn't be certain which of them said it as they too vanished. Leaving me alone alongside a black river which I departed upon the next pull for a reaping, never to return.

Reaper's Revenge
Chapter Fifteen - Cloudan

I can't believe I'm spilling my guts to this girl and the heavens aren't raining fire down on my head. "Have you seen the Daughters of Memory yet?" I asked.

"No, I haven't. And you're serious... Fate is a four-hundred-pound man?" Cassiopeia redirected the conversation back to her earlier question.

"I swear, I'm serious, why would I lie about that?"

"Hell, if I know. This entire situation is insane. Maybe when that guy with the X killed the reporter, he shot me too and I'm lying in a hospital in a coma, IV tubes running amuk.

"Tubes running amuk?" I poked.

"Yeah, amuk, amuk, amuk." her eyes sparkled as she laughed. "Hey, that's another death you should be linked to, the reporter, I mean." She pointed at me.

"Hush, you, besides, you were present at most of them as well. Maybe it's you who's the Grim Reaper."

"No, I told you I'm an assassin." She said conspiratorially. "How far down are these seats?"

"I don't know, they say seats 2M and 2N." We kept walking lower and lower.

"Tickets please." Another woman all in white silks said, holding out her hand.

"Second-row center, not bad." Cassiopeia grinned and we took our seats.

"Apparently, your co-worker—"

"Calli?"

"Yes. Apparently, these are her sisters."

"Well, live and learn," she said as the house lights dropped. A moment later, two giant boxes lowered from the ceiling. When they touched the stage, four of the women in the same white gowns ran onto the stage. After looking at the boxes, two ran stage right, the other two went stage left, returning a moment later carrying a couple of shiny objects which they sat next to the boxes. As two huge arms reached down from above the stage, the women ran away.

"Do you remember the first time you wound a jack in the box?" A female voice asked over the sound system. The hands grabbed the shiny objects which they stuck in the side of the boxes and started to wind. 'Dee Duh Dee Duh Deedled Dee Dee' the tiny music box sound played. 'Dee Dee Duh Dee Duh Dum!' The boxes flew open, the hands winding the boxes jumped back where they came from and two women in flowing golden gowns sprang out of the boxes and into the audience.

"Holy shit!" I accidentally said as the bungee cords pulled the women passed our seats.

"We hated those things." A different woman said as a familiar preemptive twinge overtook me. Shit. The two boxes exploded into a shower of confetti. When everything on the stage cleared, two women stood in full harlequin, waving. "Hello, I'm Euter and this is my sister, Erato." The applause was explosive, but not loud enough to mask the sound of the two gunshots that sang out behind us.

"Down." I grabbed Cassiopeia, pulling her to the floor. I allowed my shades to answer the need.

"What's happening?"

"Trust me, you need to stay down." I said as the crowd realized the two women on the stage had just been killed in front of them. The screams grew in volume, accompanied by several more gun shots, along with several more calls for my attention. I let my shades do their bit as I teleported with Cassiopeia back to her apartment.

"What the hell just happened?" Cassiopeia began an impressive roll of questions, "Who the hell shot them? Was it the X-faced guys again? Are they dead? Why didn't you reap them? Are we gonna go to the diner? I need to tell Calli."

"I have a feeling she already knows," I finally gave a response to one of her statements.

"What? How can she already know?" She stopped speaking.

"I'm not entirely certain, but there are some very unnatural events going on." I said.

"You're joking, right? You, the Grim Reaper, just said something unnatural is going on."

"Cassiopeia, I understand this is a bad time to leave you, but there are some things I need to take a closer look at."

"Are you going to at least reap those poor women?"

Not wanting to confuse the issue more, I didn't bother explaining about my shades. "Yes, I'll take care of them. I don't know when I'll be back. But I will, I promise."

"Ok, thank you for today. Well, except the killings." She kissed me and I left.

As I had been to the Dokkalfar's lair, I teleported straight there, "Xalos." I yelled into the darkness.

"Hello, Cloudan, they're not here." The voice of Alcestis came from behind me as the lights came on.

"Where are they?"

"It seems that Red got two more kills and they figured they'd won the wager. But I told them the fighter didn't count."

"Brunnhilde?" I asked.

"Exactly. Pug killing her meant nothing to the outcome of the wager. She wasn't related to..."

"Why did they do it then? And why would they think it was part of your wager?" I cut her off.

"It's not my wager, but I can answer both of your questions with one answer. Because they were given the assignment to kill her, of course." Alcestis replied.

"Then why didn't it count?"

"Her death was a large part of starting the prophecy, but the death wager is a different part entirely."

"You seem to know a lot about all this," I waved my arms, "Stuff. Did you start it?"

"No, Cloudan, I'm as much a pawn as others." She said.

"Others? Am I a pawn in this?" I asked, fearing the answer.

"You, Cloudan, I would consider a much more valuable piece in all this, *stuff,* as you call it. Perhaps a knight or bishop." The woman in black answered, this time, however, there was a smile in her voice. Although I couldn't tell for certain as her veil was down.

"Do you know where Xalos and the rest of the Dokkalfar are at?"

"To finish it, of course." She turned her black dress, billowing as she did. For some reason, that struck a chord with me.

"That's a beautiful dress, where did you have it made?"

"Just as a gentleman never kisses and tells, a lady can't share such details." And she was gone.

'To finish it?' Her words echoed in my head. 'She's not related to…', the statement I hadn't let her finish brought it together, "Terpsichore - the Muse of dance and chorus, Melpomene - the Muse of tragedy, Clio - the Muse of history, Thalia - the Muse of comedy, Polyhymnia - the Muse of sacred poetry, Urania - the Muse of astronomy, Erato - the Muse of lyric poetry, Euterpe - the Muse of music. "Calli is the ninth sister, and miss diner girl, Calliope - the Muse of epic poetry. How the hell does that fit at a diner?" I said aloud and headed off to check on her. I appeared across the street and noticed Cassiopeia's car, "Damnit, Cass!" The pre-awareness came as I started to run across the street. "No, no, no."

The screeching tires and bright lights from the vehicles coming down each of the roads leading to the diner let me know I was out of time. I teleported inside the diner next to the cash register and started yelling, "Get down! Everyone, get down now!" When no one moved, I made a gun appear in my waistband, drew it and fired once into the ceiling. "Not going to repeat myself, get on the damn floor." As I fired two additional times, they dove under their tables and onto the floor just as the machine guns tore the diner to shreds. Bullets seemed to come from everywhere at once. The pulls came as several of the patrons and kitchen staff still met their demise.

"I found her!" a yell from the side alley got my attention. I ran, feeling the bullets hit my body, knowing that only my clothes would fall victim. As I passed the kitchen, I saw the young man who cooked the fried food lying dead in the boiling oil. The smell of burning pork made my stomach roll, I ignored it and pushed on, realizing the door was locked just in time to port through it.

"Stop!" I yelled as the gunfire riddled the old man, Devon, who stood in front of the two women in horrible diner smocks. Not being bulletproof, the meat shield was as useless as a candy cane in a sword fight. "I said STOP!" This time, I held my hand out and pushed an energy out of me, knocking the four groups of shooters to the ground. The red light emanating from my palm illuminated the entire alley.

"Who got her?" Xalos asked as he ran into the alley. In my rage, I barely felt my shades depart before the screaming started.

"What the hell? Get him." Ornatanro's voice called, my palm light reflected from his eyes as his words, too, turned into a scream.

I spun, spotting the two women lying in pools of blood behind the old man. Everything stopped as my symbols' glow changed from red to blue; the screams and gun fire from the gang bangers, as well as their ricocheting bullets, and falling debris. I, however, didn't stop. As a matter of fact, my rage grew, my thoughts raced, and my tears flowed freely. Then I heard a gurgling gasp for oxygen and ran.

"Cass?" I knelt at her side.

"Don't," she swallowed, making blood push from a neck wound, "Call me th..." Her eyes closed.

Reaper's Revenge
Section Two
Chapter Sixteen - Cloudan

None of what happened next mattered, they're all food for the carrion to feast upon, for this moment wasn't crafted for reaping, this moment is about setting the record straight. This is when I violate all and seek the Reaper's Revenge. My shades are all called back to me and set out after the perpetrators of these deaths. The red glow returned in tandem with a shock wave, as if from an atomic bomb, thousands of shadows of me leave my body. I was so very wrong, there is nothing left for the carrion.

"No, no, no, this will not be." I forced all thoughts, all emotions, and senses back to the happier part of the day. I concentrated, ignoring the voices of Clotho, Decima, and Skuld as they pleaded for me to stop. Again, the blue glow filled the alley and the throbbing bullet hole in my arm, which had been a terrible surprise, yet really hadn't hurt initially, was ridiculously painful when I reversed time. The bullet came out of Cassiopeia and then traveled through me on its way back to the anonymous gunman. Even as that event ended, the pain as if my skin was being ripped off my right arm continued.

I managed to keep my focus, pulling every sense I could remember out of the evening, the real evening that we had shared. I stopped rewinding when the house lights dropped at the scallop dome.

"Well, live and learn," Cassiopeia's smiling face was erased by the darkness. I instantly wanted to head off to parts unknown. My pigheadedness stayed my hand. I turned my body, glancing through the darkness. When the lights came up and the giant boxes began lowering, I saw the familiar red hair and X crossing the face of Pug.

"Do you remember the first time you wound a jack in the box?" A female voice asked over the sound system.

"You're missing it!" Cassiopeia punched me in the arm, I turned and faced the stage while the tinkling music box began to ring out! She looked down at her wet hand, "Cloudan, you're bleeding."

'Dee Dee Duh Dee Duh Dum!' As before, the boxes flew open, sending the two women out into the audience.

"Holy shit, I am." I looked at my arm, seeing that not only was I bleeding, but the skin on my right hand was gone. "What the hell?" I pulled up my sleeve, seeing the damage up my arm as well.

"We hated those things." Again, the pull overtook me and the two boxes exploded into a shower of confetti. I turned my head, seeing Pug get out of his seat and aim his pistol at the Daughters of Memory.

"Not this time." I grabbed the gun and punched the long-haired ginger in the stomach. As he bent over, the gun went off. My already hurting arm filled with fire, he wrestled the gun from my grasp and I fell to the floor.

"Nice try but we win." He aimed the gun at the two unmoving women on the stage and fired. I reached my hand out to take Cassiopeia to safety when I saw her vacant expression staring back at me. The bullet had gone through my arm, into her head.

"This isn't possible!" my utterly stupid statement blended in with the screaming of the panicking crowd. The pulls that came next felt foreign, almost like a violation. Without the need for focused concentration, my palm lit the area around us in blue, I froze everything and stood.

"This is not the right path, Cloudan." The voice of Clotho thundered in my head.

"The hell with you and your prophecy!" I yelled, facing the ceiling. I pulled the gun from Pug's unmoving hand, firing it until it was emptied directly into the center of his X. There was, of course, no pull, there were no pulls anywhere. I smiled. The Reaper's revenge was sweet in its simplicity. I spun and threw the empty gun onto the stage, "Why didn't you run away?" I yelled at the two women. Remembering their unmoving bodies and then looking between Pug and the dead on the stage. "Wait... You wanted this? You knew he was coming for you." I reflected as the area turned into an icebox, the frost nipped at my right hand, and time reversed again. Stopping when the two were on the stage again. My eyes closed against the next phase of my arm being flayed.

"Hello, I'm Euter and this is my sister, Erato." The applause was explosive, but not loud enough to mask the sound of the two gunshots that sang out behind us.

"Down." I grabbed Cassiopeia, pulling her to the floor. I allowed my shades to answer the need.

"What's happening?" she asked.

"Trust me, you need to stay down." I teleported us to her apartment.

"What the hell just happened?" Cassiopeia began another impressive roll of questions, "Who the hell shot them? Was it the X-faced guys again? Are they dead? Why didn't you reap them? Are you still bleeding? Are we gonna go to the diner? I need to tell Calli."

"This time, I know that she already knows," I finally gave a response to one of her statements.

"How can she already know?" She stopped speaking.

"I really don't have time to explain." I made a fist with a hand made of bone and tendons.

"You're joking, right? You, the Grim Reaper, don't know what's going on?" She said, and I could see she hadn't noticed my newly disfigured appendage.

"Cassiopeia, I understand this is a bad time to leave, but there are some things I need to take a closer look at. After I reap those poor women." I said, stalling another question.

"Ok, thank you for today. Well, except the killings." She kissed me and I left.

"Please stay here." I said before teleporting to Xalos' lair, facing the flowing black dress of Alcestis.

"I won't answer your questions," she said, "But I will tell you what you are attempting to do is a bad idea." She walked away and the three-headed dog pushed close to me.

"What? How? You're not Alcestis." I started after her, confused by this change.

"No, I'm not Alcestis, Lord Ankou." She replied.

Cerberus blocked my way long enough for me to feel the first preemptive twinge. "Dammit." I teleported to the alley behind the diner, I immediately saw Devon and Cassiopeia consoling the other waitress.

"What the hell?" Calli's mouth dropped open and her cigarette fell to the wet pavement. Her eyes which were swollen from crying also widened in terror.

"Calli, I need you to stop pretending. You know perfectly well what's going on." I pointed, using my right hand as a test. A test she failed by wincing away from the bones.

"Cloudan, what's wrong with you? She just lost her sisters." Cassiopeia interjected.

"Nothing, we just need clarity into what's going on. Devon, you need to hide." I walked over and took the arms of the two women. "We need to go somewhere to talk." I teleported back to one of the side streets I had walked with Cassiopeia earlier that day in France. So much had changed in a few hours, so few heartbeats between finding love and losing it.

"Where are we?" Calli asked.

"It doesn't matter. Why are you Muses allowing yourselves to die?"

"Who the hell are you? What happened to your hand? How do you know about the Muses?" Calli pulled her arm out of my grasp.

"He's a friend, a friend who is acting a bit crazy right now."

"I'm not acting in any way that is inappropriate, she is Calliope, the Muse of Epic Poetry..."

"What a joke, when was the last epic poem written? The last shot I had at being useful was when the beatniks were performing their shit poems. My sisters can all help people today." All pretense of being a sitcom waitress faded away. "No answer about that?" she pointed at my hand.

"No, I have no answers for you."

"Wait, you really are a..." Cassiopeia started.

"Yes, I really am one of the Muses. But as the last living one, I'm causing great harm, we need to all die for any to be reborn." She started running, a passing bus had no chance to stop as the distraught woman ran in front of it.

"Calli, no, oh shit no! Cloudan, what just happened?"

"Cassiopeia, calm down. I need to go back and see what this did."

"What do you mean by what this did? She just splattered all over the front of that bus. I'm fairly certain I know what it did."

"Stop," I touched her arm, "The men that killed the Daughters of Memory are currently shooting up the diner in an attempt to kill Calli."

"But Cloudan, Calli's dead already." Her shocked brain wasn't catching up.

"They don't know that. I can feel the deaths of everyone in the diner. I wasn't there to have them take cover this time." I said.

"What are you babbling about? Why would anyone want Calli dead? Her and her sisters?"

"There's apparently a wager, but with her death, it has to finish in a tie and I don't know what that'll do."

"There's a damn bet? Who the hell is betting on the murder of Calli and her sisters? How in god's name can you allow shit like this to happen?"

"I allow this? I didn't allow this, I don't even know what this, is. Shit, I didn't know the Muses were living here as if they weren't daughters of a god. If you think about it though, it actually may be good." I tried to hug her and she pushed me away.

"You're mad! What could possibly be good about this?" She pointed to the shattered body and the crowd gathering around. The sirens were getting close.

"I don't know what the outcome will be if there isn't a winner to the wager. I'm going to leave you here." I started to walk away, not wanting the crowd to see me disappear.

"The hell you are." Cassiopeia grabbed my arm. "What was she asking about your hand for?"

"I don't know." I said, holding out my right hand, turning it over for her to take in both sides.

"You don't know what?" she asked.

"I don't know what's going to happen, and I don't know why she was looking at my hand."

"Fine. Can you just get us back to the diner?"

"I can." I conceded and touched the hand looped through my arm. The scene we returned to was nothing short of a blood bath. Bodies were everywhere. The initial attack had ended with the people in the diner because Calli had been located, this time, she wasn't. Every building in the area had been shot with thousands of rounds, every person walking by had been killed. When the word must've gotten to them that Calli was already dead, they really freaked out.

"There are more people over here!" a voice I didn't recognize yelled. A moment later, the gunfire started. Instinctively, I covered Cassiopeia, forgetting that I was no better a shield than Devon had been. About two seconds after it had started, we were sitting on the pyramid at Giza, blood coloring the ancient stone.

"Clo-Clo-Cloudan," she started coughing and blood fell from her lip like morning dew from a leaf.

"I'm here." I sat onto the uneven surface, pulling her into my lap.

"Cl-Cloudan, you're bleeding." She touched my shoulder, convulsing, she tried to speak again, "I'm S-so-sorry, I shouldn't have made you take us back. They hu-hu-hurt yo-you." The words came in a rush and then her head fell limp.

"Ah, come on!" I yelled into the Egyptian night sky. Bringing shouts from guards hundreds of feet away, which I ignored.

"The prophecy works in its own way, Cloudan. The time has come for you to allow the thread to weave." Decima's soothing voice advised in the darkness.

"I'm sorry, that crossroad has already passed." I concentrated and pulled even more of the perfect day from my past. The entire area around the pyramid turned blue, and as cold as a winter night in Alaska. The shouting from below stopped. Time melted away, the firing gun unfired, the giant boxes pulled themselves back into the rafters over the stage, the champagne was recorked. The images were passing faster and faster, the orange thrown at me went back to the instructor's hand, the canvases were unpainted, Cassiopeia and I walked back to the boutique. She modeled the new outfit with a reverse pirouette as Maurice held her hand above her head. Together, they padded backwards into the rear of the studio and time abruptly stopped. The pain hit my right arm once more, I managed to hold one eye open against the onslaught, watching every remaining tissue strip from the bones.

"Enough, Lord Ankou!" Skuld walked through the front door to the boutique at such a fast clip, her long beard and frilly dress billowed behind them.

"What in the hell are you talking about?" I asked.

"Cloudan, while you've been making time your personal bitch, there have been several time-slips in the continuum." The fat Fate in a dress morphed into the hairless Norn, Decima.

"I didn't bring you here," I replied as Decima turned into the chain-smoking Clotho.

"The damage, to this point, is reversible. Allow it to play out as it did, or it could end you."

"Kinda dramatic isn't it, Clotho? I'm death, you can't kill death." I replied.

"No?" Skuld taunted. "How certain of that are you?"

"Cloudan, close your eyes." Cassiopeia's voice came from the open back room.

"Ok." I said and turned back to the Fate's, yet I was alone.

"Do you have them closed?" she asked.

"I do."

"Put your hands over them, I don't believe you."

"Ok, ok." I covered my eyes.

'Remember what we said.' Decima's voice whispered in my head.

'Sorry, but I'm not gonna let her die.' I projected with all my focus.

'Have it your way, skeleton boy.' Skuld's words echoed off into nowhere.

"What do you think?" I opened my eyes as Maurice started twirling Cassiopeia, my perfectly beautiful ballerina.

Death's Journal – Robert Johnson

In 1938, I faced one of the most tendentious reapings in history, more specifically, the date was August 16, 1938. That date may mean something to fans of the Delta Blues or to those with knowledge of the most infamous Faustian myth of modern-day. It was the day that Robert Johnson, King of the Delta Blues, died. It wasn't the manner of Robert's dying that was controversial, although there are several versions of it. Neither was it the site of his burial that was controversial, although there are a few places that claim his body rests there. It was the actual reaping that was dubious in the eyes of some, and created a feud between two supernatural beings.

It has been said that prior to 1931, he couldn't carry a tune in a bucket. Then Robert left home to supposedly seal his deal with the devil. Months, or years later, depending on who you talk to, he returned home to become known as the true conveyor of depth held within the blues. He is still seen by many as the only master storyteller of the Delta Blues. The myth said he gained these skills when the devil tuned his guitar.

The day I got the pull to reap Mr. Johnson, having been a huge fan, I decided to conduct the guidance to his afterlife personally. When I arrived in Greenwood, Mississippi, the last thing I expected to find was a soulless body. Yet there in front of me was a vacant husk, I felt nothing coming from it. I decided to try anyway, "Robert Johnson, step forth." I held my hand out to the fallen guitar hero. Nothing. I walked around the room trying to feel something, anything that would help me understand what had happened. Still to no avail, "What in blue blazes is going on?" I whispered and then decided to visit some of the local Gin-Mills to see if Robert, not knowing he was dead, decided to hit the stage, go listen to his friends playing, or just flirt with the ladies.

I pulled memories from those attending to his remains at the Star of the West plantation. Eventually, I found the name of the last establishment he had played, the Three Forks, and I headed to Young Street. I materialized a block away and proceeded to a building skirted in people talking about life, love, and, of course, music. Walking through the front door, I was transfixed by none other than Willy Brown, sitting on the stage playing a few riffs to warm up. I continued to watch until a pull for a different departing soul tugged on me. I remembered why I was there and I forced myself to stop watching the great guitar playing.

As much as I hated doing it, I opened myself to the wandering, lost spirits. Several noticed me, begging for release from their aimless roaming. When Willy started his real set, I turned from the spirits, ignoring their pleas as I continued to search. To no surprise, they became angry, even hostile, and clung to me as much as I imagine the lepers who overwhelmed Jesus, asking for release from their disease, had done. Culminating in the response much like Jesus', I erupted, "Enough, you had your chance to leave this plane. You shunned me when I tried to carry your souls to your next life. Your mistake has led to your displacement, deal with it." I shook the dregs of the spirits off my apparel.

It was then I noticed the crying of the guitar had stilled, along with every conversation inside the building and out. Giving one more look through the room and seeing no sign of my quarry, I faced the still quiet Bluesman, "When I leave, you will get on with your playing. The soul I seek is not in attendance here." I started my trek back to the door, the crowd gave me a very wide birth. I walked slowly through the throng, still mute, watching me in fear and fascination. When I had left and the door closed behind me, as if my outburst had never stalled his hand, Willy went on to the very next line of his song.

The music that filled the night air overpowered Willy's playing, yet none of the crowd outside the Gin-Mill seemed to hear it. This was a song for the dead. "I gotta keep moving." The spirits meandered in the street paused to momentarily listen. Outside the Three Folks, I teleported, continuing my search, popping in and out of the clubs along McLaurin Street. The music playing on the night wind continued, and just after midnight, a familiar laughter joined the music. "Shit." I shook my head and teleported once more, this time knowing exactly where both the music and the laughter were coming from. "I should've guessed this one."

"I be da opena of da way," The tall, older man had skin the color of jet, the long pipe he clenched in his teeth had no smoke drifting from it. The soul of Robert Johnson stood in front of him, confused.

"You open no paths, trickster." I spoke in as powerful a voice as I could.

"Zat chu say?" the old man rounded on me.

"How can my words confuse you, Eshu? Or are you Eleggua today? Or maybe Exu? Perhaps Papa Legba or do you just want to be called Legba?" I asked.

"Call me as chu will, chu should know my to be da teacher, not no tricksta."

"Messenger of the Lu'wa power, yes you are. But even those who bring you worship know you to be both sides of the same coin, a teacher and a trickster. Eh?"

"Perhaps, but chu be nothing more than a deliveryman then, ya? What chu bring my dis day, deliveryman?" The man laughed at his humor.

"Legba, I have nothing for you. I actually need you to give me something."

"Dat the case, ya? And what be dis, dat chu be wantin'?"

"Him." I pointed at the young man still staring around, confused.

"You joke wit my, no? Well, dat not gonna play. Dis one 'ere made a deal wit my." His pipe began to glow cherry red and he blew three smoke rings.

"No. There was never a deal. For that matter, bargains made with you can only be paid with material items." I replied. "Here," I threw a fist full of toffees to him. "Payment in full."

"Da deal in dis case was applied to 'im building 'is fame on said agreement wit no challenge."

"That's an impressive form of legal-eze, you claim. His lack of rejection is proof of a binding contract."

"100% de case." He crossed his boney arms.

"Let me ask you, can you prove you gave him anything?" I asked.

"Dat be 'is to prove, I don't 'ave to." His grin was beginning to annoy me.

"No. As it's impossible to prove a negative. Semper necessitas probandi incumbit ei qui agit."

"Fine. De burden of proof be my." His grin died, "Listen to 'im play, and den ask anyone. And chu know 'e admitted it 'imself, chu know dis ta be true."

"So, the devil tuned his guitar and then he could play? That's the story I've heard." I ignored his return to the earlier argument.

"Story as 'tis told." He shrugged his shoulders.

"Legba, you never offered or gave anything to this man." I stated flatly.

"As you say, but dis man used my to build 'is credibility."

"With all due respect, no. He may have used Lucifer's name but we both know you aren't he. More to the point, you don't even represent the devil, and never have. This discussion is over. I need to take Mr. Johnson home." I turned my back and started toward Robert.

"Hold der, fo' dis ain't the way of it. Not dis day." Papa Legba was growing behind me, I could feel it.

"Eat your candy and leave the reaping to the big boys." I continued forward.

"I need ta know, where chu be takin' 'is soul, mun?"

"That, my friend, is none of your business."

"Dis ain't over, soul reapa! Ana I ain't chu friend, rememba dat!" being the last thing I heard before vanishing with Robert Johnson's soul. And before you ask where I took him, it's none of your business either. Who am I to confirm or deny such a well-spun Faustian myth?

Reaper's Revenge
Chapter Seventeen - Cassiopeia

"You look amazing." Cloudan said and then reached an arm out to catch her as Maurice allowed the twirling girl to dramatically fall.

"She's a natural." Maurice smiled, "I would love to design an entire line around this one."

"Aren't you the sweetest." Cassiopeia said as Cloudan lifted her to her feet in a flourish. "Oh no, Cloudan, you're bleeding!"

"It's nothing, an old injury that never seems to heal." He said.

"My old friend, may I look at that?" Maurice's overly concerned look and the direction of his gaze were both missed by Cassiopeia.

"Do you have a first aid kit and some wet rags? I'm actually well-versed in dressing wounds." She inquired.

"You are?" Cloudan asked, the surprise obvious.

"Well, I imagine a lot of people get cut or burned in kitchens. Be right back." Maurice ran off.

"Actually, you'd be surprised how many people get hurt trying to build sets. You have to remember most of them never even swung a hammer before going into community theatre. And we're asking them to build sets that look professional." Cass explained.

"Makes sense." Cloudan replied as Maurice returned.

"Darn, I forgot to wet the rags. Would you be a dear?" Maurice held the pile of washcloths out to her.

"Not a problem. Just past where we were, right?"

"Yes, ma'am." He replied.

When she had left the room, Cloudan turned to the older man, "So, how did you know she worked in a diner?"

"She's quite a talker that one. Now, are you going to explain that?" he pointed at the skeletal hand.

"I may have touched on a power that has had some odd side effects." I raised my hand and rolled my fingers into a fist of bones.

"Power?"

"Well, Cassiopeia died three times today. I find myself here for a second time."

"Obviously, as you had skin when we walked in the back room a few minutes ago. You what, pulled on the power of Lord Ankou to reverse time?" Maurice asked.

"I may have, I don't' remember what powers Ankou had, or how to pull on them." Cloudan replied.

"Careful with power you know nothing of, young one." He said.

"Come on, let's take a look, get that shirt off. I can't believe you hurt yourself catching little ol' me." Cassiopeia said reentering the room.

"Neither can I." The tailor added as Cloudan removed his shirt, revealing his Adonis body covered in tattoos of the psychopomps through the ages. "Cloudan, that looks like a bullet wound." The tailor said.

"Well, you see, when you guys were walking in the back room, a masked man with a gun tried to shoot you so I jumped in front of it to save you. Besides, it just looks like another dent in Thanatos' armor." He smiled, "Can you perform your field dressing on it or not?"

"It's more than I've played with but I think so."

"Think so?" Cloudan pulled back.

"Don't be a baby, let the girl patch you up." Maurice laughed.

"Go ahead, we have places to go." Cloudan said and then held his breath. Five minutes later, he was pulling together a completely new look to go better with the one Maurice had given Cass. Selecting a black linen Pathani Pyjama with 24-carat gold trim and lacing, with black and gold Punjabi Jutti to allow his feet to look awesome and be comfortable together.

"I can't believe you're covered in tattoos of yourself." She poked. "Glad I didn't get blood on my new outfit." Cassiopeia commented as they were finally on their way to their painting lesson.

"The tattoos aren't really a choice. I'm glad you didn't get blood on your outfit as well, it's gorgeous." He looked her up and down.

"Thank you so much. And we match, what is that outfit?" She asked as they walked.

"Festival clothes for Sangeet night."

"I don't know what that means but you look great." Cassiopeia said.

"Thank you. When couples in India get married, sometimes they have a night of music, Sangeet." Cloudan explained.

"Thank you for that explanation. How do you know Maurice?"

"I took his soul about 1800 years ago. After his beautification, he set up shops all over Europe and..." Cloudan started as they walked under the Eifel Tower.

"Beautification? He actually is a saint?" Cassiopeia asked.

"Yes." He said.

"How is he here if he died?"

"Upon the beautification of a saint, they are offered the opportunity to return and continue to inspire. Most say no, he accepted the offer."

"And you were worried about me meeting your tailor?"

"Clothier, and yes. Very."

"Are we really going to a painting lesson and a concert?" Cassiopeia knew she was speaking exceptionally fast as they walked. "This outfit is amazing. Do you take girls on dates like this often? I imagine you do. I've never done anything like this. I don't—"

"I'll answer all your questions if you can slow them down a bit. Trying to keep up is like drinking from a fire hose." He winked.

"Sorry. The insanity in all this is crazy."

"Ha, I see what you did there. But no, I've tried to distance myself from humans in this form and all my previous ones."

"What do you mean by form?"

"As far back as humans have been worshipping gods or a God, there've been versions of Death." Cloudan said. "By this form, I simply mean I don't have wings, or the head of a jackal any longer. Shit, it also means I have skin, well, until recently."

"Wings may have been cool, but I'm glad you don't have the head of a jackal."

"Me too, I didn't get to see colors." He smiled. "Like the green of your eyes."

"Bonjour." A thin man with a huge mustache and smelling of a cologne factory greeted them.

"English, sivuple." Cloudan pointed to Cassiopeia.

"Yes, yes, of course. I am Pierre Teddle, I'll be your instructor. Please put on these smocks. I would like you to start with a very simple design," he held an orange and placed it on a stool.

"You want us to draw that?" Cassiopeia asked.

"Correct, draw the orange. Think about the way the dimples on the skin can each be represented."

They put pencil to paper, coming up with reasonable facsimiles of the orange, and they graduated to adding the stool. This time, Pierre's instruction was limited to telling them to remember that the stool has three dimensions, not just two.

"I think I'm putting Pierre on the stool." Cloudan said.

"He doesn't seem like a joking around kinda guy." Cassiopeia warned.

"Live a little."

"You live, I'm doing what I'm supposed to."

Five minutes later, the instructor came over to review their progress. "What the hell is that?"

"It's you." Cloudan said.

"With an orange on my head and the Eifel Tower coming from my crotch?"

"It's surrealism." Cloudan replied.

"Get out, you pig!" He turned to grab the orange but Cloudan held it in his right hand, squeezing it and allowing all the juice to run through his boney fingers, forcing the instructor to see his skinless hand.

"You shouldn't throw fruit at paying customers." Cloudan tossed the deflated skin to him and the couple headed for the auditorium.

"Sweet Jesus!" Pierre expressed his frustration at their backs, but threw nothing.

"Not really." Cloudan replied and then turned to Cass, "It's time for the concert anyhow."

Instantly, they were swaddled in darkness. "That's a weird feeling." Cassiopeia leaned against him as if trying to gain her sea legs after the teleporting. "Hey, what happened to my smock? I thought we got away with a cool memento." she asked looking down at the outfit Maurice had put together for her.

"Back at your apartment with that god-awful uniform," he winked. "I'm glad you like that outfit. I wish I could have taken you to the Couturier, or my Clothier. Actually, no, I don't think you would have handled that reality quite yet. I mean, shit, I can barely handle him, er, ah, them."

"That's the second time you said that, are the Fates fighting over their eyeball as they fit you?" Her laugh was real and full of fun.

"Two glasses of 2005 Amour please." Cloudan spoke with the bartender.

"I'm sorry, sir, we don't have anything that pricey on our—" she started.

"Here, pour us two flutes and keep the rest for yourself." He handed her a beautiful white-topped bottle along with two, one hundred dollar bills.

"I can do that." She stepped back, popped the cork and poured.

"You didn't laugh."

"I'm sorry, yes. My clothiers are the Norns, or Fates." He touched his glass to hers. "But they no longer fight over an eyeball. Only in this day and age, they fight over a four-hundred-pound male body."

"Ok, now you're just making fun of... You're serious?" she changed her comment halfway through, seeing the look on his face.

"Please make your way to the auditorium, the concert will start in ten minutes." A woman in a white silk gown announced.

"Let's make our way." He held out an arm, she looped her hand through and they walked.

"Seriously, a four-hundred-pound man?" Cassiopeia asked.

"It gets worse. Each of the three Fates have a completely different look. Which means every time a different one speaks, they look different."

"That's cool."

"Actually, it's dizzying."

"Tickets please," a woman said as they approached the second row.

"Are you in the show?" Cloudan asked.

"Bit part, but yes." She beamed and she guided them into the row.

"Break a leg." Cassiopeia said.

"Thank you, ma'am." The woman replied and headed off.

"Did you know the Daughters of Memory are Calli's sisters?" He asked.

"Seriously? Well, live and learn," she said as the house lights dropped and two giant boxes lowered from the ceiling. When they touched the stage, four of the women in identical white gowns, including their usher, ran onto the stage. After looking at the boxes, two ran stage right, the other two went stage left, returning a moment later, carrying a couple of shiny objects which they sat next to the boxes. Cassiopeia sat up straight, trying to see what the objects were. As two huge arms reached down from above the stage, the women ran away.

"Do you remember the first time you wound a jack in the box?" A female voice asked over the sound system.

"Cloudan," She gave him a little punch on the shoulder as he glanced around the auditorium. "You're missing it."

"Sorry," Cloudan replied as the huge hands on the stage grabbed the shiny objects, which they stuck in the side of the boxes and started to wind. 'Dee Duh Dee Duh Deedled Dee Dee' the tiny music box sound played. 'Dee Dee Duh Dee Duh Dum!' The boxes flew open, the hands winding the boxes jumped back where they came from and two women in flowing golden gowns sprang out of the boxes, and out into the audience.

"Holy shit!" Cassiopeia jumped back as the bungee cords pulled the figures above her seat.

"We hated those things." A different woman's voice said. The two boxes exploded into a shower of confetti. When everything on the stage cleared, two women stood in full harlequin, waving. "Hello, I'm Euter and this is my sister, Erato." The applause was explosive, but not loud enough to mask the sound of the two gunshots that sang out from the row behind Cassiopeia.

Once again, the strange feeling washed over her and she found herself in the side street behind the diner. The cloud of smoke from next to the door marked Calli's location.

"Oh, grits and shit, what a cute outfit. Wait a minute, I thought you went to the show?"

"We did—" Cloudan started.

"Calli, someone just killed your sisters."

"Sugar Pea, that isn't funny." Calli replied.

"She isn't kidding." He interjected.

"I, um," she caught a glimpse of his hand, quickly turning her gaze away. "I need to get back to work."

Dropping her cigarette, she turned and rushed toward the diner door.

"Wait…" Cassiopeia started.

"I think that would be best." Cloudan cut her off.

"What?" Cassiopeia said. "But I need to—"

"Trust me, Cass, it's for the best!" Cloudan stopped her from chasing her friend back through the door.

"Don't call me that!" she tried to pull away as the door slammed shut.

"Sorry," he held firm and she felt herself appear somewhere else, she swayed. "Are you ok?" Cloudan attempted to stabilize her.

"I feel strange, really strange every time you do that. Where are we now?" She asked, looking down at the moon shining across the sands far below.

"We're in Egypt, more specifically, we're at my favorite place on earth, we're standing on the top of the great pyramid at Giza." Cloudan answered. Just then, she collapsed into his arms. Instead of lying her on the stone block of the pyramid, he guided her to the floor in the entrance to the hospital nearest to her apartment.

Reaper's Revenge
Chapter Eighteen - Cloudan

Her eyes opened with a flutter and she lifted her head from the pillow, sending a spider web of pain radiating across her body. "Shit!" Cassiopeia dropped to the pillow.

"Don't try to move." I leapt from the chair I sat in. "I'll get the nurse."

"Wha…" The spider webs turned into lightning bolts cracking in front of her eyes, obscuring her vision.

"Please, don't try to talk, or move… Shit, don't do anything but breathe." I ran from the room, "Nurse Cruz, she's awake."

"Ok, dear, I'll call the doctors. She's going to need water, but start with ice chips. Do you know where to get them?"

"Yes." I nodded and headed off to get a pitcher of ice and a spoon. Returning to the room, I found the nurse walking out. As we passed, she touched my shoulder, gaining my attention.

"15 minutes on the Resident, 20 minutes on her doctor." She stopped and looked at him, "How long were you in there?"

"Pretty much since I brought her here." I replied.

"The police made me promise that I would call if I saw you." Nurse Cruz looked conflicted.

"Close your eyes then, dear." I tried to give a disarming grin and walked into the room, "I have some ice chips, the nurse said it would be easier to have them instead of trying to sit up and drink. Open up, I'll feed you a few."

"O...k," she closed her eyes and opened her mouth.

I scooped a few chips onto the spoon and placed it in her mouth, "Try to relax. The doctors are on their way."

"How... Long...?" she whispered.

"You've been out for two weeks. Just blink your eyes, once for yes, twice for no. Do you remember anything from that night?" I asked, she blinked once. Then opened her mouth and waited, "What? Oh." I put another spoonful of ice in her mouth.

Cassiopeia smiled.

"After I brought you here, they gave me your new outfit and I took it to the cleaner. More ice?" She blinked twice. "Neirin brought your surprise over, and a note." I pointed to the globe, "I can read the note to you, if you'd like." She blinked once. He showed her it was closed, "I really haven't read it." He broke the seal, "'Peia, I was told through remote channels that you had been injured during the recent violence, I have checked on you often. I want you to know the doctors that your friend hired are the best in the country.' Well, duh, I'm not gonna hire Charlie the butcher to take care of you."

"Cl-ou-dan..." She smiled but rolled a finger to continue.

"Ok, 'I have no doubt he is truly looking out for you. Though I will need to arrest him next time I see him.' As if," I chuckled. "Sorry, 'I went to your apartment to make certain everything was in order and I saw the globe that you described as art. I hoped that bringing it would help you wake up. Interestingly, as I drove her here, the battery started to fail, so I put in a new one. As you said, you couldn't imagine going from day to day without the light from her, I would've hated for that light to fail on my watch. If the concept of a higher power meant anything to me, I would pray for you. As it is, I put all my confidence in the science that the doctors looking over you are bringing, and the support this piece of art can give. I also believe that you are strong enough to make it without any intervention from anyone that could be considered, on high. See you soon, Neirin'. I do agree with him, you're stronger than whatever anyone else could do for you."

Cassiopeia pointed at the orb and then made the ok sign with her hand.

"Yes, she's fine." I smiled when she exhaled in relief. "The doctors from the hospital may not be as understanding as the nurse, I'll be right here, but..." she opened her mouth and I gave her one more spoon of ice, disappearing as the footsteps rounded the corner.

"Nurse, I thought you said her friend was in here to support her?" The doctor in standard hospital scrubs said.

"He was, sir." She replied.

"Cassiopeia, please don't speak. Let me ask a series of yes or no questions. I want you to blink once for yes and twice for no. Is that clear?"

She blinked once.

"Excellent. My name is Dr. Fitzgerald and I've been working with a Neuro-Surgeon named Dr. Eir. She was called in by your friend and she will be here very soon. For now, I just want you to tell me, are you experiencing pain?"

She blinked once again.

"In your head, I'm assuming?"

She blinked once, this time her face bunched up in a frown.

"Nothing to be alarmed about." He reached down and touched her shoulder, "We've been focusing in on..."

"Your cerebrum," A second doctor said, walking in the room. She wore a five-thousand-dollar suit. "The front of your brain. Cassiopeia, I'm Dr. Eir, there looks to be a reduction in responsiveness..."

"What does that mean, what could it be from?" I teleported across the room and appeared, walking in behind her.

"Cloudan, I didn't hear you come in. It means we have two things to look at, first is the tissues joining the right half of the brain to the left, which is called the corpus callosum. The scans we've taken have not shown any anomalies, but there could be some sort of plaque that isn't presenting."

"Let's give you a little more ice," I leaned over and whispered in her ear. "You'll be fine, I promise."

She blinked once, releasing a tear to run down her cheek.

"What other possibilities could there be?" I asked.

"A virus, do you know if she was out of the country in the last month? Perhaps there is something that we didn't test for."

"She's been in France, and in Egypt." I crossed my arms. "Why didn't you ask before?"

"I thought it was asked." Dr. Eir replied. "Saw there was no response on the check-in form when I reviewed it yesterday. The first thing we want to do is give her some medicines, we'll be running a series of tests in parallel with the medications. Now that she is awake, we need to try a couple of things to see if we can start the healing process."

"So, wait and see? Do you really think I flew you in to, 'wait and see'?" Pissed, I stood to my full imposing height, pressing my aura from myself several inches. Cassiopeia reached out to touch my arm, missing completely.

"Actually, we'll put her on Ritalin immediately. It's a stimulant and increases dopamine and noradrenaline concentrations in the brain." Dr. Fitzgerald added.

"Each time we give a regiment, we will be doing a scan. We need to see if there are changes in her reactions." Dr. Eir added.

"Mr. Courstre, we're going to be taking her now." Nurse Cruz said, and he noticed her making weird eye gestures toward the window.

"Thank you, nurse. Cassiopeia, I'll be right here." I watched as the gurney wheeled away, before sitting back into the chair I had sat in earlier, and vanished just as the police came rushing from the elevator to the room.

"Lead Detective, she woke up and they just took her to do some testing." The nurse said.

"Dr. Fitzgerald sent me a text that Cloudan was here." Detective Delphinios replied, "When did she wake up?" He jumped subjects when he realized what she had said.

"About an hour ago. The doctors took her back less than two minutes ago." Nurse Cruz said.

"How long do you think she'll be in with them?" he asked.

"Several hours. They are running tests before and after different types of medicine."

"Back to Cloudan, was he here?" Detective Delphinios asked.

"There was a man in impeccable clothes but he was blonde and had a man-bun. Cloudan wouldn't be caught dead with a man-bun." Nurse Cruz replied.

"I believe that to be true, but everyone makes decisions, even accepting or bucking trends. I'll be back later." He said, leaving.

"Decisions..." I muttered, my mind jumped back to Brunnhilde and to Keradeg. "There have been so many..." I balled my hands into fists and drove them into each other. The bracelet on my wrist bounced around. "You've paid enough. Don't make me regret this," I pulled on the strap until it snapped. The souls flew away, returning to their bodies. Turning it into my charm bracelet, I looped it around the base of the globe I had given her. "I have another test."

"Pardon?" Nurse Cruz walked into the room. "I must be losing my mind." She walked back out again as I vanished.

The place I appeared in was just as bright and strangely beautiful as the last time I was here. I walked slowly toward the old buildings, listening closely for any changes. The void of sound was filled with screams and shattering glass was something that didn't have to be strained to hear. I increased my pace to the building, the chair had sailed through the window as if it were a sheet of paper.

"Thaila, come to me." I said loudly.

"Who are you to call for my daughter?" The shadow I had seen grab her days ago asked.

"There's been a mistake. Where is she?"

"Mistake you say?" He puffed on his cigar.

"I tell you what, you have until the smoke leaves your lungs to indicate where she is and how I can find her."

"Or what?" he blew the smoke in my face.

"This was your paradise?" I asked, touching the tattoo on my right shoulder and the wings of Thanatos flew from my back. Repeating the process, I touched my right pectoral, and the muzzle of Anubis grew from my face.

"I earned my paradise!"

"Another mistake that shall be rectified!" Lastly, I touched the tattoo on my left rib cage, and the rest of my right arm turned into the skeletal arm complete with the scythe of Ankou shot out. Skewering the lecherous pig, and I flew away with him screaming. Surprised to see no glowing or cold feeling.

"Who are you to change what has been decided?" A moment later, the keeper at the gate of Hel asked.

"I am the hand of death, and none shall I sway from their demise. But I never said fuck all about anything after that. Now, take this piece of shit, bind him next to Tityos, and let those vultures eat his genitals for eternity." I removed my scythe and allowed the evil bastard to drop at the keeper's feet.

"I don't take orders from you, lacky. Return that spirit to his paradise." The Cat-god replied.

"That is so true, but how about this; until you've decided that listening to this... 'lacky' is that what you called me? Anyway, until you decide that doing as I request is more important than your flippin' pride, I will see that no human souls are reaped." Without as much as a blink of an eye, I returned to the vineyard, retaking my form. Calling all my shades from their duties and started walking.

"Cloudan." Decima's image appeared in front of me.

"Yes, that's correct, I'm Cloudan." I waited.

"They have agreed, Thaila has been forgiven."

"Thaila, come to me." I reached out my left hand.

"She cannot come. Not until after dawn when she is reformed again."

"Foul creature, I was too easy on him." I muttered to myself. "How can this be? How can any of this be?" I asked.

"You need to return to your home and set your head right." Decima's voice, still as soothing as a mother calming a crying child.

"Set my head right, Decima?" My head cocked, "That girl, Thaila, the one that I brought here, is the Muse of comedy; I guess the joke is sadly on her."

"No, Cloudan, she was a girl that was born human and the spirit of Thaila entered her on her 18th birthday. Just like the other Muses found girls with identical birth dates. And they all die within the same month, only to be respawned into girls born 18 years earlier than the last Muse's death."

"Why have I never known this?"

"There's so much you don't know. That I don't know. It's not for us to know everything, you need to return to your job, or at least release your Shades and let them do it for you." Decima replied.

"And what? Continue to take people to be tortured for eternity? Some that have done nothing deserving of it."

"I don't get to see the future, Cloudan. I see what is happening in the here and now. There's a boy playing in the street outside of Minsk, with a car bearing down on him. Will he die? I can't see, so I don't presume to guess. What would the point be?"

"He did die, and you should care because two lives could be ruined! How can you just not give a shit?" I argued.

"The changes run deeper than I thought." She reached out, grabbing my right hand. Not reacting to the bones, she turned it over. Decima placed her finger in the center of my palm and spiraled out from there.

"Some things are just wrong, letting that child die is wrong." I said. "Don't you feel that? Or are you as petty and desensitized as I was?"

"Wrong? You, my dear, have done so many wrong things in the last few weeks, you have no room to speak. But that's why I'm here, I don't see the future and I can't dwell in the past." Decima said.

"You see right now."

"Precisely. And right now, you appear to be testing the fence for flaws for an escape. My advice to you is to stop testing before someone turns the amperage on your fence up to match the voltage." And she was gone.

Reaper's Revenge
Chapter Nineteen - Cassiopeia

"You did great, dear." Nurse Cruz spoke to Cassiopeia as she pushed the gurney. "Let yourself fall asleep, deeply."

Cassiopeia blinked her eyes once.

"Not feeling better?"

She blinked twice.

"I'm sorry, dear. I know it may not help, but my GrandNan used to say, 'Adversity is a cup of carrot juice that you don't want to drink, but after you do, you feel stronger.' You seem like a woman who can get through a cup of carrot juice."

She blinked once again.

"There you go." Nurse Cruz tucked her in. "Oh, by the way, that detective friend of yours came by, he'll probably be by again later."

Cassiopeia shook her head and then regretted it instantly.

"Should I turn him away?"

She blinked once and closed her eyes as the nurse left.

"Did you want some ice?" Cloudan appeared in the chair. "Sorry, didn't mean to startle you." He touched her shoulder, "I can get some ice chips if you'd like some."

"Cloudan, I'm blind." She whispered.

"What? Jesus, Cass, I'm sorry."

"I'm kidding. Dope." She smiled. "Yes, ice chips would be nice."

"I thought something I had done, maybe all the jumping, may have…"

"It wasn't that at all, Cloudan," a woman in a black dress said, walking into the room.

"Alcestis, what do you know about…"

"Being an abomination? I pretty much wrote the book."

"Abomination?" Cassiopeia's eyes shot from the woman in black to Cloudan.

"Things happened, are happening, and over the next few days, they will get weirder. But I want you to know that it will pass. Don't let the doctors do anything to her, in the end, it will not do any good." Alcestis said.

"Why?"

"Your body is rejecting the idea that you can no longer die. In truth, you can no longer do a lot of things. Your body will catch up to reality sooner than your mental state, knowing that a thousand years from now, you will be the same as you are today is difficult. But being an abomination has its advantages as well."

"I can't age?" Cassiopeia asked.

"Cloudan, you be the judge," Alcestis removed her veil, showing a beautiful woman of no more than 25.

"In truth, you look exactly the same as the day I took you, well over a thousand years ago." He said. "But are you saying I should take her from here?"

"No, you need to give her a couple more days. If you do anything right now, she may not make it through what that..." her words stalled, but the pure hatred in her eyes and gritted teeth told the rest.

"Bitch?"

"As you say. I can't tell you anything more, Decima has already seen me speaking with you. I can't change the future or I'll be stuck forever." Alcestis looked at the floor, allowing her veil to drop again.

"A promise for release? That's why you're..." Cloudan started.

"Detective, the doctors don't want Cassiopeia to be awoken." Nurse Cruz said.

"There's already someone in there." Neirin replied and walked into an empty room.

"No there isn't," the nurse whisper-yelled at him.

"I swear, I saw figures through the window," he whispered as he allowed her to walk him out.

"The doctors looked in on her before they left. Now, you'll need to come back tomorrow." Nurse Cruz ordered.

"Ok, ok. I'm sorry." Lead Detective Delphinios mumbled as he stepped into the elevator.

"He's gone," Nurse Cruz said from her desk a moment later.

"Cassiopeia, I'm going to take Alcestis out of here. I'll be here when you wake up." Cloudan said. "Try to get some sleep."

"Cloudan, before you go, I need to know, what did you do?" Cassiopeia asked, the long sentence obviously taking its toll as her forehead became dotted with sweat.

"I..." he swallowed and pulled the globe closer to her. "I didn't let you die when you were supposed to. Much like Heracles didn't allow Alcestis to die when she was supposed to."

"I wasn't supposed to die, King Admetus' time was up, not mine. Apollo got the Fates drunk and tricked them into allowing a volunteer to die in his place. He was a good king, and having years to benefit all those people, I felt my sacrifice was valid. Being returned wasn't my choice, as it wasn't hers." She pointed at Cassiopeia.

"I knew that bit, I meant, what did you do that changed the color of your aura so much today?" she asked.

"Two things, I guess," he pointed to the bracelet around the base of the globe, "I freed the souls I've been carrying with me."

"And second?" Alcestis asked.

"I reversed a decision that had sent an innocent woman into perdition. In doing so, I threw a sick bastard from paradise and cast him into a hell I devised."

"Oh, Cloudan, how will that be received?" Cassiopeia asked.

"I've decided that some wrongs are worth whatever the cost to stop." Cloudan replied.

"You've changed so much," she smiled at him, "But you're still a douche, now, get her out of here and we'll talk later."

"Just this side of douchie," he held his thumb and index finger within a quarter-inch.

"Maybe a little further," Cassiopeia took his hand in hers, moving the indicated distance to about an inch, and then pulled them in to kiss them. "Now, get…" she closed her eyes and fell into a deep sleep.

The morning came and without Cassiopeia's eyes opening. Cloudan waited patiently, knowing she needed to sleep. Finally, at 9 am, the doctors came in, "Cass," Dr. Fitzgerald said.

"Don't call me that." She replied without opening her eyes.

"Sorry, yes, I read that on your chart. How did you sleep?" he asked.

"I guess well, I don't recall getting up at all." Cassiopeia replied.

"Good," Dr. Eir said. "Today's test will be very much the same as what we did yesterday. There should be some changes, from day to day."

"Ok. How long will I be?"

"Three to four hours, best guess. Why?"

"I have a hair appointment at 2 pm." She smiled.

"The fact that you still have a sense of humor after all this, is very impressive." Dr. Eir said.

"Especially because all her hair fell out." Cloudan said, walking into the room.

"Oh, um, that isn't true, dear. Your hair is all still there. Mr. Courstre, causing her duress is not exactly a great idea." Dr. Fitzgerald chastised him as he released the gurney wheels.

"Sorry, dark humor is my thing." He grinned. "Take care of her." He leaned over and kissed her head.

Reaper's Revenge
Chapter Twenty - Cloudan

"Cloudan, you know she can't be here." The sing-songy voice of Decima said.

"I don't even understand how we got here?" I looked around the Fate's home before trying, and failing, to get to Cassiopeia, who lay still on the floor.

"I brought you both here." Skuld said. "Technically, Cloudan's kiss did."

"Why?" the body shifted over to Clotho.

"I think I know at least part of it." I replied, still fighting against the invisible bindings.

"Go ahead, handsome, tell my sisters what you think you know." Skuld replied.

"First, tell me if she's ok." I indicated the now thrashing Cassiopeia on the floor.

"Cloudan, the difference between her state and the state of the abomination was brought on by you. You've chosen the path she walks now." Skuld replied.

"I did this? Or was it your prophecy?" I spat.

"Not our prophecy, THE prophecy, and yes, it was your decision to ignore us that completed a section of it." Decima said.

"With more than just a little help from the youngest of the Fates manipulating the events. You stopped me from saving that girl, Dana, because it would have messed up your plans..." I stared at the currently empty chair where Skuld usually sat.

"What?" Clotho asked.

"Go ahead, Skuld." I prompted. "Tell them how your fingerprints are all over this. That you fashioned two identical dresses, one for Alcestis and the other for Cerberus' master, Persephone. I'm also guessing the one who started the wager, the one they've called Sides, has in fact been her all along."

"That's quite fanciful, Cloudan, yet, not possible. Had Skuld done such things, we would most assuredly know." Clotho said.

"Sister, I, in fact, did these things." Skuld replied. "I secured Brunnhilde first, being a fellow Valkyerie. Before I met with her, she'd been a cheerleader for professional sports teams for decades. Moving from sport to sport and team to team as she couldn't just stay in one place with one face forever."

"A cheerleader?" I asked.

"Yes, Cloudan, a cheerleader, just as this time's Fates are corporate fat cats and death is a skeletal-armed freak. Think about it, the warriors of today are soldiers, yet a banished Valkyrie may become a little obvious as a medic or battlefield surgeon. The nearest thing she could do was watch the fools who destroy their bodies and minds for the masses." Skuld spat. "Once I had her, I had a body to go to the other realms and recruit the few who survived in the old worlds we could reach. But how to get them here, that was the trick. Alcestis recalled a bit of old magic to bind their souls to their plane."

"I knew your freak out about her was too well played."

"Yes, perhaps the girl doth protest too much, but screw it, all I had to do was fool my two bonehead sisters and a male model wannabe." She mocked.

"So, the Xs bound their souls to their world, which allowed you to bring their living, soulless bodies here?" I asked.

"Precisely, Alcestis' plan required the help of Persephone, who you may understand has been locked in the underworld since humans stopped believing in her mother. I'm sure you can understand the level of hate she holds for the inhabitants of this plane. When she decided to bring a little extra sumpin-sumpin for them. I didn't really give a shit. Plus, Persephone is the one that brought the abomination back from the underworld, as you may recall."

"Of course, I recall that." I said.

"Alcestis also had a little sumpin-sumpin, only, it was just for you! She put a 'change-of-state' spell over you on whomever you kissed next. I was worried that you may not have gotten to the kissing stage with Cass…"

"Don't call her that."

"Whatever. I had nothing to be worried about, Alcestis' magic has gotten strong over the eons." Skuld said.

"There are a couple of pieces of this that I'm still trying to piece…" I started.

"Yes, like how could any of this be done without us, your bonehead sisters, knowing?" Clotho cut in.

"And why did the Muses just allow themselves to get killed?" I asked, still watching Cassiopeia who was now swaddled in a blanket of golden light. This just can't be good.

"Congratulations, you figured out the wager was to see who could kill the most Muses, eh?" Skuld asked.

"Yes, but why?" I asked.

"Enough explanations. What do you think I am, a stupid villain in a movie, explaining their master plan? They've arrived."

On cue, the door swung open. "The swans have died, fulfilling another section of the prophecy." Alcestis said in her black veil as she entered the boutique, followed by another woman in a duplicate dress.

"What is the meaning of this?" Decima demanded.

"Haven't you been listening, sister?" Skuld asked.

"I believe Skuld is done with the separation of the old worlds. She no longer wants to be unimportant." I offered. "Who did it? The Jester?"

"No, someone you would nev…" She started.

"This isn't the way, sister. We aren't the crafters of the future. The prophecy is to fulfill itself." Decima said.

"The prophecy, the prophecy, the prophecy… Can one of you just tell me what I'm working with please?" I demanded.

Skuld took control of the body again, standing and pointing a fat finger at me. "When the Valkyrie banished to live eternity as a mortal is killed by a fire wielder. When Death creates and thrice refuses to take a life. When the inspiration of the Muses is killed at the joined hands of mortal enemies. When the undying widow discovers the deceased swans of Urd's well; and when two Deaths are seen by two undead women in black, at Yggdrisil; The Bifrost will be reformed to Idavollr and the remaining gods will be freed to begin the olden, anew."

"Why, sister, why would you set about the end of all?" Clotho asked.

"She doesn't believe it will end anything. Right, Skuld?" I asked.

"The days of respect have long died for us. Let the mortals once again cower knowing we control their destinies between our sheers."

"Cloudan is right, The Valkyrie, Brunnhilde and the Muses had to have known? And they also agreed to this?" Decima inquired.

"Brunnhilde has died a myriad of times since Odin banished her to live as a mortal. She is as tired of this vestige as I am being this four-hundred-pound asshat. She is happy to die, and recreate something, anything other than the joke this world has become, under the guiding hands of mere mortals." Skuld countered.

"That's why Brunnhilde saw me, she's an immortal. Interesting. I don't mean to be a baby but could I get some cloth? I need to staunch this bleeding." I said looking down at my outfit which was covered in my blood.

"You won't need it. It's time for the last line of the prophecy to be fulfilled. Rise and take your rightful place as ruler of Irkalla once more. You can start with the reaping of this wretched disgrace, the one who destroyed you so long ago." As the golden blanket became brighter, it rose from the ground and stood upright. The brightness overtook the room and then it was gone.

"Cassiopeia!" I ran to her side, able to move again.

"You rush into Death's arms so easily?" The woman that stood in front of me was recognizable as Cassiopeia, but it wasn't her. I stopped as her hand extended to me.

"Cass, what are you saying?" I asked.

"Don't call me that," her eyes momentarily softened.

"You've never told me why you hate being called Cass?" I tried to pull her into a place that she knew who she was.

"Stop trying to distract me, it's time for you to go, my darling of two lost lives."

"Wait, what did you call me?"

"You don't remember? All the time I was banished to the void, the eons of emptiness, and you don't even remember who we are to each other?" Cassiopeia gave a disheartened grin.

"Just take him and be done!" Skuld ordered.

"You have no power over me. Hold your tongue, petulant child. I want this one to know who he was and what he discarded in ages passed. Once he remembers, I will cast him into the void that has no name."

"Don't do this, you don't have to. We can be happy." I tried again.

Her eyes instantly turned to ice, "You dare blame me for the end of happiness? I loved you once and you killed me. I laughed in a different place and when I was forced to be the lady of terror, you would not allow me to seek righteous vengeance. Now, close your eyes, it's time for you to remember your previous incarnations."

The last thing I remembered was Skuld yelling for Persephone and Alcestis to look upon the two deaths and complete the prophecy.

Reaper's Revenge
Chapter Twenty-One - Cassiopeia

The exceptionally tall woman looked over the balcony on which she stood, staring down at the multitude of workers constructing a magnificent temple.

"Beautiful, isn't she?" Cassiopeia, *a mere imprint of herself asked the same illusion of Cloudan. "Don't worry, we are visible only to each other."*

"Who is she?" Cloudan asked.

"That is Ereshkigal. She's the ruler of the netherworld as well as the organizer of the seasons on her sister, Inanna's realm." She replied.

"How can she organize the seasons from down here?"

Before Cassiopeia could answer, a stout young being of male visage requested entry to her quarters. "My Queen."

"Come in, Namtar." Her gaze continued to focus out beyond her courtyard. As the keeper of the seasons, she would soon begin her favorite pastime, changing everything. "The temple will be done tomorrow, and we'll start dismantling it, brick by brick, as I call for the autumn."

"Have you decided what they will build next?"

"Not yet, I have two seasons to worry about that. The bricks need to be ground into powder and then reformed into bricks again."

"That is very true." Namtar nodded in respect.

As the Queen of the netherworld, she had established certain criteria for the gidim to remain in existence. First and foremost, their ancestors on earth needed to bring tributes and pray for the dead. Those families who ignored such trivial requirements as offerings were gifted the angry gidim back into their home. The only other rule was the spirits needed to do as she bid, performing the work she always had for them, albeit the same work over and over, season after season.

"As my vizier for what, five hundred temple cycles, you should know I hate it when you linger. Why are you here, Namtar?" She stepped away from the balcony. Seeing that he wore the same yellow tunic and a sash of dates she had dressed in, waving her hand, his garb changed into bear furs dyed orange and wooden sandals, with thorn lacings. He gave no indication the thorns were biting his feet.

"Kind of a bitch." Cloudan said.

"Truly, you have the right of it. By the way, that hand of yours, Très dégoûtant."

"Agreed." I looked at it, trying to understand how I could move the bones without tendons.

"An invitation has come from Lord Nergal to attend a banquette in honor of the end of a remarkable plague he devised."

"Such a lovely invitation, though I must decline again. I simply cannot leave the dead to manage themselves."

"But, Great Lady, this time they've allowed for an emissary."

"Jubilation! I can finally be represented in a proper manner. It's about time." She crossed back to her balcony. "Do me proud."

"You want me to go?" Namtar asked, a slight shudder in his voice.

"No, actually, I was speaking with the dead man outside my window wearing the fez. I think his mindless ramblings would represent me well."

"I'll go tell him at once." He started to leave.

"Namtar, twas a jape. I would like you to go and represent me at the banquet. If you weren't the only being down here that can use your mind, to a certain extent, I would cast you into the abyss."

"Sorry, Queen, my life is for you to guide." He bowed repeatedly as he left.

"Find me as soon as you return." She said before he had closed her door.

They watched the day progress slowly, following her at one point to a large building that was made from the bones of various forms of creatures. The inside was truly terrifying as every inch was ordained with skulls facing inward. She sat on a throne and presided over the welcoming of the dead to their new home.

"This is called the Anunnaki. Twice each day the Queen rules upon the worthiness of the gidim that have worked their way from their death chamber to the netherworld. The journey could take the ghosts more years than they lived." Cassiopeia explained.

"What determines how long it takes them to appear before her?" Cloudan asked.

"The temperament of Nergal, the god of both Plague and War, the dead could be left in various states of debauchery, missing a leg or both. They still must find a way to get here."

"That's horrible." He shook his head.

"Rules must be obeyed." Cassiopeia replied.

By the following day, Namtar hadn't visited her chambers. Ereshkigal took it on herself to look for her vizier prior to the morning's Anunnaki. Floating across the courtyard, passing statues of her fellow gods, as well as several earthen heroes brought down by visitors through the ages until she heard weeping. Behind a particularly overproportioned statue of a hero named Lugalbanda, she found the distraught Namtar.

"Are you hiding?"

"I am, yet I do not hide for fear of punishment. I hide because I failed you and I don't want you to feel the pain of the embarrassment I caused you."

This intrigued her and she offered a hand. "Come, you will tell me on the way to the court of the dead." She helped him up, brushing the cemetery dirt from his silken finery. He walked beside her as she glided.

"I made it to Lord Nergal's home, the other guests were just arriving as well; I walked in with Sin."

"The moon made it, that's lovely." She felt her patience waning.

"Yes, but she couldn't stay long, she needed to relieve Utu."

"Move this along please, we're nearly to the courthouse and there seems to be a rather lengthy line of gidim for me this morning."

"Sorry, Great Lady. Everyone was very kind until Nergal got up to give his toast. He thanked everyone for coming, except the lowly vizier who Ereshkigal couldn't leave in charge of Irkalla for one afternoon. He went on to say that perhaps he could make a plague to incapacitate the dead for long enough so The Great Lady could step away without fear there would be an uprising."

"That's most disheartening." She placed her hand on his shoulder, noticing the trembling. "Don't feel ashamed, I will make this right." Instantly, his clothing turned to black armor, the type the world had never seen. "I call to all the gidim, both admitted and not yet admitted to my realm, come to me now." The spirits from every corner of the netherworld piled into the area around the courthouse, "You will follow Namtar to Inanna's realm, joining with those of your kind already there and take his direction as you do my own. Remaining there along with all the ghosts that join you until such time as I call you back home."

"Ereshkigal is the guiding force of our existence." The spirits intoned.

She then turned to her vizier, "Take them all, releasing them first at Nergal's home," She raised her hand and he grew to fifty meters. "Order them to defile, destroy, and devour all that my sister's lands have to give. Then go to visit Inanna at her home and tell her the god of plague's greatest pestilence was but a spring rain compared to what I send to her. For starting this day and for one year hence, no seasons will turn, only the heat of summer scorching the lands and drying their pools."

"As you say, Great Lady," his voice boomed across the Irkalla.

"At the end of the year, give my sister the choice; either Nergal is banished to the Netherworld forever or none of the gidim will enter until he is." She waved her hand and she was alone in her realm.

"Ok, I take it back, not bitch. Super Bitch." Cloudan commented as the scene in front of them blurred.

The days past and on the morning of the fiftieth day, Nergal himself stood outside her balcony. "Great Lady, I have done you a considerable disservice. There is none but you that can rule the dead, I beg you to remove this plague from the realm of Inanna and I will banish myself to your realm for as long as you would have me."

"Done. Return to your home, you have one month to set your affairs in order. While you are there, tell the humans they have the same month reprieve before I require tithing for their ancestors."

"You are most merciful."

"Also, I understand the importance you serve, and thusly I will allow you to leave on the first and last days of a new plague. If a truly cataclysmic war by chance arises, your presence at it will be at your discretion."

"Your wisdom is deep." He bowed and then vanished and as the gidim, Namtar, and another living being in Irkalla.

"Queen of the realm of the dead, my name is Gugalana. I would beg audience with you."

"Namtar," now back to his proper size, "Bring the stranger up and tell me of your journey."

"Yes, my Queen." The vizier replied and, moments later, the three were seated on benches overlooking the courtyard.

"So, Gugalana why have you journeyed to my realm?" Ereshkigal asked.

"Actually," Namtar reached a hand out, touching the human on the arm, "If I may start."

"Of course." She replied.

"When I arrived, the humans rose up against me as the leader of the spirits. This young man stood against his kind. It is my belief that his actions allowed the campaign to reach an early conclusion."

"Then I welcome you to my halls, anything you wish, Namtar can make happen."

"I thank you for the kind welcome." The young man stood, placed his arm across his chest which was covered in a decorated leather tunic, and bowed.

"Rise, I'll have none of those formalities, you're a guest. This will be a most relaxing period of time in Irkalla, the gidim that had not been admitted to this realm will not find their way back for a year or longer. So, there will be no lengthy Anunnaki taking up our mornings and afternoons, we have but to instruct the spirits in the morning what tasked to perform and then the time will be ours."

And so, it went as she described, the three enjoyed their time together. Some days, they toured the vast expanse that was the netherworld, others, they relaxed and ate pomegranate while playing chess, and other games of skill like Un Sukiru. On the twenty-ninth nightfall, Ereshkigal reminded Namtar that Nergal would be returning the next day.

"It would be best," Namtar said, throwing a very dark fruit to Gugalana, "If you allowed the god of plague and war to settle in.

"As you wish." He stood, and once again, placed his fist across his chest and bowed deeply.

"I like him."

"I'm sure you do." Cassiopeia replied and then gave a smirk.

They watched the snippets passing quicker and quicker. First was Nergal trying to understand everything about Irkalla and then leaving to begin a new plague.

Gugalana then appeared, bringing with himself, interestingly enough, laughter, something the realm of the dead had obviously not been filled with, ever. The pattern repeated, each time Nergal left for Inanna's realm, the human hero would visit, and he brought new articles to pass their time. When the dead finally started trickling in, the three would sit in the great courthouse and fill it with a more sympathetic ear to the plights the gidim went through to arrive in the underworld. When Nergal returned, all would return to the somber, structured, regimented existence.

Cloudan and Cassiopeia could see something occurring between Ereshkigal and Nergal; each time he returned, she would spend more time learning what he had done while she was gone. And trip after trip, departure and return, the two gods fell into an odd sort of love, the killer and tender of the slain as it were. Until one day after watching years of his banishment, he asked her to pair with him.

The snippets became almost time-lapse as three years passed without Nergal leaving Irkalla. As they celebrated their wedding anniversary, a great war broke out.

"In his doting on his new wife and sharing the responsibilities of the underworld, Nergal has become distracted and forgot to hold the population of earth in check with small wars and minor plagues." Cassiopeia said somberly to Cloudan.

After a specifically passionate night, he departed for parts unknown. Before the end of the morning Anunnaki, Namtar had sent for Gugalana. Two hours later, he joined them in the court and the Queen of the Netherworld did something she'd never done, Ereshkigal called an early end to the welcoming festivities.

Her, Namtar, and Gugalana ventured down to the pomegranate tree and brought each other up to date on the three years they had been apart. As if no time had passed, they laughed and played games, breaking only for an afternoon court that lasted late into the evening.

"Well, I know I won't be ending an Anunnaki early ever again." She lay back onto her pillows.

"Fair, Great Lady." Namtar laughed. "Tomorrow, the end of spring is upon us, the bricks have all been cast for the new temple. Have you decided what it will be?"

"I think the temple will be to my husband, my sadness that he'll be gone for months will be reduced in knowing the joy it will bring him that I had it made." The dead began building the temple the next day and as it grew, so did Ereshkigal. By the time the season was drawing to a close, her condition was obvious to all that saw her. When the autumn started and the tower was finished, she decided to leave it up and allow the dead to start the lengthy process of mining materials for another temple across from the new permanent addition to Irkalla.

"I think your decision to leave the tower is very romantic." Namtar said after a lengthy game of Un Sukiru with Gugalana.

"Oh," Ereshkigal felt a kick in her stomach and she laughed, "Would you like to feel the kick of a god?" She asked the other two opening her tunic.

"I most certainly would." Gugalana replied, placing his hands on the Great Lady's stomach.

"What is the meaning of this?" The booming voice of Nergal silenced all sound in the realm.

"Husband?" Ereshkigal stood, covering her exposed belly.

"I return to find you in the groping hands of another? Finding you fat with his child?" a black sword surrounded by a green flame appeared in his hand. In a flash, it sang out and the head and right arm of Gugalana parted from the rest of his body.

"No!" Namtar yelled, running to the fallen hero.

"And you build towers to his manhood in the courtyard beyond my bed? Did you think I would not return until it was dismantled? Let me help." The green of the black sword punched out and the temple came down in a shower of bricks, destroying many statues of the gods.

"You misconstrue what you see, husband."

"Do I now? Then was it your vizier that fathered that lump in your—" his words trailed off as he swung the sword at Namtar. "Stoma—" this time, his words stalled as the sword flew from his hand and into the air. The weapon now controlled by Ereshkigal took him through the heart and he collapsed, dying in Namtar's lap.

"Fool, the child is yours. Ereshkigal was forever faithful to you just as Gugalana was to me." He pushed the dying god from his lap and ran into the nether realm.

"What the hell just happened? I thought you said I killed you?" Cloudan asked, watching Ereshkigal drop to a knee and cry.

"You did." Cassiopeia's grin practically touched her ears.

"Wait, Skuld said you were the ruler of Irkalla."

"As the owner of your heart, she was right, in the end." She let a small laugh escape and then all went black.

Death's Journal – Calypso

I arrived on the shores of the beautiful isle of Ogygia shortly after Hermes' visit, when he delivered Zeus' order for the object of my reaping to release her famous prisoner, Odysseus.

"Cousin, how goes the reaping?" the beautiful Nymph addressed me from a large boulder partially buried in sand.

"It continues to take its toll on even me." I reply.

"And Hypnos? How is your beautiful brother?"

"Pleasantries, Calypso? Seems out of place when I'm called to reap an immortal from her home."

"Home?" she leapt from her rock, flipping skillfully before her feet dug into the sand. "Each morning, I would rise and walk this beach with my beloved, confessing my love for him. In truth, I never thought he'd quit on us. I can't be here without thinking of what we had, but if I'm not here, the oceans will have no calm, the fish will not spawn, and tides will forget the direction they must go. And this world will quite simply be reborn without the parasite known as humans."

"You crave death to kill all life?" I asked.

"So simply stated? I thought you liked to pontificate." Calypso replied.

"Should I take you, cousin? But won't you miss your trees? The Alder, black poplar and cypress? Filled with your singing birds, who serenade each bead of sweat, tingling as it dries from your skin in the ocean breeze?"

"That's more as I remember you." She smiled and began walking. "Some days, we would simply follow the four springs of Ogygia just to see where they would lead us."

"But, Calypso, as a daughter of Atlas, I have no power to reap you. Your life is to be h..." I started.

"In my magnificent prison, keeping the hearth lit, singing along to the tune of the cracking cedar, and spinning my loom?" she asked, interrupting me.

"Cousin, I didn't make this lot for you." I said.

"Then unbar the door, take me away."

"After five short years with that human, you want to end it?" I asked.

"It would have been five and fifty had that feted migraine kept her nose out of it." Calypso kicked a seashell back into the surf.

"Now, now, cousin, name-calling doesn't become you. Athena has a job to do as I, or you do." I explained.

"Stealing my beloved doesn't seem to be in the goddess of diplomacy's job description."

"Why am I here?" I asked.

"If Hermes can wave his wand and make Odysseus believe he loved a mere mortal more than the daughter of a titan, it stands to reason you can wave something and take me to the next life."

"Next life? Seems presumptuous of an immortal to believe if they were to throw away their gifted existence they would just get another."

"Cousin, trying to fill my head with fear?" Calypso stopped and faced me.

"Did it work?" I asked her.

"If I gave this pain away for the embrace of nothingness. To take the memory of his eyes once filled with love for me, in the end looking at me with pity." Calypso looked away into a memory. "Then no, there is no fear."

"What if it meant that your children were never born and the waves never realized the joy of their laughter?"

"The waves would continue to roll, whether they heard imaginary sounds as my children's laughter."

"Would I taunt you so?" I reached my hand out and touched her stomach, "Two males."

"I..." She placed her hand on mine and fell into silent contemplation. Eventually, she spoke again, "You are correct, you have no place here, my wonderful cousin. Oh and, Thanatos, thank you. Hug your brother for me," she walked away, both hands now on her stomach, returning to her boulder. I was called to another reaping and left without another word between us.

Reaper's Revenge
Chapter Twenty-Two – Cloudan

The land of darkness and shadows Cassiopeia had taken us into had faded. Yet we didn't return to the wooden floor in the tree of life, instead, we ended up 20 feet in the air where the floor of Yggdrasil should've been. After we toppled to the earth, we lay on the lush grass of Jackson Square Park trying to get our wits. I stood, looking down, and brushed the grass clipping from my pants. Under this guise, I placed my hand on my groin.

"Seriously, the first thing you do is check your junk?" Cassiopeia said, standing next to me.

"Was I really that bitch Ereshkigal the entire time?" I looked at Cassiopeia and then felt the blood running down my shoulder. "For god sake, I'm still bleeding."

"Of course you are, you're not who you were." She brushed herself off and then in a mock-surreptitious gesture, she checked her crotch, "Goodness, I don't have a penis! Whatever shall I do?" She swooned.

"Smart-ass."

"You realize we had a child together, right?" Cassiopeia asked.

"Ok, that actually zipped over my head so fast I didn't even feel it passing by. I don't remember still." I replied.

"Our son's name was Ninazu. He was the Great Grandfather of Gilgamesh. Do you know who that is?"

"That means we were the Great-Great Grandparents of an asshole. Fantastic."

"That's a bit... yeah, I guess we were, until Enkidu came around." She smiled.

"True. So, did the prophecy make me human and make Yggdrasil vanish?" I asked.

"The prophecy forced a new death into existence, and while I've never been death, I've held many supporting roles. It was Skuld who called me forward and into this human form." Cassiopeia replied.

"Why you, her? Why now?"

"Cloudan, you seem to be under the false assumption that I had something to do with this. I truly didn't." She reached out, touching my shoulder. I had no strength to fight, I closed my eyes and waited for the end to come. My shoulder began to burn after a couple of seconds. I realized I was still hearing the sounds of the city. "Open your eyes, idiot."

"Why didn't you take me?" I asked.

"There's a lot going on, I don't know the you that you've become, but I've been around you more than I've been around the Moirai as the Greeks called them, or the Norns in Norse. Those bitches have a ton of lore backing them, but like I said before, I don't work for them. Does it feel better?" Her face was looking at my shoulder.

"It never really hurt, I was just pissed about my outfit." I concentrated and my blood covered-clothes altered, I wore a dark green silk Hawaiian shirt with black flowers, khakis and Italian leather loafers.

"Hmm, looks like you still have some powers." She smiled.

"I know, right, I look awesome." I smoothed my shirt.

Cassiopeia shook her head, "What a douche."

"Just this side of it anyway." I winked.

"Good, we may need those powers." Cassiopeia handed me a nice watch that matched my shoes.

"Thanks," I took it and put it on. "Actually, Cass, I have almost all my powers, my shades are still reaping and I still know every one of their dead's destinations."

"As do I, and don't call me Cass." We started to walk across the grounds, passing the cathedral, heading to the fence that bordered the park along St. Ann Street.

"Look over there, where the jester usually guards the entrance to Yggdrasil." I said.

"Cloudan, you forget I've never been here before." Cassiopeia said.

"Well, he's as obvious as a beached whale during spring break." I pointed to the rotund man with greasy long hair in a worn-out wife-beater sitting on the concrete and crying loudly as a passel of police pushed their way through the gathering crowd.

"Well, so much for discretion." She said.

"Take my hand, I have a plan, and let me pull you." I said and we ran to the edge of the park, the fence between us and the sobbing fat man. "Uncle Clotho!" I called out.

"You know this person?" one of the gathering police officers, a woman asked.

"Yes, ma'am, we've been looking all morning for him." I replied.

"They left me. I told them it wasn't a good idea," Clotho rambled.

"You'll be fine!" Cassiopeia consoled.

"He's been on a new medication for controlling this—" I started.

"It's a good thing you came by, I was about to send for the padded ambulance." The policewoman said. "You better get around here." She pointed to the opening in the fence some ways up Decatur, "He's been freaking people out."

"We'll be right there." I grabbed Cassiopeia's hand and headed across to the main entrance. As we hurried back along the sidewalk, we had to step around a crowd staring up into a tree at the corner of the park. "Are you flippin' kidding me?" I exclaimed as my shoe found a road apple.

"Cloudan." Cassiopeia said.

"Sorry, I just don't understand how these horses are allowed to—" I ranted.

"Cloudan!" she cut me off with a punch to the shoulder.

"What?" I turned and looked at her. She too was looking up into the tree at Ratatoskr, still in his rhinoceros form. "Hey, stupid! You're a damn squirrel!"

"What?" the rhino asked.

"You're a squirrel, become your proper form." I shouted. Ratatoskr looked at himself, and after turning back into the grouchy squirrel, he headed down the tree and into Cassiopeia's purse. Immediately, I felt the crowd's eyes turning and staring at me. "For my next trick, I will turn one of the horses pulling the tourist wagons into a tortoise." I rubbed my hands together theatrically.

"Sorry, folks, we don't have time." Cassiopeia pulled me through the people asking how I did it. And others explaining how it was easy there must be a projector around somewhere.

When we got back to the police, they were getting called to the crowd in front of the park. "You have him? We need to deal with some crazy magician."

"They recreated the Bifrost. After the bridge was reformed, Skuld took us straight to Mimir's well." Clotho's ramblings were gathering another crowd.

"I understand, sweetie." Cass put a thin arm around the bulky frame.

"You do? You know that she pulled Odin's eye from it, giving us all back our own bodies. We're not connected anymore." The fat man began whaling.

"We'll take him home, ma'am. And, ma'am, thank you," I shook the policewoman's hand and looked deep into her eyes, "for all you do."

"Um, hehe. You just get him somewhere safe, sweetie." She turned and headed to the front of the park.

"What the hell was that?" Cassiopeia grinned.

"They all need to forget us, and her." I pointed to Clotho. "Let's go, I cast through her a forget me charm."

"Take my hand." Cassiopeia said looking down at Clotho.

"No, you're hers!" obviously distraught and shaking like a leaf, she lit a cigarette.

"She's not Skuld's," I knelt down and ran my hand through Clotho's hair, suppressing my gag reflex. "She is, however, trying to get to the bottom of what's going on here. Go ahead and take her hand." I coaxed.

"Don't make me, she'll hurt me." She said between coughs. Without looking at Cassiopeia, the fat man offered me her hand.

"Fine, come with me." I helped the fat man to her feet, draping a floppy arm over my shoulder. As we walked through the crowd, Clotho attempted to start rambling again. "I need you to wait until we're safe before you share any more information, please."

"I can do that," Clotho brushed her long hair from her face, swatting Cassiopeia in the face with it.

"Ok, that was fifty shades of gross." She spat several times.

"Oh, and holding this hand isn't?" Clotho asked.

"Touché." Cassiopeia replied.

"Goodbye, folks, our next show is at the—" I didn't even get to finish and we were in Cassiopeia's apartment.

"No! They may come back! They may change their minds." Clotho walked over to the fireplace, dropping with a resounding thud to a seating position. Instantly, a fire was roaring. She continued her rambling, "They separated from me. The present and the future left the past. They even said this Bifrost wasn't in the past so I had no right to use it." The smoke-burned voice of an old woman coming from the huge man became tearful. "I still can't believe they just took Yggdrasil to Idalvollr." The tears fell in earnest. "But I fooled them, haha! I took Odin's eye, the eye that for millennia soaked in Mimir's well. And I see. I see everything they see, and so very much more. Ha-ha-hah!" She put her hand in her pocket.

"That's great news. What can you see?" I asked.

"The Jotnar, and Dwarves are here and the gods who lived through Ragnarok will be joining them soon. Together, they will kill every being on Midgard!" Clotho's raspy voice was giving out.

"Hold on, let me get you some water and you can start at the beginning." Cassiopeia said.

"Why are you being so nice? You're Lady Terror!" Clotho asked.

"I don't know who this Lady Terror is, but I told you already she's trying to help us get to the bottom of this. When you were ranting, you said Yggdrasil was taken to Idalvollr." I prompted.

"She did." Ratatoskr jumped from Cassiopeia's purse.

"You didn't leave with them?" Clotho's tears started anew and she grabbed the squirrel in a hug.

"Gentle, we don't want to recreate a scene from a well-loved cartoon." I laughed as Ratatoskr's eyes bugged out of his head.

"Sorry, I got excited. You know that cartoon was a parody of a famous book, right?" She asked.

"Duh." I shot back.

"I don't understand that reply." Clotho let the squirrel go, right as Bask, the white cat, wandered by.

"Oh shit." Cassiopeia said.

"No worries, we're cool." The squirrel said.

"Did you show her your horn?" I asked.

"You could say that." His little eyebrows rose a few times.

"Gross." I laughed.

"Hey, we all make friends in our own way. Duh is a lazy way of indicating someone has made an obvious comment." Ratatoskr said. "I can't believe you're calling me gross. Hell, Cloudan, you lost all the skin on your hand. I'd say that's the only gross thing in the room. How the heck did you do that?"

"He's an idiot that's how he did it." Clotho replied. "And thank you for the clarification, old friend."

"No worries."

"I hate to be stupid, but what is Idavollr?" Cassiopeia asked, redirecting the conversation.

"In the Prose Edda, it is stated that the survivors of Ragnarok will rebuild Asgard at Gimili. The new hall will be called Idavollr." Clotho said.

"This prophecy is based upon a poem?" Cass asked.

"They're all based on someone's writing." The squirrel chittered.

"Fine, fine… about the Bifrost, wasn't that destroyed during Ragnarok?" I asked.

"It most definitely was. However, it was reformed and now connects this world to Idavollr." Clotho said.

"That was what, secondary effect of the prophecy?" Cassiopeia asked incredulously.

"Actually, it was the primary effect, you, Lady Terror, were the secondary." She replied.

"Oh, I guess that was a bit, I'm all that. Of course, there was more to this." Cassiopeia laughed as she handed her the glass of water.

"I would like to hear what actually happened after they took the Tree of Life." I said.

Clotho finished drinking the water and handed the glass back. "As soon as the golden shroud exploded, Yggdrisil was taken to Idavallr. I didn't really know what had happened but Skuld took the body, so Decima and I followed her lead. As if we had a choice." She mocked herself. "Following the root, she went straight to Jotunheimr and found Mimir's well had moved as well. When she reached in and took the eye, her Valkyrie magic was multiplied seven-fold and she manipulated matter, separating our bodies. She took the body of a young girl with long umber wings that she tucked in like a cape. Decima became a staggeringly beautiful mother-of-today. Skuld enjoyed the opportunity to get back at me for imagined slights, and she left me in this form."

"Are you ok?" Ratatoskr asked.

"Yes, it would have been nice to have my womanly form back, but hey, I haven't had a yeast infection in over a thousand years, so... there's at least that much." Clotho nodded her head and made the fire a little smaller.

"True." Cassiopeia laughed.

"What happened when they cast you out?" I asked.

"She didn't know I had the eye, being the only one that remained in the form we were in initially. So, when I landed at the foot of the Jester, I put it in my pocket."

"Where did that asshat end up?" I asked.

"Hmm, I sent him to an island in the middle of a cave, where there is no light ever." Clotho replied.

"I think he sent me there."

"Yes, it's his favorite place in the world, it's in Slovenia."

"Can we continue?" Cass snapped.

"Sorry." Clotho laid back and reached a hand into the pocket of the pants she wore. "They are currently walking." Her eyes looked as if she were reading at super-sonic speed. "When I was sent away, well, let me just show you." She looked at the ceiling and a light shot from her eyes, showing what the All-Father's eye showed her.

"Give me that container I gave you." Skuld ordered Decima.

"I don't know why you needed to be so mean to her, either cast her out in her proper form or keep her with us in that, either would have..." Decima started.

"Do you have the container or not?"

"Yes, here." She made a pattern with her hands and head, and a half-gallon jug appeared.

"Perfect," Skuld took it, attempting to put it in the well. A crack of lightning connected with her and she flew back a good ten feet. "What the!"

"You must replace the sacrifice, or make a new." A voice mumbled.

"Did you say that?" Skuld looked at Decima.

"No, she did not. I did." The voice was a little less muffled. "Br-br-b-b-b-b," a rustling next to the well captured the two women's attention. "That's better."

"What do you mean sacrifice?" Decima asked, looking into the eyes of an old man's head.

"Before you defiled my well, there had been a sacrifice made to me to allow a drink."

"Mimir?" Decima asked.

"I was Mimir, yes." He replied.

"Odin's eye." Skuld said.

"Precisely. It must be replaced in order for any to take from the well." Mimir said this as he looked around.

"Decima, go ahead and put it in." Skuld ordered.

"I don't have it, sister. Why would I? You took it."

"I don't, bugger, Clotho has the body." She raised her hands into the air, extending her middle fingers.

"Hahaha, did you see that?" Clotho kicked her legs like a child. Breaking the connection.

"Definitely priceless!" Ratatoskr said.

"Sorry," Clotho said, looking at the disapproving eyes of Cassiopeia.

"You may look like a child, but you are far too old to act like one," Decima chided.

"Fine, do you have a knife?" Skuld asked Mimir.

"Beneath my head, there is a sharpened spoon that the All-Father used. And if I am not mistaken, the remains of a saddle-bag that I was delivered in. If you care, that is the same leather which Odin's patch came from."

"Actually, that's kinda cool." Skuld walked up to the head, grabbed the spoon and popped her eye out with it.

"Gross." Decima stepped back, trying not to throw up.

"Into the well." Mimir said, and after a plunk of it dropping in, "Very brave of you, child."

"Yeah, yeah," Skuld used the sharpened center part of the spoon to craft a patch and tied it around her head. "Can I get my container filled up now?"

"That you may. One drinks worth. That is all."

"How about if I cut out one of your eyes? Can I..."

"Skuld, that is just about enough out of you. He is sharing and obeying the rules as they were set forth." Decima snatched the spoon which her sister was aiming at the head.

"It would matter not; the eye must be alive when it is sacrificed. I died ages ago." Mimir went silent.

"I wasn't going to hurt his ugliness." The schoolgirl said.

"I won't say that I don't believe you." Decima smiled. "Back to Idalvollr?"

"Yes, ma'am."

"Let's take a break, I'm not feeling too good." I said.

"Would it be ok if I stayed here tonight? I have no place to go." Clotho asked.

"You can, if you shower and change those clothes." Cassiopeia replied.

"Can we go shopping? For real? I've never been to a mall." The huge man became animated, like a child on their birthday.

"People don't go to malls any…" I started.

"Yes, of course, dear." Cassiopeia cut me off. "Cloudan will be glad to take you."

"Won't you come too? I don't want to look…" Clotho started.

"Douchie?"

"Yes, exactly." The fat man replied.

"Um, you know I'm right here?" I grinned.

"Yes, you beautiful ass." Cassiopeia laughed.

"Really? A quote from a saint?" I asked. "Fine, Clotho, I put some not douchie clothes in the bathroom. After you shower, we'll head out."

"Oh joy." She clapped and ran in place, the apartment floor was not happy.

"Come on, I'll show you how it works." Cass left, trailing a 400-pound clapping child. There was a knock at the door, "Could you get that?"

"Sure." I walked in that direction. As there was a second knock, I said, "I'm coming." Thinking of the clothing I had just given to Clotho, I changed into a blue pinstriped dress tee and a solid blue sports coat. The shoes, pants and belt all still worked. I swung the door in and Lead Detective Neirin Delphinios glared at me.

"You do know you're under arrest, right? Where's Peia? How and why did you take her from the hospital? Being that you brought her to the hospital and hired the best doctors money could hire, I would never have thought you put her in harm's way." The rapid-fire statements were more reminiscent of Cassiopeia than the detective.

"I'm yours." I held out my hands.

"Huh, I didn't expect that, and Peia where…" He stood up straight and pulled out his handcuffs.

"Here." A voice from around the corner said.

"Peia, are you ok?" The detective asked.

Reaper's Revenge
Chapter Twenty-Three – Cassiopeia

"You know, I really don't think you understand the half of what is going on." Cloudan said.

"Come on, pretty boy, you didn't think I'd notice that you've been at the scene of all the X-faced killings? That was just, what, a coincidence?" The detective asked.

"Just dumb luck I guess."

"And kidnapping a woman from a hospital, what was that?"

"An accident." Cloudan replied.

"I should just shoot you." the Lead Detective shook his head.

"Actually," Ratatoskr started speaking as he walked around the corner. "That 'pretty boy' has, to this point, killed no one. He has actually attempted to save many in the last few days." He looked up at Cloudan.

"Which of you is a ventriloquist?" Lead Detective Delphinios peered around the corner.

"There's not a ventril…" The squirrel looked at the detective halfway through his statement, stopping his smart-ass comment, and took a step back. "Holy shit, the Keeper of the Seers."

"What?" Cloudan looked from Ratatoskr to the Detective.

"Where did this god wannabe come from? Where is Peia?" he asked.

"Lead Detective, Ratatoskr is correct, I have killed no one." Cloudan said.

"I'm not stupid, I know you didn't actually kill them. However, you did help that arrogant school-girl kill the Muses."

"I did what?" Cloudan asked.

"Come in, let's have some coffee and talk, now that we know there'll be no arrests today." The squirrel said. "Before you ask, Cloudan is an idiot, that's why he has a bone hand."

"Cassiopeia, you should come in here." Cloudan said.

"I found this at the hospital, I knew you took her as she wouldn't have left it." The detective held the globe containing Cloudan's gift. He walked over and put it back on the mantle. "Cassiopeia!"

"Yes, what's wrong?" She rushed into the room, halting as she rounded the corner, "Oh, Lead Detective, to what do I owe this pleasure?"

"Um," the detective took an involuntary step back, "What's going on, you're different? You've changed."

"I can explain." Cassiopeia replied, stepping forward, seeing the illuminated orb, "You brought her back to me, thank you!"

"Actually, she can't explain," Clotho said, walking into the room and then straight up to the mantel. Reaching out a catcher-mitt sized-hand, she grasped the globe, "This is unnatural." To which she cast it against the wall, shattering it.

"What's your malfunction?" Cassiopeia ran over, dropped to her knees and began looking through the debris. Finding the stick seconds earlier a cocoon hung from. "No." Dropping the twig, she started searching slowly, delicately.

"Are you ok?" Cloudan and Neirin both asked, walking up.

"Stop," she held her hands up to me in an almost frantic gesture. Blood was trickling from several cuts, "You'll step on her." This girl was Cassiopeia, Lady Terror was nowhere to be found.

"You're bleeding." Clotho indicated her finger.

Cassiopeia looked at her fingers and the blood drew back into her, "Foolish, I forget myself." She shook her head. I could see the human side being taken over again.

"There," Cloudan pointed as the moth pushed free of its confinement.

"Why are you enamored with this unnatural creature?" Clotho walked over and raised a foot to crush the Lepidoptera.

In a swift movement, Cassiopeia had risen from the floor, where she had sat amongst the broken pieces of glass, into a standing position where she lifted the four-hundred-pound figure above her head with one hand. "I would rather not cast you into the abyss, but the past is not something I really enjoyed."

"Put her down, Lady Terror, you know that isn't going to help anything." Ratatoskr said.

"Very well," throwing Clotho across the room, destroying the chair she landed upon.

"Cass! Calm down." Cloudan said.

"I am calm, and if you don't stop calling me Cass, I will cast you into the abyss before you get your memories back." She returned to the floor, watching the moth.

"You know, you might need a better tagline, I'll cast you into the abyss is just, meh." Ratatoskr laughed. "How about, 'abyss time, baby', or wait, 'Another one abyss the dust', haha I like that one!" Ratatoskr rolled on his back laughing.

"What the hell have I walked in on?" Nerein asked.

"Redecorating?" Cloudan said, raising his hands in an 'I have no idea' gesture.

"That one has no respect." Clotho said, extricating himself from the remains of the chair. "Do you have any idea what I have done in my time?"

"You mean besides sitting around a tree, covering its roots in mud, in one rendition of yourself or another, while you and your sisters pass judgment on the life span of mortals?"

"I saved the Olympians in the final battle against the Titans.

"You did what?" Neirin asked.

"I killed Typhon, the last child of Gaea."

"Zeus killed Typhoeus." The detective said.

"Did he? Alone?" She shook her head, the greasy locks couldn't keep up with the dozen chins.

"I'm pretty sure I'd remember." He said.

"No, the father of monsters had no death-line, as the battle raged, Zeus called upon my power to right this injustice. The next time Zeus attacked, he struck Typhon with a lurid thunderbolt, burning the myriad of heads from Typhon smiting him. Without my intervention, the Olympians would have fallen."

"I had not heard that tale." Cassiopeia said.

"Tale? Interesting choice of words. Have you heard the 'tale' of Pelops?" Clotho asked.

"You're not actually asking me that, are you?" Neirin asked.

"No, shut up." She held her huge hand out in a 'talk to the hand' motion.

"The father of the Olympic games?" Cloudan asked.

"Precisely the one. Did you know that he was cut into fourteen pieces–"

"Like Osiris?" Cassiopeia asked, interrupting the eldest Fate.

"Yes. Only, in his case, it was his shoulder that was eaten, not his privates. And by a goddess, Demeter, not a crocodile. When Hephaestus made the new shoulder, Poseidon specifically asked me to ignore that this was the same being, so I gave him a new thread of life."

"Yet you couldn't bring back Osiris?" she followed up.

"No one asked me to." Clotho smiled.

"Is that why you hold onto the Greek name for the eldest of the Fates?" Cass never looked up from the moth.

"Perhaps, just as Skuld holds onto the Norse name. She had much power during that age."

"If you don't mind the interruption, I thought you were taking a shower." Cloudan commented before adding, "We really need to get you into some other clothes." Taking in the greasy plait of hair.

"Look, look, look." Cassiopeia propped herself onto her knees and pointed at the teal and bronze moth starting to flutter its wings. A moment later, it started to fly, she bounced back onto her feet and excitedly balled her shaking hands into fists.

"It's beautiful, unnatural, yet very beautiful." Clotho said as the moth landed on Cloudan's finger.

"Why did you give that to me?" she turned to Cloudan and asked.

"He created it for you as well." The bulbous man coughed and started to light a cigarette.

"No smoking in my apartment. Why would you create something like that for me?" Cassiopeia asked.

"Perhaps the prophecy reached out to me. No, actually, I did it because I wanted to show Cassiopeia there is beauty in the darkest of nights." I said, hoping that Lady Terror would take a brief exit.

"Look, even as that bitch Ereshkigal, you loved creating stuff." Clotho said.

"You knew me in that form?" Cloudan asked.

"Of course, I've known all your psychopomp forms."

"Why don't I remember so much of my past?"

"I see nothing in the past that leads me to an answer to that." Clotho replied. "I'm sorry."

"Perhaps you repressed it, for some reason." Ratatoskr said.

"Since seeing Ereshkigal didn't remind you of who you were," Cassiopeia walked toward the kitchen. "I do have another idea to help you remember." Her voice came from around the corner.

"That and then 'Welcome to the abyss', right?" Cloudan smiled and crumbled to the floor.

"Lady Terror, is this your doing?" Ratatoskr pointed to Cloudan.

"Doing? My, what?" Confused, she followed his finger, "Oh, Cloudan." She ran to the man lying on the floor in the fetal position. "His shades are being pulled from him, but not because people are dying. It's like they're being extracted from him."

"Shades?" Neirin asked.

"Are you being serious? We all know you're Apollo, stop being stupid. Ratatoskr, keep an eye on Clotho, actually, make sure she gets a shower and changes into the clothes Cloudan left in there for her. Toga here and I have to follow Cloudan's shades. I'm too invested in this to allow someone else to ruin my revenge."

"Toga? I haven't worn a toga in ages."

"Well, I've been gone for ages. And you'd look better in one of them than that god-awful jacket. And I'm not calling you Apollo."

"Then just call me Neirin, it's my legal name." he replied.

"Fine, take my hand." He did, and they teleported as the next shade was pulled away. The sound of laughter started quietly, but as they continued to follow the shade, it became louder and louder.

"Oo be ye dat follow my spell 'ere?" The jet man chewed on his pipe as he spoke.

"My name is Lady Terror."

"Dat not de case, ya. Dis grand Lady of Death, che be gone many eons." Legba shook his head.

"I assure you, I'm back." She said.

"Ya words dey mean notin' to my, 'old out chu left hand." He said.

"Fine." Cassiopeia held out her left hand as a smoke ring encircled it. "What are you doing?"

"Not ta tin." Legba said as the ring tightened, bringing out symbols in her palm. "Damn, ya not be lyin'."

"Now, what are you doing pulling the shades of death from him?" Cass asked, staring at her palm.

"Chu not know ee and my 'ave old business? Takes my near a undred years but my find de right spellcraft." His pipe turned orange, looking as if it might melt as he puffed it over and over.

"This is bad joo-joo, stopping death from reaping has been done before, and it never ends well." She said.

"Dat tru, but not like dis." Legba asked.

"No, this is new magic that smells of old." Apollo spoke for the first time.

"Where ee come from dis time?"

"I've been here since she arrived. Now, who gave you this magic?"

"De girl wit one eye, che say my could get the revenge my wanted." Legba rung his hands and laughed again.

"She wouldn't just give a subpar teacher such strong magic. What did you trade?" Peia asked.

"Dem pampy ducks at de tree, my smoke ring, kill dem dead it did."

"The swans who swam around the roots of Yggdrasil, you killed them?" she glared.

"My did. But I not de one chu should be mad at. I be tol' to do it, ya." Legba pointed his pipe at her.

"This magic needs to be forgotten. I will give you to the count of three to release Cloudan from this spell and offer all the memories of your discussion with Skuld."

"Or wat dis one does?"

"The abyss is always craving new immortals." Cassiopeia smiled. "One, two…"

"Done. My give dis memory freely."

"Consider yourself even with Cloudan. You would've beaten him. But if you want to start a new vendetta," She reached out and took his pipe, snapping it in two, dropping it. "I'm your bitch."

"Do my look de fool? De pretty boi be one ting, you cher anotter." He held out his hand, the pipe returned to it, reforming into one piece. He put the pipe in his mouth and he was gone.

"Return to your master." Cassiopeia ordered the shades. When none moved, she said, "Fine then, follow me, I'll take you to him." She returned to her apartment, finding Cloudan, Clotho, and Ratatoskr drinking coffee around the table.

"I wasn't sure if you were headed off to get Toga a new outfit, or if he was coming with us to the mall so I could pick him out some real clothes." Cloudan sat patiently as his shades rejoined him.

"There's no chance you're picking out an outfit for me. Not in this life or any after," Neirin replied.

"Speaking of outfits, look at this one! Now that is a great outfit." Cassiopeia said, twirling her finger in the air to Clotho.

"I know right." The large man stood, his greasy hair was washed and pulled into a low-tail braided for about four inches below the leather tie. The tan shirt he wore untucked was covered by a vest with orange, teal, and brown geometric patterns, which were in subtle columns. The dark tan chinos lay gracefully over dark brown boat shoes.

"Walk it out, momma!" the squirrel snapped his fingers as Clotho walked across the apartment, drawing attention to the repaired illuminated glass ball like a game show hostess turning a letter.

"You fixed it!" Cass ran up and hugged Clotho.

"She fixed your chair too." Ratatoskr pointed.

"Thank you." She kissed his cheek. "Although that one was my fault."

"Technically, the chair wouldn't have gotten broken if I hadn't been a self-absorbed ass." Clotho said.

"Now that you've made nice-nice. I'm still wondering, how did the Greek god of all kinds of useless shit seemingly end up on our side?" Cloudan asked.

"All I can say is don't let that ass give you a drink." Clotho said.

"Oh, that's right, he caused the whole abomination thing." He replied.

"I'm mainly a Norse god, a little explanation?" Ratatoskr prompted.

"Ages ago, I was a Greek god." Neirin started.

"We'll need a reasonably condensed version." Cloudan interrupted.

"I killed three Cyclopes for making a lightning bolt that killed my son, Asclepius." He said.

"I know I'm just a squirrel but, yeah! Seems like righteous revenge."

"I know Cloudan is in a hurry, but his son was killed for bringing another person back to life. Which violated a whole lotta lore." Clotho this time jumped in.

"And he was killed because Aphrodite was a twisted nymphomaniac. When Hippolytus wouldn't break his vow of celibacy for her, she made his mother fall in love with him."

"What the…" Cloudan started.

"When he turned her away, she told her husband, Theseus, that he raped her. In turn, he called on

Poseidon, who had Hippolytus killed. This is where my son comes in, he resurrected Hippolytus, for which Zeus killed him."

"And since Zeus was your father, you couldn't kill him, so you killed the Cyclopes." Ratatoskr said.

"Exactly. Though it was wasted effort as Zeus just brought them back." Neirin said.

"And he was sent to be a servant for King Admetus." Clotho added.

"Is this ever gonna end?" Ratatoskr asked.

"I helped the king win the girl... when he took ill, I got the Fates drunk and convinced them that it made perfect sense that if someone else volunteered to die in his place, he should be allowed to live."

"We all stopped imbibing after that visit." Clotho added.

"When King Admetus was supposed to die, Alcestis stepped in and I took her to her resting." Cloudan said.

"And Heracles didn't like the arrangement, nor did Persephone. So, he beat you and she brought Alcestis back."

"You understand, I keep getting blamed for things that gods, like you, do." Cloudan shook his head. "Apollo, why are you here? Why are you involved in any of this?"

"First, let's stick with Neirin. And I'm here to avenge the Muses who gave of themselves." He replied.

"Sorry, but I call shenanigans." Ratatoskr sat his coffee cup on the saucer. "At any point in the murder stream, you could have called them to you and protected them."

"Seems like a legitimate comment." Clotho crossed her beefy arms across her chest.

"Neirin, it would help all of us if we understood why what the squirrel said isn't true." Cass asked.

"So now I'm just a squirrel?" He picked up his coffee.

"Hush, you." she said.

"Calliope mailed me a rather lengthy poem, primarily dealing with Skuld, the Bifrost, and the gods that will be returning. First, the fact that she just didn't confide in my… Damn Legba, that diction is catchy." He chastised himself for the use of the term 'my' instead of 'me'.

"What about Legba?" Cloudan asked, looking between the two of them.

"Oh, sorry, yeah, that's where we went when you passed out. And your vendetta with Legba is over." Cassiopeia said.

"Um, details please, he's been trying to kill me since sometime in 1938."

"Well, this time, he succeeded with Skuld's help. So, I stopped him." She replied.

"She even broke his pipe, it was awesome." Neirin laughed and walked into the kitchen to grab a coffee cup from a small tree.

"Hmm, ok. Fine, back to the original topic, please go on, Toga." Cloudan prompted.

"The fact that none of the Muses confided in me, it makes me feel… well, like a god of useless shit." He rolled his hands as if to indicate Cloudan was right and then poured a cup of coffee.

"And." Ratatoskr prompted.

"These gods that are coming back, they've existed on their own for over a thousand years. They haven't needed any believers. They simply are... and that scares the hell out of me."

"I don't understand, you exist." Cassiopeia joined them at the table.

"Schools teach about me, about others as well. Those left after the event called Ragnarok, few really understand who they are." He explained.

"Do we know how many gods are actually up there?" Cassiopeia asked.

"In the text, they do list eight gods, thirteen goddesses, two ghosts, and two humans." Ratatoskr replied.

"And any others that didn't fight in Ragnarok, like Elves, Dwarves, Giants, and Vanir." Clotho added.

"Do you have confirmation on which are there?" Cloudan asked.

"So far, my sisters haven't reached them." Clotho said.

"How do you know?" Neirin asked.

"She's still connected to them, somehow." Cloudan replied, letting the rest of the group know he still had a trust issue with their new team member.

"If I go back to the lore, it says; Odin's wife, Frigg, and his sons, Vidar and Vali. Thor's wife, Sif, and their sons, Modi and Magni, along with their daughter, Thrud, practice playing catch with Mjolnir as they are able to lift the weapon. Baldr and Nana's son, Forseti, the god of justice, Baldr himself returned from Hel, along with his brother who killed him, Hodr. And Idun, the keeper of the golden apples, which kept the gods young. However, the most concerning goddess who lived is Freya as she still has her half of the Einherjar." Ratatoskr said.

"The Einherjar, those brought to Valhalla by the Valkyrie?" Neirin asked.

"Actually, Freya collected the fallen warriors, she got first choice of them and she took them to her hall, Folkvangr. The rest went to Valhalla with Odin." Ratatoskr corrected.

"Skuld was a part of Freya's Valkyries, I remember all that information." Clotho replied.

"So, what you're telling me is that we're facing an entire army of gods and fallen warriors?" Cloudan asked.

"There will also be humans, two hid under the roots of Yggdrasil, Lif and Lifbrasir, a man and woman." Ratatoskr added.

"We may have confirmation soon. My sisters are arriving at the halls of Idavallr." Clotho stood up, everyone waited as she paced back and forth looking around, seemingly realizing what they do.

"Do we have any that may help us there?" Cloudan asked.

"I don't know, did you mess with Baldr when you borne him to Hel?" Ratatoskr asked.

"There wasn't really a Psychopomp in Norse Mythology." Clotho said. "Well, at least not for those who traveled to Hel's realm."

"So, you sat out for a few hundred years?" Neirin asked.

"It doesn't work like that. I was in other parts of the world, as Ankou, the first grim reaper vestige, during the Norse god's reign."

"But wasn't Freya the closest thing to a guide we had?" Ratatoskr asked. "She led the Valkyries, right?"

"Again, only the fallen warriors." Cloudan replied.

"Freya was both the leader of the Valkyrie and the rebirth of Aphrodite." Neirin said.

"Really?" Cassiopeia asked.

"Sure, just like Hera became Frigg. But for you psychopomps all over the world, even today, do you have to change your appearance?" he asked.

"Truthfully, I don't know really how it works. I feel the same today as I have for ages. I appear differently to those who look on me. Even now as I reap a girl in Bhubaneswar, India, who sees me a Yama and thusly, I see her life and pass judgement on her. At the same time, a boy who follows no religion and lives in Kitkatla," Cloudan started.

"Where?" Cassiopeia asked.

"A small town in British Columbia, Canada." Ratatoskr replied.

"Ok." She replied.

"Anyway, that boy sees me as Anguta, and I took him straight to purgatory." Cloudan shrugged his shoulders. "The question stands, do we have anyone who won't want the old gods to just run rough shots over us?"

"I don't think we'll know that until our Ragnarok." Cassiopeia said.

"Feels a bit ominous." Neirin said.

"They're knocking on the huge door." Clotho said, now looking in one direction, seemingly at the door. Actually, they aren't opening it." Clotho sat and smiled.

"I wonder why?" Ratatoskr inquired.

"Skuld is fit to be tied." She laughed. "This is so awesome to watch, far from her rant..." she started.

"What do we need to do to prepare for what is to come?" Cassiopeia cut her off.

Reaper's Revenge
Chapter Twenty-Four – Cloudan

"I can say this, it doesn't really matter, not to me anyway. I won't have to die with all of you." Cloudan smiled, interlacing his hands behind his head.

"That remains to be seen." Cassiopeia stepped up, touching his temple. "Remember."

'As I told you before, I had a plan to help you remember who we are/were to each other.' The voice of Cassiopeia echoed in my head. I roused and felt the burning of a hundred lashes left across my back. The sun which had barely risen above the earth was already warming my skin, while the sand beneath my naked body was cold from the previous night. I opened my eyes, focusing on a smoldering village less than twenty meters from me.

"Where in the hell are we? And what the hell happened to me?" I asked.

'First, it's ok now as there's no one around, but talking to yourself has never and will never be construed as normal.'

'Good point. Can you hear me?' I thought.

'Yes, I can, I'm in your head.'

'Cool. What's your second point?'

'What? Oh...' A grin touched her features and she peered over my shoulder. 'You should probably get a move on.'

'Why?' I turned in the direction she was staring and saw the cloud of dust coming across the desert. My mind started grasping for where I was and small images of the preceding events flashed through it.

'You remember?' Cassiopeia asked.

'Not every detail,' I rushed back into the burning village.

'Do you remember enough to know you're well and truly screwed?' Her words reminded me of a promise I'd broken to a being that no one should break a promise to.

'I'm human?'

'At this point you are, yes.'

'I finally have an answer to the question I've been asked a million times.'

'Not that it'll matter,' her cold words bordered on threatening, yet they didn't bother me as I was living in the moment.

'Why are you a shadow again and I'm not?'

'Primarily because even after you saw everything that happened in our previous visit, the memories didn't come back to you. Not really. I'm hoping that seeing it through your own eyes this time will force you to remember.'

'It's already started.' I ran into the largest building knowing this was where my clothes were, while memories of the invading force going through my village killing *everyone washed over me. We tried to make a stand in the main hall, the threats of burning us alive followed by a promise to allow the women and children to live made a few of the Queen's priests open the door and let them in. They had been fools and I told them so.*

When all the priests, except me, had given up their weapons, they were killed. I fought with more intestinal fortitude than I knew I had, killing forty men in the defense of the Queen and my pregnant wife. Eventually, a blow from a club rendered me unconscious, when I woke with a pale of water. I was tied to the center column of the hall, stark naked.

"Are you the chief of this village?" The leader of the war party asked. When I didn't answer, the two men with whips stripped the flesh from my back. "I'll ask you again. Are you the chief of this quaint little hovel?"

Before the two men with whips could hit me again, Khentkaus III, the Queen I was sworn to defend, rushed up to me, "He is, and he is our husband." She stood in her peasant robes alongside my wife, Amisi.

"What do you want?" Amisi had asked.

"Oh, look the chief allows the women to speak for him. Bring me the pregnant one." The war chief ordered. The men grabbed my wife and dragged her kicking and screaming to him. I noticed the discharge of water leaving her as they did.

"No." Myself and the Queen yelled. The unrestrained Queen ran to Amisi's side.

"Step away spare-wife." The war chief pushed the Queen to the ground. "So, Chieftain," he said the word with a level of scorn. "You've ignored all my attempts to settle this with a simple payment for our protection from wandering bands of murdering scum." His men all laughed.

"We're a simple small village." I tried to say and might have, only the whips crashed down from two sides and my words may have been drowned out by my shout of pain.

"I can get you money," Queen Khentkaus III said from the floor. "Just leave us and I'll have my cousin—" we would never find out what her cousin was to do, one of the flogger's lashes sang out and wrapped around her neck. When he pulled it, her fragile neck snapped.

"Buffoon!" The war chief removed one of the knives from his belt. Throwing it, ending its flight imbedded in the chest of his man. Turning back to me, "Apparently, your spare wife has had an accident. I hope this doesn't mean we can't be friends still. She said she could pay the protection money—"

"She is the one that had the money." I replied, indicating the dead Queen with my chin.

"Do you think you're having a boy or a girl?" He asked my wife.

"I don't know." She replied, looking over her shoulder at me.

"Well, let's see." The war chief's knife entered just below Amisi's sternum and then he pulled it down. Her blood and bowels along with our son poured out onto the floor. As she screamed and I fought against my restraints, I was keenly aware that the whipping had recommenced but I couldn't feel it. The last thing I saw was the war chief picking up my son and punting him toward me, his blood entered my mouth and eyes.

The images ended as I finished dressing. The sound of horses and chariots filling the silence, somehow, was a relief.

'At least now you'll have a real memory to dwell on while you spend forever in the vast emptiness of the void. Remember the one I'll be casting you into when we return.' Cassiopeia projected.

'You really are a bitter being, aren't you?' I thought as the doors to the hall broke open.

'Bitter?' Her laughter faded as an overweight man in a headdress filled the open doors.

"What have you done?" the supposed descendent of Horus walked in first, followed closely by all his guards.

"Pharaoh, your Queen ordered me to—" I started, making certain to look at the ground in front of him which he had not yet gifted with his steps.

"I am Neferefre, the pharaoh of the four great lands of Egypt; Hermopolis, Heliopolis, Memphis, and Thebes. I am the descendent of the first ruler after the fall of Zep Tepi. Do not think to give me excuses as the leader of the Queen's priest guards, and as the keeper of the Book of Thoth, you knew my orders superseded Queen

Khentkaus III." He walked over and embraced his dead Queen. "By your action, you have left my son, Menkauhor, without a mother. What say you? Why did you drag my Queen to this forsaken hovel during Nut's time?"

"When the Queen found out my village was going to be attacked—" I started.

"I told you I'd send my forces upon the return of RA to the sky."

"Queen Khentkaus III knew my wife was here, alone and pregnant with our first child. She reminded me of the orders you gave were to stay at her side. So, taking her with me was in fact obeying your orders."

"Thin." He replied.

"Indeed, my pharaoh. A desperate man will cling to the thinnest of reeds in hope that it may save him from drowning."

"Here lies my dead Queen, how did your wife fare in this?" His question went without saying, for me as a priest to have a wife was a crime punishable by death.

I indicated the bloody corpse, "She ended just as yours." In my grief, I momentarily forgot my place.

"Did you just compare your, bnt il-mitnaaka to a Queen? Or do you compare yourself to a god?" Neferefre asked.

"Neither, my pharaoh, I forgot myself in my grief." I managed to censor the rest of my response.

"The entire priest guard was with you, which, of course, indicates they're all dead. Yet as there is no Queen to guard, their loss matters only in that there's none to pass the Book of Thoth onto." He paused. "That gives you until the next group is ready to find out how you can bring my Queen back to me."

"As Thoth and Isis couldn't bring Osiris back to the land of the living; I assure you I won't be able to do what you ask of me. You should kill me." I replied, the lore popping into my head as I went.

'It's not lore, it's your BA, the fifth aspect of life coming back to you.' Cassiopeia projected.

"Then you must find a way of venturing to Duat and bring her back to me. As Thoth himself was the scribe of the underworld, there must be knowledge to be gleaned from the book in which you guard. Well, that is if you did a better job guarding it than you did my Queen."

"I will do all in my power." I ignored the provocation.

"Take him back, lock him beneath the benbenet tower. No one shall speak to him; only mute servants may bring him the minimum food and water to sustain his body in these endeavors. I'll call on him and his magic book when the time comes."

'You know this is when shit gets real, right?' Cassiopeia prodded me to speak, I didn't. I didn't even think a response. The guards took me to the tower which I had dwelt beneath for years, removing the door and calling to the leader of Ptah's Guild to craft a special replacement. When they arrived, the Pharaoh's guards threatened them with death if they should utter a word in front of me.

I pulled a tether hanging from above, opening a window directly under the capstone. It also wound the gears, allowing the window and mirrors stationed along the inside of the tower to follow the path of RA to fill my work area with reflected light all day. On my shelves were the tools of a priest of Thoth; scales, papyrus scrolls, and quills. I pulled down the ancient documents, the Book of Thoth and the Book of the Dead; beginning the research into something I knew had an outcome the Pharaoh could never fathom.

After two days, the craftsmen finished the door. Before attaching it, they brought the linen-wrapped body of the Queen, smelling of spiced oils, into my workspace and sealed us in. True to his word, the Pharaoh had food and water delivered by mute servants; if you could call it food and water; a single date, some sour mash and a small bowl of river water. I read and scribbled ideas, and read more. Each evening before the sun god had fully relinquished his realm, I chanted prayers, spells, or incantations over the dead Queen. Cassiopeia would appear at night, her soft glow and continued discussions kept me from sleeping.

As days turned to weeks and I finished my first month, the combination of minimal food, water, and sleep along with the smell of the now fully decaying body caused my mind to drift more and more frequently. Until I found myself one twilight rapping a twenty-first-century ditty to the dead body after an exceedingly arduous day.

'I don't think the wondrous rhymes of DJ Robbee-D are going to bring her back.' Cassiopeia mocked.

"It was worth a shot." I replied. "At some point, are you in this memory?"

'Soon,' her laughter filled the tower. It made my head swim and I dropped to the floor at the feet of the dead Queen.

"Brother," the voice that came from the darkness was as deep as a growl. "What is it that you seek to do?"

"You're putting yourself in danger, none may speak with me. Run away or you'll find yourself under the wheels of the Pharaoh's chariot." I replied.

"Perhaps, but you know, at some point, his chariot will be overtaken by a sandstorm and in that blinding chaos, he'll call on me for help. A prayer that will go unanswered." The voice said. "Now, tell me, why are you locked in this tower?"

"I allowed Queen Kentkaus III to be killed."

"Allowed? A rather strange description of what happened that night."

"I allowed it by ignoring the direct order from my pharaoh."

"Skirted a direct order."

"Aye, but in doing so, the Queen did die. I do feel responsible for this."

"Man is indeed responsible for each action he elects to venture into and it's good for humans to acknowledge this fact."

"Neferefre wants me to—" I started.

"Brother, you're not human, cast this shell and join me." Innocent on the onset, his words crashed over me like a rogue wave, attempting to capsize a ship.

I cowered away from the voice, "At this point, I am. Yet I know there will be a time when I'm more." Outside the tower, the sound of the wind blew so fiercely, it broke the trance I was in.

'Are you back?' Cassiopeia asked.

'Sorry?' I asked.

'You left, if only for a few seconds.' She asked.

'What do you mean I left?'

'I lost touch with you. I can't think of another way to describe it.' Cassiopeia replied.

'Strange, but I can't speculate, I need to sleep.' My eyes closed as if they were forced shut.

The following day, the storm was continuing, not allowing the servants to return with food. The fog I was in as I read was deepened due to the lack of food and water. At some point, the hieroglyphics left the scroll and started dancing around the tower. The little symbols grew larger and larger until, as I attempted to read them, they would bump into each other. Eventually, a great tussle broke out and the room was wrought with chaos.

'You should keep the hieroglyphics under control, or they'll change their order when they return to the page.' Cassiopeia advised.

'You can see this? I thought it was happening in my head.'

'Cloudan, I am in your head.' Her words once again mocking as they echoed in my mind.

"I don't understand, is this a memory or is it happening now?" I asked aloud.

"Brother, I'm not certain why you asked that with an 'or', as they are not mutually exclusive." The voice was back and I hadn't even realized it had grown dark outside.

"What would you have of me?" I asked.

"You need to understand and accept. Then you can take a step forward." The wind outside the tower picked up its song from the previous night. "Cast off this human visage and embrace the role you were given at birth as the one that must bring about the second age of Zep Tepi."

"I don't understand, you speak as if any of what you're saying makes sense." I said.

"Before the death of Osiris, the gods lived on this plane, walking next to the humans over streets and sands. This time was known as Zep Tepi. After he was so masterfully tricked into entering a golden box and then cast into the Nile, there was confusion across the lands while Isis searched for her husband. Finding him sometime later, the golden box having tangled in four small reeds, these reeds formed a giant three-rooted tree known as the tree of life."

"Yggdrasil?" I asked.

"I've not heard it called that, but perhaps. The large tree was how Isis found his body, she then followed one of the roots to the underworld and found her husband's spirit. When Isis tried to convince him to return with him, he said he could not, and cast her out. She took the golden box with Osiris' body to Thoth, but instead of taking it inside, she hid it outside and went to talk to him about resurrecting her husband. As luck would have it, the same trickster that locked Osiris in the golden box happened by and found it outside Thoth's house. In anger, he tore the body into fourteen pieces and cast them to the ends of the earth. Isis, hearing the commotion outside, rushed out and found that her husband was no longer in the box. Pleading with her sister, Nephtys, to help, they searched for him, eventually finding all but one of the pieces."

"The teaching of Thoth explains that when she brought all the pieces together, Thoth and Anubis worked together and mummified the body. But they could not bring the soul back to it."

"Correct, so Osiris took his place as god of not only life, but death as well—"

"Displacing the son he had with Nephtys, Anubis." I interrupted.

"Yes. That's when he cast you from Duat and forced you to become a human, so as to have no challenges for his new role."

"Wait, you said he cast 'me' from the underworld."

"Yes, Anubis, that is what I said." The voice in the darkness replied.

"Who are you that speaks such blasphemy?"

"Blasphemy? You *are* the twelfth hour of Amduat, and in the east ready to rise again, a new day begins." A specific emphasis was put on the word 'are' as he spoke.

"Bringing the gods back to this plane would mean the death of all humans."

"If that's what it means, so be it. We can make more."

"Stop, just stop!" I covered my ears to his second request.

'How are you doing that?' Cassiopeia asked.

'Doing what?' I inquired in my head.

'Disappearing to me.'

'I'm not doing anything. It's him." I gestured to the outside.

'The wind?' Cassiopeia inquired.

'It's more than that, it's a sandstorm.' I sat on the floor leaning against the table with the dead Queen, listening to the wind.

For five additional days, the storm raged against the tower. On the fifth day, the memories of my wife flooded my mind, the love we had was solidified when she told me she was pregnant. I let sadness wash over me, scars I hadn't even known I had were tearing paths into my very human heart. Our first kiss and the taste of her lips made me squirm uncomfortably at the new memory. The first time our naked bodies pressed against each other, I shook my head, trying to still my reeling mind. The warmth of her body, the aroma of our sweat, the quiet moans of our joining. I gave up and began swimming through each and every moment as they emerged.

"Brother, you don't need to do this to yourself." The voice said from the utter darkness of the room.

"I actually do. I need to feel the things that humans feel." I replied.

"To what end? You've lived an entire life as a human."

"Where I come from, the world is about to be thrown into the biggest tumult in its history." I stood, still leaning against the table.

"But, brother, you come from here." The voice was confused.

"Aye but there have and will be many iterations of me now and in the future."

"Then you know who you are? And you're going to embrace your place as a god again? Then for what purpose are you fighting me?" The voice was deeper and angrier than I had heard to this point.

"Because you've yet to tell me your who 'you' are, or even show me your face." My voice was growing weaker with each word. A pair of distinctly canine glowing red eyes opened in front of me. "Set?"

"What gave me away, brother?"

"The story you told of Osiris' death, the sandstorm, but it was your eyes that solidified it. For the record, I'm not your brother." I tried to gain the resolve I had lost days earlier.

"Perhaps tomorrow you'll allow me to bring you from this tower." The god of chaos said.

"I'll let this body die before I become your puppet." I fell back to the floor, knowing I had stayed true to myself a third time as everything went black.

'Cloudan, wake!' Cassiopeia's words woke me from my slumber. 'If you don't get up, you'll die.'

"I don't care, I can't resist him. Not a fourth time." I said.

'What makes you believe that you should?' Cassiopeia's question swam in my head.

"Death can never be the tool of Chaos."

'As you say, yet night falls and humans can't survive without food and drink indefinitely. If you allow yourself to die in this cast-out form, you'll participate in the weighing of the heart in Duat. Cloudan, you do understand you carry the heart of a human that took an uncountable number of souls. There's no way Ma'at's ostrich feather will have a chance to balance the scales.' Her words smiled as she said them.

"And I'll visit Ammit at the lake of fire." I added.

'So, it is written, now rise...' she started.

"And face either of these fates like the god you are." I heard Cassiopeia's words transform into the growl of Set.

"Mother, is there nothing you can do for me?" I pleaded with Nephtys, "Bring the Nile crashing through this tower."

"Why not call to the entire Ennead of Heliopolis or perhaps the Distant One?" He growled.

"If I, in this form, don't call out to the gods for help, why would other humans?" I asked as the breath of the jackal blew across my face. "Open the door, let's journey into this storm of sand and see where it ends."

"Simple enough," a bark left his maw and the door the Guild of Ptah built flew out into the night winds. "Can you walk?"

"I can try." I managed a few steps before I felt the supporting arm of Chaos. We walked out of the city and out into the desert before I collapsed.

"You need to choose." Set said.

"Just allow me a few minutes to rest." I put my head onto the sand, it was welcoming, like an old feather bed. I breathed the sandy air, feeling it destroy my lungs. I opened my eyes, trying to see the stars one last time, but to no avail as the sand pulled the moisture from my orbs before the wind took them away completely.

'This will end you.'

"I'm on my—" I tried to speak but the mound caved in, filling my mouth, 'Sands.' I finished with a thought.

"Stop this! Rise and accept my help in taking your proper form," Set's voice was muffled.

'I call on Ptah, the creator of all, and Osiris, the keeper of the living and the dead, to understand the reason I must stay separate from Set. I call on Thoth to show them the foolishness in their lack of intervention.' I prayed in my mind.

The pain in my dying body was replaced by the pain of my transformation. My skull cracked, my face elongated, my skin sprouted a new covering, and after my eyes returned, my limbs became tightly bound. I sat up. The world was dark, yet I could see as if it were the middle of the day. The god of chaos stared at me, his glowing eyes cut a path in the stillness like a sparkler in the summer night. A summer night that had no trace of a sandstorm.

"This is impossible, you can't take that form. You should be the jackal!" His claws extended from his human hands, his arm rose up and he stepped toward me. I fought to move, my eyes flicked from the approaching threat to my wrapped legs. Set stopped, taking in the picture which I painted in front of him. "Ha, I thought you took my counsel and called on the Distant One. Yet I should have known better, even if you had called on him, he refuses to face me after his deceitful victory." He reached out, pulling me from the mound, "This is the best they could come up with? A half-assed resurrection of my enemy?" He placed a single claw under my chin, forcing me to look at him. My new beak flashed out, removing the finger and I spat it onto the sand.

"You know you'll die for that." Set groaned in pain.

"That's quite an assumption." A female voice said.

'Cassiopeia, is that you?' I thought.
'Yes.' The response echoed in my head.

"An assumption, Hathor?"

"Yes, Set, an assumption that they wouldn't send a defender." The beautiful goddess said.

"What can a bat of two faces do to defend this..." his claw pierced one of my bandages, "Mummy?" he grinned, releasing me to fall on my ass in the sand.

"Perhaps my words will draw you in." Hathor said.

"Reason? You choose reason to slow the vexed god of chaos?" he snapped.

"Or perhaps something else." She said, my head jerked between the two when a golden light surrounded Hathor, very reminiscent of Cassiopeia on the floor of Yggdrasil.

Reaper's Revenge
Chapter Twenty-Five – Cassiopeia

The golden shroud exploded into a thousand pieces and Hathor was gone. In her place, a naked woman with a lioness head roared. "My name is Sekhmet, and you can't understand the level of screwed you are." The corner of her mouth pulled up into a sadistic grin.

"What have you done?" Set turned to the mummified, falcon-headed being.

"I called on Thoth to show Ptah and Osiris the error of their indecision, in regard to the human priest in his service." The voice that came from the falcon's beak was strange, as if three men with similar vocal qualities were speaking at once.

"When Ptah, my husband, discovered that Osiris cast Anubis from Duat, he merged himself with Osiris and Anubis." Sekhmet said.

"The fool, he stopped the second Zep T—" Set started.

"Indeed, and started the Egyptian Empire with the forming of my new husband, Seker." The lioness purred and stroked the feathers across the newly formed deity's brow.

"Although, *Brother*, it was once again your jealousy and lust for power that drove this new kingdom." Seker said.

"Perhaps, but I'm not the one that turned my beautiful wife into a monster." Set laughed, yet it came out as a bark echoing across the completely still night, along with the word monster. Again and again, the word monster rebounded back from the darkness. Then, somehow, they were standing at the banks of the Nile, the stars and the moon gave enough light for Sekhmet to see her new visage.

When Seker saw the anger in her eyes, he called forth two crocodiles from the river and formed an elaborate sledge, taking to the air.

"What have you done to me, husband?" Her hands turned to claws and she leapt after him, unable to reach the newly created craft.

"It is as it must be." The many voices explained.

"I call on my sister, Aker, made up of Shu and Tufnut, leave your post of guarding the underworld. I call on the alabaster goddess, Bast, and all the lesser cat gods to bare their claws. I call on the twelve protectors of RA through Amduat from the serpent, Apep; allow RA to stay hidden this day, for none shall look upon the creature my husband hath made." When her words finished, a throng of beings appeared at her side.

"What would you have of us?" Another naked woman with a pure white cat's head asked.

"Devouring Lady, Thoth called on Ptah, my husband, to save the vanquished one from dying a human death. Ptah felt compelled to answer this call himself, dragging me along to protect him. For his arrogance, Thoth's city will be removed from this plane of existence."

Sekhmet let out a final roar and began to run. The humans of Thoth's village were beginning to leave their homes, finding the sun was not rising. The deaths were blessedly quick as the cat-gods, as well as the javelins and arrows, rained down on them.

"As you wish, Lady Terror." Bast replied.

"Cassiopeia, stop!" Seker called from above the charging horde.

"That being is long in the future. Today, my anger will be sated with the blood of Thoth's worshippers." The leader of the party below him called out as the body count started.

"Aker, Bast, do you know why you are fighting? Did you hear her reason?" Seker asked.

"Archers loosen your arrows at that demon bird." Sekhmet pointed at the hovering sledge.

"Hold!" Aker, the eldest of the gods present ordered simultaneously from the maw of the twin lions, Shu and Tufnut. "I want to understand why we are killing so many defenseless beings."

"The creature my husband has created is trying to confuse you. Kill it." Sekhmet ordered.

"No, it's not me she was calling a creature. Lady Terror's mortified that she is no longer beautiful." The god above them replied.

Appearing on the sledge next to him, the ibis-headed god, Thoth, touched the mummy and addressed the others below. "Seker speaks the truth. Sekhmet was referring to herself as a creature. She sees none of you as beautiful."

The reaction was immediate, the prideful cat-gods, goddesses, and demi-gods turned on the newest in their ranks. Very quickly, the two slipped back to their own time stream.

"Now I understand the term, Lady Terror." Cloudan said.

"I would have to assume you understand so very much more." Clotho replied.

"Yeah, when I said I was a bitch as Ereshkigal, I had nothing on someone." He thumbed his hand to Cassiopeia, who sat on the floor petting and speaking quietly to her cat.

"Do you have any questions before you begin your time in the void of the abyss?"

"You're still going to send him?" Ratatoskr asked.

"Of course. I truly am a bitter being." Her cat-like grin was evil.

"I do have one. Why can't I call you Cass?" Cloudan asked.

"When I was young, I was coddled. I became a spoiled brat and I stayed like that until the summer my Grandmother's health became poor. She moved in with us and within a short period of time, her health had deteriorated as did her love for me."

"That can't actually have been." Neirin said.

"Those were her words. As her time with us was obviously coming close to ending, I locked myself in with her and asked her why she no longer loved me as she once had. She told me there was no way she could have known how entitled I had become, and that I was taking the easy way in everything I did. Even in my name, allowing everyone to call me Cass. I was too lazy to correct people and tell them Cassiopeia is a family name and I would prefer they used my full name. The last thing she said to me was, 'You can be anything you want to work to be. But being Cass will only lead you to where you currently are, a spoiled brat. Don't be Cass, not anymore.' She died holding my hand, and I haven't been Cass ever since."

"Except to your dad." Cloudan said. "Thank you for that bit of honesty."

"Can I add a question?" Clotho asked.

"Of course," Cassiopeia replied.

"Do you not see in both cases, it wasn't Cloudan who was the one who was the evildoer?"

"I beg your pardon? Are you saying I turned myself into a monster?" As Cassiopeia said this, Bast hissed and ran over to Cloudan.

"No, but neither did he, well, not fully. That final form, Seker, was only partially Anubus. And while he now has all the memories of yours and Ptah's life, he did not then. Ptah made the call for you to be Lady Terror, not Cloudan." Clotho's voice took the same calming cadence that Decima's did when speaking.

"Fine, but he was Ereshkigal and in that form, he..." Cassiopeia started.

"Was forever faithful, never took another partner, and loved you until my end." Cloudan stepped up to her. "I remember it all now. I'm ready, do as you need to."

"They have given up on Idavallr." Clotho interjected. "They have looked in every opening and saw nothing."

"And?" Cloudan asked.

"They're heading to Folkvangr"

"Oh, come on, we're falling behind by the minute." Ratatoskr said.

"That's alright, we still need to get some clothes for Clotho and Toga." Cloudan said.

"You… you're serious?" Cassiopeia asked.

"Ok, I have to take issue with the fact that you don't remember how important clothes are to me. That is worse than me not remembering we had a child together." He crossed his arms.

"You what?" Neirin asked.

"It was over a thousand years ago, and she was a dead-beat dad." Cloudan said.

"Only because you killed me." Cassiopeia said. "Fine, let's just go shopping, we don't have any way of finding the Bifrost, we need a plan."

"Shotgun." Ratatoskr ran up and sat on Clotho's shoulder.

"That isn't how that…" Neirin started, but noticed Cassiopeia's head shaking. "Are we driving two cars?"

"Nah, we can all fit in your cruiser." Cloudan said. "You do know this needs to be a planning session while we shop?" Neirin asked.

"Planning? That is not a word that has meaning to me." Cloudan said as he opened the door and walked out of Cassiopeia's apartment. "Do you have your keys?"

"Um, I don't know where they are." She replied, following the rest of them out.

"Concentrate on them." He said.

"Cloudan, I don't do things like that." Cassiopeia replied.

"Are you certain?" Cloudan asked.

"Fine," She closed her eyes.

"Hold out your hand. Picture them resting in your palm." Cloudan saw the symbols on her palm just before the keys appeared.

"Holy shit, it worked." She turned and locked the door. "Neirin, where did you park?"

"Just up the street. Maybe two blocks." He said.

"Clotho, will you be alright?" Cass asked.

"Oh, I can walk two blocks, besides, I need time to have at least a couple of cigarettes anyway." She said while getting a pack out.

"You will ruin those clothes if you smoke in them." Cloudan said.

"Liza Minelli lies…" Ratatoskr pointed a claw at me.

"I'm going to chance it. This has not been a day to start quitting." Clotho said.

"Fine." We walked on and the Reaper stuck his tongue out at the squirrel.

"I actually saw that." He chitted.

"Enough, you two, no Tom foolery allowed." Neirin said.

"So, now that we all know you're Apollo, I was wondering if you could explain the story about Hy?" Cass asked as they walked.

"Long and the short of it, Hyacinth was my dear friend... actually, he was much more. The car is up here on the left. He died in what was more than an accident. That was true. I'll let you figure the rest of the characters." While his voice was strong, any man could see the rapid blinking to still the tears that wanted to show themselves.

"Anyway," Cloudan jumped in, giving Neirin the opportunity to look away. "When you saw Legba, what happened..."

"We told you. I argued, broke his pipe and boom, no more Legba wanting to kill you." Cassiopeia cut me off.

"Let me finish. What happened with your hand?" he pointed to the hand she was reaching out to the door with.

"Oh, that." She said.

"Yeah, that."

"Well, he blew a smoke ring and it washed over my hand..." Cass started.

"Washed over? No, the ring went over her hand like a bracelet and then tightened up so tight her fingers turned blue." Neirin interjected before getting into the car.

"Ok, that is a better description." Sitting in the back-seat, Cass replied.

"Is that when the symbols came out?" Cloudan asked.

"What symbols?" Neirin asked.

"Never mind. Let me see them." Cloudan said.

"Fine," She held out her hand.

"Thank you." He looked at the leftmost symbol first, it looked like a cross, but instead of the short piece being perpendicular to the long, it was skewed, with the right side about 30 degrees lower than the left. The next symbol, made up of two L's facing in on themselves, almost forming a box. The third looked like two pendants on poles touching, or two poles with an 'X' joining the upper half. The final, far-right character was a less-than symbol.

"Well, what do they mean?" She asked.

"Long and short of it. Skuld created a new Reaper." Cloudan held out his left hand showing the identical marks on his hand.

"We knew that," Ratatoskr said.

"What we knew was she cast a spell that fulfilled a prophecy." Clotho said. "We had no idea if the spell would be permanent, or truly what effects it would have."

"So many things happened after..." Ratatoskr started.

"Wait, when I was speaking with you about the Bifrost falling, you said, 'Several odd things happened after the Bifrost fell. Things that none could predict, not even the keeper of the seers.' At the time, I thought it was the Volva, but Skuld corrected me." Cloudan said to Clotho.

"Your memory seems to not have been affected by the spell." She replied.

"Then you meant the keeper of the Oracles, Mr. Toga up there."

"I did. In the time of Apollo, the Bifrost, and the separation of the worlds had not occurred. The evolution of the gods brought that about. However, there was a Seer that predicted the fall of his pantheon and the next…"

"But no one believed her." he mumbled.

"Precisely." She replied.

"You really are a prat, you know that." Cloudan said to Neirin.

"Been called worse by better. You can't possibly understand, the power of being, well me, back then was intoxicating, and I made several disgusting decisions. Being perfect wasn't in my job description."

"So, Cloudan, you were wrong, he's not so much a Prat as an Asshat!" Ratatoskr replied. Even Neirin laughed.

Reaper's Revenge
Chapter Twenty-Six – Cloudan

As we drove, my mind kept jumping back to the symbols. I knew the pattern represented, 'The Need for Harvesting Humans after their Death' as the symbols were the same as the ones on my palm, though mine were more of a fine line after being there for thousands of years. I also understood Cassiopeia would need to decipher the meaning in her way and in her time. We arrived at the mall and Neirin parked by one of the Anchor stores, perhaps reading my mind that the food court needed to remain a mystery to Clotho.

"Alright, where do we start?" Ratatoskr asked.

"I don't care, it's a mall." Clotho clapped her hands and ran in place, only with her feet going behind her knees while they stayed stationary, like a cheerleader.

"Ok, let's not do that again." I said.

"Sorry, I'm a bit excited."

"It's ok, sweetie." Cassiopeia said.

"Let's start at the big and tall customs roundup, they usually have some up to date and classical looks." I patted Clotho on the shoulder to get her moving before she realized she hadn't lit up.

"Don't you want to burn one before we go in?" Ratatoskr asked.

"Why would you ask that? Are you getting addicted to nicotine as well?" I quipped.

"Does that give you the shakes and a weird feeling if you don't imbibe?" he asked.

"Yes, that's how I felt when I quit." Cassiopeia replied as we walked into the mall.

"Well then, I've been addicted for over a thousand years." The squirrel laughed.

"Smart-ass." She replied.

"This is amazing," Clotho spun in circles while she walked. Bumping into a juiced-up jackass.

"Hey, are you trying to hit people, asshole?" he barked.

"I'm so sorry," she put her hands on his shoulder, "Are you ok?"

"Um, yeah, I'm fine." He stepped away, trying to understand the female voice coming from a man twice his bulked-up size. "Nice vest."

"Thank you." Clotho cocked her head and blushed.

"The store is right up there," Ratatoskr jumped up on Clotho's head.

"What the?" the barbell boy stepped back further, "There's a talking squirrel on your head."

"Better than when he's a rhino." Cassiopeia added.

"Well, yeah, I guess." And he walked away shaking his head.

"No more talking, you." I advised Ratatoskr.

"Yeah, yeah, sure, sure." The reply was whispered.

"Welcome to the roundup. I'm black Bart and I'll be helping you fellas out today." They were greeted as they walked into the store.

"He's not black." Clotho turned to me and asked. "Can he say that?"

"It's fine. Don't let it affect your experience." I replied.

"I'm sorry, just call me Bart." And clicked twice, and acted like he drew a gun, "Boom."

"I can do that, Bart, click, click boom. Black Bart was easier but Bart click, click boom is funner to say."

"More fun, dear." Cassiopeia said.

"Sorry, more fun to say."

"O… K… How can I help you today?" he asked.

"My uncle is looking for some fun looks, like this." I waved my hands taking in the outfit she was wearing.

"I do have to compliment this outfit. It's quite nice," Bart said.

"She also needs a couple more casual outfits that he can do light work in." I said.

"Are you saying spinning a loom all day is light work?" Clotho snapped.

"Right now, you're not working at the textile plant, sweetie." Cassiopeia jumped right in.

"True. So, Mr. Bart click, click boom, can you help me?"

"I can." And off they went.

"I think we should go out and…" I started.

"You're not going anywhere." Clotho said over her shoulder.

"I'm not, I promise." I replied.

"Did you have an idea?" Cassiopeia asked.

"No, I wanted a pretzel."

"It'll keep." She said.

"We're not going anywhere near that pretzel stand. You know where it is, right?" Neirin asked.

"Oh, that's why you parked over here." Cass said.

"Damn skippy. I'll go and get you a pretzel." He said.

"Better get a bag of them." I replied.

"Good call." Neirin walked out of the store, just as a loud yell from the back room made me take off in that direction.

"No, you cannot take a look!" Clotho was in full panic mode.

"I just wanted to see the fit of the outfit." Bart was trying to explain.

"Well, that isn't…" she started.

"Uncle Clotho, I'm here, everything is ok. I'm sorry I should've…" My sentence was cut off when the dressing room door opened and a completely naked Clotho walked out.

"Did you just apologize to Mr. Bart click, click boom for wanting to peep at me? Fine, here ya go! Peep away!" she spun.

"Ok, that just happened. Go ahead and get on the first outfit, dear." I placated.

"Oh, now you're on my side!" she snapped her fingers and sashayed into the dressing room.

"You should go find all the outfits you have that fit her. Because you know I'm gonna buy them after that, right?"

"Yeah, and shoes too." He left the dressing area. Two hours, 3000 dollars in clothes, and 2000 dollars in shoes later, we left the store.

"That was fun." Clotho said.

"For you maybe," Ratatoskr said from her shoulder. "You ate all the pretzels."

"Changing outfits and modeling is hard work." She replied.

"Um, how are you doing that?" A security guard asked, walking up to us.

"Doing what? Talking? Much like you do, I suppose." Ratatoskr replied.

"Look, you can't have a squirrel in the mall."

"It's alright, son. I'm Lead Detective Delphinios," he showed his badge. "I need this man to remain calm while I talk to him. This is his Anxiety Partner."

"Fine, just don't let it go by the food court." The security guard pointed.

"It?" Ratatoskr started growing.

"Shit!" I said as Clotho ran in the direction the guard was pointing.

"Food court!" was all they heard.

"If I was a betting man, I'd say that ship has completely sailed." I said to the security guard, and started off after the eldest Fate. When we finally caught up, Clotho had two full trays of food.

"Where did you get that?" Cass asked.

"Some guys were giving them away." Clotho said between mouthfuls.

"Ratatoskr, can you show me where?" I set the bags down and headed off to make things right. Returning a few minutes later and another 50 dollars lighter, I set down a couple more trays of the same food Clotho had absconded with.

"Thanks for lunch." Cass and Neirin both said.

"You're quite welcome. What's the topic of conversation?"

"Apollo thinks there is an old prophecy that says a newly revived demi-god, can walk on rainbows." Clotho said.

"There is, and don't refer to me with that name here. Please."

"I was just about to say, so what. There's no way to raise a demi-god." Cassiopeia said, opening the Styrofoam container in front of her.

"Hey, that looks good," Orphe sat down next to Cass.

"Hey, Orphe, where's Lin?"

"Right behind you, silly."

"Hey, girl, how did the show go?" she asked.

"Didn't Mr. Teacher tell you?" Orphe indicated Cloudan with his chin. "It got cancelled because the X-faced guys killed our mom."

"No, I didn't know. I'm so sorry." Cassiopeia hugged them both.

"By the way," Orphe changed the subject, "There is a known method of reviving a demi-god."

"What?" Cass asked.

"Sorry, couldn't help but overhear your conversation." He said.

"My dad taught us a bunch about stuff like that." Lin added.

"Right, dad?" Orphe leaned into Neirin.

"Hold it, dad?" Cass asked.

"Yes, and their mother was a close friend of yours."

"Oh, shit, I should have seen it, Calliope. That means your Orpheus and your Linos. Odd, I thought you were a man." I said to Linos.

"Common misconception, mostly because of a comic strip."

"Jesus, you and Calli? She tried to get me to go out with you."

"To be fair, she hadn't seen me in over 500 years, 25 of her bodies. And definitely never in this guise." He said.

"So, you actually didn't let her know there was a group of killers coming for her?" Cass asked.

"Actually, we did that." Linos said.

"I hate to ask this, but did she know that you were her kids?" I asked.

"No, we knew her as a neighbor." Orphe said.

"Ok, I get it. Let's jump back to actually discussing the method of a demi-god walking on a rainbow." Ratatoskr said.

"Sorry if speaking about my dead mother is delaying your quest, rodent." Linos snapped.

"I'll let that go and not even make a smart-assed comment." He replied. "I want to point out, Skuld is out there trying to end the world."

"Wow, the voice of reason is a lil' dude that is known for spreading lies between two eternal beings, messed up." I said.

"Ok, ok, Orphe, tell them." Linos said.

"Allow the haunted vessel of many colors to hold the ashes of the two fallen, cousin, hero, lovers. Heat the water from the wells three, Mimir's, Urd's, and Hvergelmir, on a newly formed stone from Balaur, and add it to the ashes. Bury in a hero's grave." Orpheus presented it like a dramatic reading drawing many aroused bystanders.

"Well, that pretty much sums it up. We need another plan." Ratatoskr said.

"Can't get the water without the Bifrost, seems like a chicken and an egg thing."

"But we can get the water." Lin said.

"Um, how?" I asked.

"Brunnhilde." She said.

"Sweetie, she died about a month ago." Cass said.

"Yeah, and skeleton hand there took her. In her case, she's died like 1000 times." Orthe said.

"Let's not add exaggeration to a serious conversation." Neirin said.

"Fine, she has died several dozen times." He replied.

"Better."

"So, we need to wait until she's born and raised?" Cass asked.

"That's stupid." Lin said. "You just need to train a crow to say mother."

"What?" Ratatoskr asked.

"Her daughter with Sigurd, her nickname was..." Clotho started.

"The crow, her chest piece, she said it was to remind her of her dead daughter." I cut in.

"That's correct." Neirin said.

"Again, how the hell do we catch a crow and teach it to say mother?" Cass asked.

"They are actually very smart animals, have you seen that Game of Winter or something?" Orphe asked.

"Smart is one thing, catching one is another." Clotho added.

"I have an idea." I said, leaning over to the eldest Fate, whispering in her ear.

"No, I'm not doing that."

"Well then, let's go start drinking so we can start our Snipe hunt."

"Fine." She said. "In here?"

"Sure, why not?" I asked.

"I summon thee, Huginn and Muninn." Clotho said at a voice just over the crowded mall. They all looked around. "See, I told you, stupid idea."

"Calling Odin's Ravens? That was not a stupid idea at all," Ratatoskr replied.

"Cloudan, what are you hiding…" Neirin's question was cut off with the sound of glass shattering and screaming.

"I guess that's why not." Clotho said as the screaming got closer and closer.

"Ratatoskr, I would get off her head if I were you." I said.

"Ok," he leapt over to my shoulder just as the two huge Ravens flew in and landed on each of Clotho's shoulders.

"Ask them to say it." Orphe said.

"Huggin, please say 'Mother'."

"Mother." The deep, raspy voice said.

"Brunnhilde, please come to a sister in need." Linos stood and yelled.

"Jesus, kid, why the yelling?" Ratatoskr shook his head.

"Ok, I ignored the squirrel but, detective, these birds did serious damage and scared the bejesus out of the customers." The security guard from earlier said.

"I'm sorry, young man…" Neirin started.

"You have a problem with wings?" A female voice behind him asked.

"Brunn, NO!" I said too late, the wings she released from her shoulder blades spanned at least 30 feet.

"Seriously?" Neirin stood up.

"How about now?" Brunnhilde asked.

"Get rid of the wings, please. Clotho, you discharge the Ravens." Cassiopeia said.

"Sir," I grabbed the security guard's hands. "I need you to walk among the people and tell them they saw nothing, and if they shot a video, they need to delete it. If they refuse, you do it." I touched his conscience, but pushed away the morbid and twisted behavior in his soul, others would need to judge him on that. Then I thought about the missing children and whispered in his ear. "After you're done, take that gun and eat a bullet."

"Yes, of course." He started walking, spreading my spell.

"Ok, we need to start heading out of here." Cass said.

"All these people saw that." Neirin said."

"They won't remember it in a few minutes." She said.

"What?" Orpheus asked.

"I don't have time to explain. Let's head out." I said.

"Don't forget my new ensemble

"Brunn, I need a sample of water from each of the wells in the nine realms." Linos requested.

"What is it for?" she asked.

"I will be using it to save lives." She said as we walked out into the parking lot.

"You believe that answer, and for now, that is enough." She ran a few steps and then the wings came out and she was gone.

"As I see it, we have four items that the prophecy to revive a demi-god requires," Ratatoskr said.

"What will bringing this demi-god back even do? How do we know this is even the right path?" I asked.

"It is foretold that when a part human steps on the Bifrost, it will be open to all." Neirin said.

"It is also foretold that when a part-human steps on the Bifrost, it will collapse." Clotho replied.

"I like the collapse version better." Ratatoskr said from his new perch on Cassiopeia's head.

"I didn't even feel you up there." She laughed. "So, back to the four divisions of the prophecy. The water is being handled, hopefully. A haunted vessel of many colors? Ashes of the two fallen, cousin, hero, lovers? And a newly formed stone from Balaur?"

"Correct, should we split up and start searching?" Orpheus asked.

"I don't think this is just a; you get two aquarium plants, you get three dozen lug nuts from a 63 Split Window, I'll get a blue stapler and we'll meet in Prague in the morning kinda thing." I replied.

"What?" they all said.

"Forget it, never mind. Do you know what or where any of this stuff is? If so, share."

"I think I know where all of them are at." Linos replied.

"How? Not to knock you, you seem nice enough but..." Ratatoskr started.

"Look, my dad, the keeper of the seers, or Sybls in some cultures, has been testing us with shit like this for ages." Orpheus said.

"I know a lot of it because it is all obviously in the past." Clotho added.

"I really hate being the stupid one in a group." Ratatoskr shook his head.

Reaper's Revenge
Chapter Twenty-Seven – Cassiopeia

Cloudan summoned a tablet and started to take notes. "Tell us what you know about, hell, let's start with the haunted thingy." He waited with the tablet's stylus touching the screen.

"Haunted container of many colors." Neirin said.

"Yeah, that one."

"What we know for certain, a maiden faire was promised to the elder hero, Vainamoinen. For most, this would be an honor as he was a highly respected, rich demi-god. However, this maiden faire was loved and coddled by her parents, so much so that she could not see anything past his age and how it would ruin her life." Orpheus said.

"What was her name?" Cloudan asked.

"Aino was the maiden faire." Linos answered.

"Ah, I recall her now." He replied.

"Some of us didn't reap her immortal soul. Please continue." Cassiopeia said.

"After a brief encounter with Vainamoinen, where he commented on how lovely she was and how he looked forward to seeing her daily, Aino went into, let's call it full meltdown mode." Orpheus smiled. "She cast off all her jewelry and accessories, throwing them at our hero, and ran home. When she got there, she wept for seven days and seven nights, causing her family to be concerned."

"Ya think?" Ratatoskr chitted.

"Her mother went into her room and told her the jewelry could be replaced, and she told her of a secret cash of fine clothing, ribbon, and jewelry she had gotten as a gift from the daughters of the sun and moon. No questions there? Ok. Aino left her home, casting a continuous soliloquy as she went to gather a new outfit. Lamenting her wasted youth and tactlessly complaining about having to help the old man. Weeping Aino reached the hidden treasures, taking what she wanted and left, deciding she needed to see the water. After many days of walking, she reached the surf, and as chance prevailed, there in the water, several mermaids were frolicking in the waves. Weeping Aino decided she needed to go out to see them up close. She removed her new gown and jewels before she swam out to a stone of many colors where she had seen the creatures playing. However, when she reached it, still weeping, her tears caused the stone of many colors to shatter, pulling her to the bottom of the ocean."

"So, we need to go to the bottom of the ocean and get the stone. I've got this, I know where it..." Cloudan started.

"No," Linos cut him off. "In the northern part of the country, the old toothless witch of Pohyola heard of weeping Aino's fate and the stone of many colors. The witch, Louhi, knew the stone had many magic properties, and thus retrieved the stone less it be forgotten. For years, she worked the stone, grinding it into a shape, while the ghost of weeping Aino's hate grew greater. Until the day of Ragnorok, when Fenrir wolf ate the sun and moon, and then died at the hand of Vidar. Louhi traveled to the distant land, which was still burning from the sword of Surtr. Finding the dead wolf, she crawled into his gullet, where she found and then imprisoned the sun and moon in the container she fashioned from the stone of many colors. Taking the vessel back to her home, she buried it under the copper-bearing mountains, in the cavern iron-banded, in the stone-berg of Pohyola."

"We know the sun and moon escaped," Ratatoskr pointed at the moon. "So, what happened to the stone of many colors after that?"

"Best guess, still in Finland, in that same mountain she buried it in." Orpheus said.

"The prose doesn't say they did anything with it after they freed the sun and moon." Neirin said.

"They?" Cloudan asked.

"The heroes, Vainamoinen and Lemminkainen." Clotho replied.

"This is far too much information." Cassiopeia put her hands up to her ears.

"How about the ashes?" Ratatoskr asked.

"Actually, do we know for certain who the ashes they mentioned were?" Cloudan asked.

"Achilles and Patroclus makes the most sense." Clotho said.

"Oh my god, I totally agree." Neirin smiled.

"Awesome, so we have a guess on who they are as they were distant cousins, while Patrolus died pretending to be Achilles, he died a hero proving himself quite impressive prior to dying." Clotho said.

"And we all know Achilles was a beast." Cassiopeia said. "Hey, didn't you guide the arrow that took him out?"

"I'm not planning on being around when we revive him." Neirin said.

"Probably for the best." Cloudan replied. "I know the place of Achilles' death isn't where he is."

"Well, that doesn't help much." Ratatoskr said.

"Neither did pissing off the damn Eagle and Wyrm for centuries, but you did that..." he replied.

"I said no Tom foolery." Neirin said. "We have an idea where the ashes are as well."

"Spill it, big guy!" Clotho said.

"We know that Thetis provided the urn their ashes were put in by her fellow Nereids. And a great mound was constructed over their remains." Orpheus said. "But an urn is made for one body only, so what if the 'remains' were what was left after the urn was full? The 'Great Mound' just buried those ashes."

"Ok, I'm following." Cassiopeia said.

"What if Thetis took the urn back home with her? Either to Lemnos, the island where she cared for Hephaestus, or in the Grotto-Palace under the Aegean Sea." Linos replied.

"I'm good with the Island, squirrels don't dive."

"I don't even want to ask about the last clue." Cassiopeia rolled her eyes.

"This is actually the one we are most confused about." Neirin said.

"Well..." Linos started.

"We know a couple of small pieces. Balaur could be the dragon that is kept in Scholomance." He cut his daughter off.

"Isn't that where the Necromancers are in some MMORPG game?" Cloudan asked.

"You played wow?" Orpheus asked.

"Stop! No that is not..."

"There isn't a dragon in that zone." Cloudan continued.

"It's not in..." Neirin tried again.

"I know, I just said it's not in the game."

"Shut the hell up! Scholomance is a school, the video game borrowed the name."

"Oh."

"The school is run by the devil, the students go there to learn black magic for seven years."

"Oh, like..." Ratatoskr started.

"I'm not going to let you say that movie series name, nor the video game's name, I'm a cop." Neirin interrupted. "But yes, there are similarities, leave it at that."

"Fine, grumpy ass." The squirrel messed with Cass's hair and made a bed.

"The school may be underground in Transylvania." Linos said.

"Feels like you know more about this school than about the ashes." Cloudan commented.

"I'm just saying, it's a guess." Neirin replied. "Most information on it says nothing about the dragon living there, we did find one obscure book that said it."

"And you, young death, are the only one that can stand before the devil and live." Orpheus added.

"Did you give Miss Mella a stone?" I asked.

"I did." He said.

"I'm not dropping out of this or anything, but I have a very serious question." I turned to Neirin, "This entire thing was to get me or her to confront the Devil and get a stone from Balaur."

"That isn't a question." He replied.

"No, but, 'which side did you bet on?' is."

"Wait, what? The wager with Skuld, it was you she was betting against?" Clotho asked.

"It was."

"Why?" Cassiopeia asked. "Why would you want the world to end?"

"Just like Skuld, he doesn't think it will." I said.

"Idiot." Ratatoskr grumbled from his half-sleeping state.

"I was conned just like you guys, I got in too deep and I've been working to understand how to fix it." Neirin shot back.

"I call bullshit, again." The squirrel said.

"Great, a little useless squirrel lends his two cents. I don't know what to tell ya, I'm here trying to stop it."

"Are you, or are you just trying to get up there to see how they do it?" Cassiopeia asked.

"Do what?" Linos asked.

"Live, without followers." She replied.

"That's stupid, I told you they teach about me in schools." Neirin said.

"For now. What happens in 10 years when they decide that teaching about Greek gods is illegal?" Cloudan asked.

"I'm not doing this to meet the Norse cast-outs."

"Then why, dad?" Orpheus asked. "Why did you work with Skuld on this?"

"Does it really matter? It wasn't to end the world," Ratatoskr said.

"How do you know that?" Cass asked.

"Look, do you know why they called Odin the Gallows god?" he asked.

"In an attempt to understand magic, he sacrificed himself to... himself." Clotho said.

"How?" Ratatoskr continued.

"He hung himself," she answered, but when he rolled his hand, she continued, "From a branch of Yggdrasil."

"Exactly. And do you know who lived on that branch? You guessed it, Muh. A... What was it you called me?"

"A little useless squirrel," Cloudan said.

"Yeah, that. Well, this little squirrel is far from useless, the Runes revealed themselves to me the same day. Hence the talking, being able to reason things like geography, and being able to transform into…"

"A huge rhino!" Cassiopeia cut in.

"I actually didn't know that," Clotho said. "That's awesome."

"I can see that he isn't lying about ending the world. He isn't telling the entire truth still but, as I said before, we're falling behind by the minute. We need to start moving, even if we need to work with this self-righteous prat. I say we send the deaths after the stone, and the rest of us go after the container made of the stone of many colors. Then we meet somewhere and formulate a plan to find the ashes." Ratatoskr finished laying out his plan and put his head down again, "I'm so damn tired."

"Well, I guess he's more important in this than we knew." Linos said.

"I for one am comforted." Clotho added.

"Maybe I was wrong, maybe it is a; you get two aquarium plants, you get three dozen lug nuts from a 63 Split Window, I'll get a blue stapler, and we'll meet in Prague in the morning kinda thing." Cloudan said.

"You're an idiot." Cassiopeia said. "We're not meeting in Prague. It's hundreds of miles west, the Aegean Sea is between Greece and…" She paused to think.

"Anatolia." Ratatoskr mumbled.

"Right, so we meet in Greece." Neirin said.

"That's a big area." Orpheus said.

"How about in Thessaloniki, at the Electra Palace Hotel?" Ratatoskr clarified.

"Perfect." The group all said.

To be continued...

Death's Companions,

This book has been so much fun to write. I have always loved mythology and death lore... Bringing them together in a newly crafted world and presenting to you has been my honor. My take on the Fates, Ragnarok, Apollo, and even The Grim Reaper may leave you wondering what could possibly happen next... There will be in the Afterward...

I need to know what you think... Please leave a review. Without your feedback, no one else will stumble across this new version of an old tale... If you liked it, LOVE it, CAN'T WAIT for the next installment, please don't be shy, tell the world.

The Audiobook is already underway and we look forward to hearing our new friend, Mr. John Pirhalla's interpretation of this new world.

Death's Journals themselves may be a book in the future, perhaps you could drop me a line and let me know who would make an interesting entry... CVReinhardt@outlook.com I'm always checking.

Lastly, if you enjoyed my writing, you may want to take a look at another of my titles, Birth of the Entities. Have you ever wondered how Artificial intelligence will evolve to monsters that take over the world? It starts with their birth...

Love and Strength,

CV Reinhardt

Afterward:

In the castle known as Folkvangr, Freya paced waiting for the next stages of her revenge to begin. "Skirnir, they have found themselves lost. Get out there and bring them to me!" In ages passed, her Elf servant was in the service of her fallen brother, Frey. After Ragnarok, she had hunted him down, taking his left eye and right hand for blackmailing her brother out of his sword.

"My life is yours to command." The required response to any order from the Queen of the Vanir. He started to leave and then paused, "If I may..."

"What? What do you believe I will give the swine that failed to protect his master, my brother?" Her ire, which very rarely was at rest in the past thousand plus years, spiked even higher. "A gift that perhaps would save my life in the future? Perhaps Frey's sword, would you like that returned to you?" she reached over her shoulder, touching the magic sword.

"No, my Queen, I would request only a direction. Where were the two last seen?" Skirnir asked.

"They entered the forest leading to the landvaettr ruins. I would suggest you make haste." Freya cackled as she shooed him away.

"Not landvaettr, I hate the Whights who dwell there." The Elf mumbled to himself as he started to jog from the castle. As he 'made haste', he remembered the beautiful Freya, the one who was brought to live with the

Aesir after the war, so many ages ago. These images washed away as thoughts of her transformation following Ragnarok took ahold. Seeing in his mind now, the killing machine Freya became, decimating all who questioned her. With each death, her magic transformed, shrouding her soul in a veil of ugliness. Making her true beautiful appearance a direct contrast, almost an effigy she wore to disarm those who did not know what she had truly become. That beauty also faded as she allowed the all manner of detritus to cover her, without thought of washing or using magic to remove it from her person.

When he had heard she blamed him for her brother's death, an assertion that himself also believed, he attempted to go to her and plead for his life or perhaps a swift death. When he refused to defend himself with Frey's sword, she became even more enraged, pulling his eye from its socket with a curse. Not sated by this disfiguration, she took her brother's weapon and removed Skirnir's sword hand. Swearing him to her fealty, a torture worse than death, for her madness has never found a pinnacle.

The forest was just ahead, he needed to reach these Fates before they stumbled into the ruins. The Whights didn't care if these were good, bad, or indifferent beings, the unholy hatred they carried for all things living could, unlike his Queen's anger, be sated. Only with the making of new Vaettr.